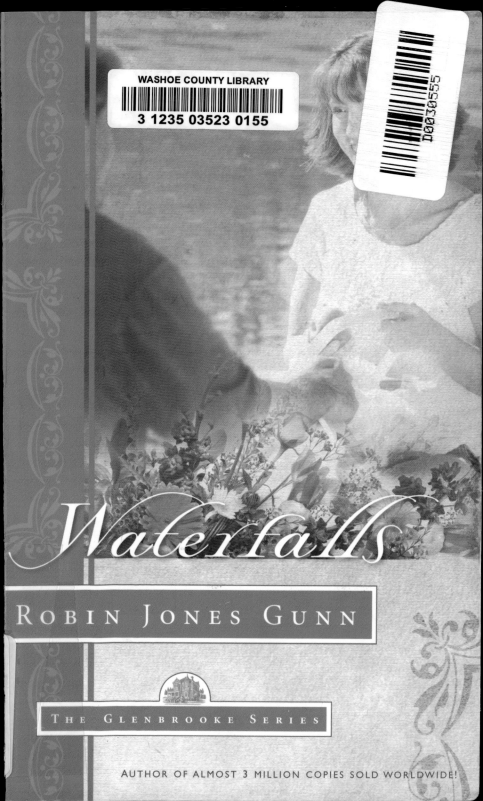

Waterfalls

ROBIN JONES GUNN

THE GLENBROOKE SERIES

AUTHOR OF ALMOST 3 MILLION COPIES SOLD WORLDWIDE!

"Years ago my daugh[...]n's stories and loving them, so I had t[...]did. Robin's characters are believable, and her stories have just the right blend of hope, broken hearts, disappointments, lighthearted fun, joy, and an eternal perspective. The Lord Jesus always plays a role, whether behind the scenes or in the thick of things. Robin lives the faith that's so evident in her books. She knows how to tell a story—and the stories she tells make an eternal difference."

RANDY ALCORN, AUTHOR OF *DEADLINE*

"When you read a Robin Gunn book, you know you're going to receive a tender lesson in what it means to belong to Christ—and you will be blessed for it."

FRANCINE RIVERS, AUTHOR OF *REDEEMING LOVE* AND
THE MARK OF THE LION SERIES

"Gratefully Robin's warmth, insight, and humor spill over from her heart onto the written page. She delights us with the well-woven fabric of a well-told tale and I'm certain Robin delights the Lord with her obvious passion for him."

PATSY CLAIRMONT, AUTHOR OF *GOD USES CRACKED POTS* AND
SPORTIN' A 'TUDE

"Robin Jones Gunn cares. She cares about her characters, she cares about her readers, and most of all, she cares about their mutual search for a life that pleases the Lord. Her novels are a delight to read—perfectly crafted, heartwarming, and fun. I'm always thrilled when one of Robin's books appears on the top of my to-be-read stack!"

LIZ CURTIS HIGGS, AUTHOR OF *MIXED SIGNALS*, *BOOKENDS*, AND *BAD GIRLS OF THE BIBLE*

"Robin Jones Gunn is one of those rare and wonderful writers who infuses her stories with bountiful doses of humor, wisdom, and warmth. Her books have touched and changed countless hearts and given a whole generation of readers a host of fictional characters who feel like dear friends!"

CAROLE GIFT PAGE, AUTHOR OF *HEARTLAND MEMORIES SERIES*

"Whenever I think of stories that touch the heart, I think of Robin Jones Gunn. They touch my heart and leave me wanting more. Reading a novel by Robin Jones Gunn is like spending time with a good friend…troubles are lighter and joys are deeper."

ALICE GRAY, AUTHOR OF *STORIES FOR THE HEART* BOOK COLLECTION

"Robin Jones Gunn writes from a heart of love. Her tender stories honor the Savior and speak truth to a world desperately eager to hear it."

ANGELA ELWELL HUNT, AUTHOR OF *THE TRUTH TELLER*

"Robin Gunn is a gifted and sincere storyteller who gets right to the heart of matters with her readers."

MELODY CARLSON, AUTHOR OF *HOMEWARD*

THE GLENBROOKE SERIES

TITLES IN THE GLENBROOKE SERIES

#1 *Secrets*
#2 *Whispers*
#3 *Echoes*
#4 *Sunsets*
#5 *Clouds*
#6 *Waterfalls*
#7 *Woodlands*
#8 *Wildflowers*

Waterfalls

ROBIN JONES GUNN

Multnomah® Publishers *Sisters, Oregon*

WATERFALLS
published by Multnomah Publishers, Inc.

© 1998 by Robin's Ink, LLC
International Standard Book Number: 1-59052-231-1

Cover design and images by Steve Gardner/His Image PixelWorks

Scripture quotations are from:
The Holy Bible, New International Version © 1973, 1984 by International Bible Society, used by permission of Zondervan Publishing House

The Holy Bible, New King James Version © 1984 by Thomas Nelson, Inc.

Printed in the United States of America

For information:
MULTNOMAH PUBLISHERS, INC.
601 N. LARCH ST.
SISTERS, OR 97759

Library of Congress Cataloging-in-Publication Data
Gunn, Robin Jones, 1955–
Waterfalls/by Robin Jones Gunn. p. cm. ISBN 1-57673-488-9 (paper)
1-59052-231-1
I. Title.   PS3557.U4866W36   1998   97–36524
        813'.54—dc21   CIP

06 07 08 09 10 — 11 10 9 8 7 6

To my dad,

Travis Garland Jones,
with all my heart.

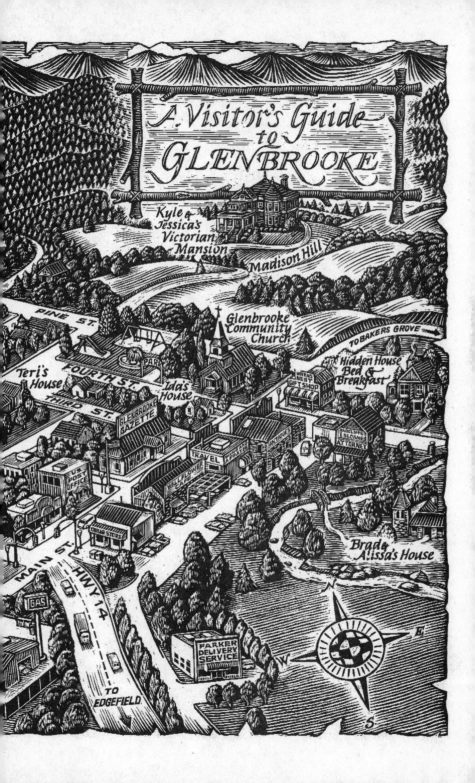

"Deep calls to deep in the roar of your waterfalls;
all your waves and breakers have swept over me."

eredith Graham ripped open the sample-sized pouch of Sweet Avocado Bliss facial mask and read the instructions aloud. "Apply generously to face and neck. Let dry for fifteen minutes or until mask begins to harden and crack. Rinse with warm water. Pat dry."

Gazing at her image in the guest-bathroom mirror, Meredith began to follow the instructions, using upward motions from her throat to her chin. She had heard once that all lotions and cleansers should be applied with upward motions as an act of defiance against gravity. Not that her twenty-four-year-old face was ready to wage war with gravity. Meredith just liked to think she had some control over her looks.

That's why she colored her hair. She had for years. One of her three older sisters, Shelly, had teased Meredith a few weeks ago, saying she was a recovering brunette. Shelly's husband, Jonathan, had added, "Yeah, she keeps re-covering the brunette roots."

Meredith didn't care. At this very moment, she had the alarm on her watch set for twenty-five minutes and wore a perky blue plastic cap over her short, soggy, dyed locks. Her face was now covered in a subtle shade of lime. And she was enjoying every minute of this royal treatment.

She raised her eyebrows and watched the lines forming on her forehead. It resembled the way her mother looked when she was worried, and Meredith didn't like that. To her, people who walked around with wrinkled, worried foreheads were people who had no imaginations.

Meredith tilted up her chin and checked on the gooey green lotion rapidly drying on her neck. She tucked the blue plastic bonnet behind her right ear and made a gruesome face in the mirror as the drying mask cracked across her cheeks. With her best cackle, Meri squinted her left eye and said, "I'll get you yet, my pretty!"

The country-western music floating from the portable radio came to an end on her third cackle, and Meredith listened closely. "It's 8:42 on this gorgeous first Saturday morning in May," the smooth voice of the female announcer said. "We're looking for a high today in Glenbrooke Valley of seventy-eight degrees. Lows tonight around sixty with some partially cloudy skies tomorrow morning. Highs tomorrow near seventy."

"Perfect," Meri muttered, her lips beginning to tighten at the corners. "I'm wearing shorts."

The radio began to blare out a song with repetitious lyrics about a girl, a pickup truck, and a dog. Meredith flipped the "off" switch and rummaged in her cosmetics bag for her travel-sized toothpaste and soap. Not that she needed to use her own. Jessica and Kyle had provided plenty of everything for the guests who were staying at their restored Victorian home for the big weekend event.

The room assigned to Meredith was the Patchwork Bedroom. Some of the women of Glenbrooke had made the patchwork quilt that graced the large brass bed. A framed square of patchwork fabric over the bed was part of a quilt made by a pioneer woman who had migrated west on the Oregon Trail more than 150 years ago. Jessica had been given the treasured piece by the pioneer's great-great-granddaughter.

This turret room was originally a storage place until Jessica transformed it into another guest room. Kyle had recently built on this small adjacent bathroom where Meredith stood, checking the timer on her watch. Four more minutes until she could hop into the shower.

The big kickoff at the camp wasn't until noon, but Meredith had promised her sister Shelly she would show up early to help with all the preparations. Shelly and her childhood sweetheart, Jonathan, had married in Seattle a year ago this weekend. They moved to Glenbrooke, where they worked side by side to develop a conference center in the woods. Kyle and Jessica owned the property and had had the original vision for the camp. About six months ago, in a broad stroke of generosity and trust, Kyle and Jess turned the whole project over to Jonathan and Shelly. And today was the grand opening of Heather Creek Conference Center.

Meredith squirted some toothpaste onto her toothbrush and made another wild Martian grin in the mirror. As the sample packet had promised, her face felt cracked. Time to hop into the shower.

Right before she turned on the water, Meredith realized she didn't have her clothes in the bathroom because she had been trying to decide what to wear. She had made the bed all sweet and tidy, almost as if she were afraid her mother would come in to check on her and scold her if it wasn't made yet. Then

Meredith had tucked her luggage neatly in the corner of the room and decided that if Mom did come in for a room check, she would have nothing to criticize.

Meredith stuck the toothbrush in her mouth and began to scrub her teeth, grinning at her own gruesome appearance in the mirror. The blue-tinted "skull cap," lime green cracked face, and foam now dripping from the corner of her mouth added up to quite a sight. If Mom checked on Meredith now, she would be in for a life-altering shock.

Opening the bathroom door, Meredith stepped into the guest room and headed for her suitcases in the corner. The cooler air of the bedroom chilled her legs under her big blue nightshirt as her bare feet padded across the room. She unzipped the bag with both hands, sucking on the toothbrush in her mouth, and pulled out her underwear, a white cotton shirt, and a pair of shorts.

Rising with her arms full, Meredith was starting back to the bathroom when she froze in place. She dropped her shorts and unwillingly swallowed the toothpaste foam in her mouth. She couldn't move. She couldn't scream. All she could do was stare.

A man was asleep on her bed. He had on all his clothes—even his shoes—and he looked as if he had dropped on the bed in a dead faint with his arms straight out to the sides and his palms up.

The man opened his eyes, then closed them. Suddenly his large brown eyes sprung open again. He shot straight up in bed. He stared at Meredith and let out a wild yelp that sounded like an animal caught in a trap.

Meredith screamed, too.

"Who are you?" he yelled.

"Who are you?" she yelled back, grasping her toothbrush like a dagger.

"What are you doing in my room?" The poor guy's face looked terrified.

Meredith realized her face looked, well…"This is my room!" she shouted. "What are you doing in my bed?"

In a confused stupor, the man tumbled from the bed and frantically grabbed his garment bag by the door. With one last bewildered and horrified glance at Meredith, the Avocado Alien, the tall, sunny blond male scrambled out the door.

For dramatic effect she slammed the door and locked it with a snap. She stood still, her back to the door, listening. Waiting. Her heart pounding. Wondering if anyone had heard them or if he would come back. She scanned the room for any more of his belongings. It appeared he had taken everything.

As soon as her pulse slowed down, she moved away from the door and gathered up her strewn articles of clothing. *I can't believe that just happened! I probably shouldn't have yelled at the poor guy. He looked awfully confused. What am I saying? He invaded my privacy! I should have thrown something at him.*

Marching into the bathroom, Meredith turned on the shower with a twist of the handle. Her hands were still shaking. *It really was my fault. I should have locked the door. But how could he have gotten the wrong room? And why would he be asleep at nine in the morning?*

Meri adjusted the shower curtain so the water wouldn't drip on the tile floor. *What if he was waiting for me? Maybe he does landscaping around here, and he heard that a lovely young princess was staying in the corner turret, and he wanted to meet me so…*

Meredith looked at herself in the mirror, and the fanciful fairy tale vanished with a poof. She smiled. Then she let loose her silvery, wind-chime laughter, spilling it all over the bathroom floor. "Look at you, Meri Jane Graham. You are a fright to behold! You scared that poor guy to death."

She slipped into the warm shower still laughing. It felt great to rinse out the cold, smelly hair coloring and to liberate her cracked face.

He didn't exactly look like a landscaper. Meredith thought about the intruder's hair. The color was too nice to be natural, she decided. The sun streaks and flecks of gold couldn't have gotten that way this early in the year without a little help from a peroxide bottle. Unless he lived someplace where the sun had already been working its mischief. He did seem pretty tan. She tried to remember what he had on. Jeans. Sloppy, camel-colored loafers with no socks—she remembered that part of his out-fit. And a short-sleeved cotton shirt with an island print. She liked the shirt. Maybe he lived in Hawaii. Or the Bahamas. Jonathan's parents lived in the Bahamas. Maybe this guy had come from the Bahamas with Jonathan's parents.

Wrapping a towel around her hair and stepping out of the shower, Meredith realized something painfully inevitable. She would see this man again today. He was obviously friends with Kyle and Jessica; otherwise he wouldn't be here. And he most likely was friends with Shelly and Jonathan or he wouldn't be here this weekend. He was possibly even a relative on Jonathan's side. She didn't remember seeing him at the wedding, but then if he was a lifeguard in the Bahamas, maybe he wasn't able to take the time off from the resort.

No, not a lifeguard. That would be too teenish for this man. He had a certain polished look, even in his frenzy. The resort golf pro. Yeah, that was it. He was a golf pro at a remote island resort, and he used to work for the CIA.

Meredith stopped drying her legs and wondered why that sounded familiar. She was quite comfortable with the way her imagination kept her endlessly entertained with story lines. They were usually far-fetched, fantastic tales loosely based on all the plots she consumed daily in her job as an acquisitions editor. For a year and a half she had filled her noodle with the creativity of hundreds, maybe thousands, of writers who had pitched to her their best ideas for children's books. The huge amount of input had taken its toll, and she was experiencing her first occupational hazard. She was never alone. A story line was always within her grasp to amuse her or confuse her. In this case, it confused her.

But this wasn't a children's story. This was a plot from a movie. She knew this plot. The CIA agent tries to get back his normal life; so he hides on some ritzy island at a French resort where he is hired as a golf pro. Then that new actress…what's her name?…the blond one with the thin lips, comes to the resort and…

That's it—Falcon Pointe! *I loved that movie! The Goldilocks guy in my bed looks like the actor in that movie. It was the shirt. The CIA guy in the movie always wore shirts like that.*

Meri took the towel off her head and checked her roots in the mirror. Not a pinch of brown showed through.

Recovering brunette, am I? Well, no one needs to know. Especially when my hair turns out this good. I have to remember this shade. Honey cream. I'm buying this one again.

Meri gave her face a careful examination. The mask didn't appear to have helped or harmed. Maybe that was the best anyone could ask from an experiment.

She began to comb out her hair and had a sudden pleasant realization. The mystery man might not recognize her. They would inevitably see each other again, but she might be introduced to him, and he wouldn't even know she had been the screaming creature under the blue bonnet. It was possible. Maybe. Hopefully. At least in her imagination.

He was pretty good looking, for a man who was in the middle of a freak-out. Meredith dressed and then coaxed her dried hair into place with a part on the side. She smoothed the sleek ends under with a curling iron and smiled at the results. She loved rare days like this when her hair came out perfect. The makeup was a snap. A little brown eyeliner, some mascara, a quick swirl of the lipstick tube, and she was ready. All she needed was her hiking boots and socks, and she was on her way to Heather Creek Conference Center.

Unless, of course, she ran into some poor, distraught houseguest wandering the hallways. Some tall, brown-eyed male in a tropical-print shirt who had a frightening story to tell about a creature from the green lagoon who had so rudely disrupted his nap. Then she would stop to listen sympathetically and suggest a cup of coffee to chase the nightmarish thoughts away.

Meredith smiled to herself. It wasn't every day she got to be around men who reminded her of movie stars. And she had a thing for movie stars. It started in elementary school when she used to sneak a peek at her friends' movie-star magazines. She had used her hard-earned allowance to buy posters from her friends, and then she had had to hide them from her father, the respected minister, who wouldn't approve of such items being in the house.

She loved movies, too. Now that she lived alone and worked out of her home office, Meri took herself to the movies at least once a week to get out of the house. She remembered how much she had liked *Falcon Pointe* when she saw it four months ago. The star magazines at the grocery-store checkout line had touted the new, unknown actor in that movie as "the next Tom Cruise." What was his name?

Meri had just finished lacing her boots when someone knocked on the door. *Come back to apologize, have you? Apology accepted. Now how about that cup of coffee?*

"Who is it?" she called out sweetly before unlocking the door.

"Meredith? It's your mother."

Meredith rolled her eyes as she unlocked the door. As she grasped the knob and was about to open the door, the name of the actor leaped before her. She yanked open the door and excitedly spouted to her mother, "Jacob Wilde! That's his name! The guy in my bed was Jacob Wilde!"

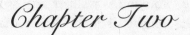

Chapter Two

I'm not even going to ask," Meredith's mother said, holding up a hand as a gesture for silence. "I don't want to know what you're talking about."

The creases in Mom's forehead were not attractive. Meredith tried to swallow her giggle. "I'm not saying it *was* Jacob Wilde; I'm just saying he *looked like* Jacob Wilde. The guy in my room, I mean."

When her mom didn't respond, Meri added calmly, "It was funny, that's all. This guy was in my bed, and he looked like Jacob Wilde from the movie *Falcon Pointe*. Did you ever see that movie?"

What am I saying? Of course she never saw that movie.

"Never mind," Meredith said in a little-girl voice. It seemed the best way to get Mom to erase Meredith's ramblings.

"I came up to tell you that your father and I are ready to go over to the camp, in case you want a ride," Mom said.

"Sure. I'm ready," Meredith said, following her mom out

into the hall. The two women walked side by side in silence. Ellen Graham was only four inches taller than Meri, but it could have been forty inches the way Meri felt right now. Things between the two of them had become unusually tense in the last six months, and Meredith's only way of coping was to play the part of the ditzy blond baby girl so Mom would ignore her. Ever since Shelly had married and Meri's oldest sister, Megan, had moved to Brazil with her husband and two daughters, Meredith felt she had become her mother's project. Meri had worked hard for her independence, but now she was the only daughter close enough to experience what she called a drive-by whenever Mom felt the need to riddle one of her daughters with questions or to re-mark her old turf.

Meri had hoped this trip to Glenbrooke would help them smooth out some of the tension. Maybe by sharing together in Shelly's success, they would be able to go back to the way things had been for the past five years. So far it didn't seem to be working.

"Did you have breakfast?" Mom asked.

"No, but that's okay. I'm not hungry. We'll be eating all day at the conference center, I'm sure."

"Jessica has a wonderful buffet set up," Mom said as they went down the winding staircase in step with each other. "You should eat a little something before we go."

"I will," Meri promised, knowing that Mom would watch to make sure she did.

"Ready, ladies?" Meri's dad stood at the bottom of the stairs in his new slacks and plaid shirt. Mom had insisted he wear something new, and they had stopped at Mervyn's on their drive down the day before.

Funny, Meri thought, *Dad looks more natural in his clergyman's collar than he does in these sports clothes.*

He was balding, brown-eyed, and had a tender smile. His appearance fit his role of minister, which he had ably filled for more than thirty years. Meredith liked her dad.

"We're ready," Meredith answered.

"After you greet your hostess and have some breakfast," Mom said in a low voice.

Meredith knew the direction this day was going, and she didn't want to go there with her mother. "You know what?" she said. "Why don't you two go on over to the conference center, and I'll come over with Kyle and Jessica."

"All right. Would you like me to drive, Perry?" Mom said.

"No, dear. I'll drive."

"See you," Meri said as her parents exited the grand entry-way.

"Yes, in twenty minutes, then," Mom called over her shoulder.

Twenty minutes? Where did that come from? I never said anything about twenty minutes. She has to have everything so neat and defined. She's driving me crazy!

Meredith drew in a fresh breath of patience as the door closed behind her parents, and she headed for the kitchen. Nothing, not even her controlling mother, could ruin her terrific-hair day. There was sunshine to be had and celebrating to partake of.

"Good morning!" Meredith greeted Jessica, who stood at the counter of the spacious, modern gourmet kitchen. "How are you feeling?"

"Pretty good, actually," Jessica replied. She was a tender-hearted woman with fair skin, a regal look about her, and a half-moon-shaped scar on her upper lip. She was also four months pregnant. Even though her frame didn't yet appear pregnant, Meredith knew Jessica felt heavy. She hadn't lost weight after her son, Travis, had been born almost a year and a half ago. Jessica had experienced morning sickness much longer this pregnancy and was just beginning to get over it.

"How did you sleep?" Jessica asked, motioning to the pitcher of orange juice before her.

Meredith poured herself a large glass and said, "I slept well, but…" She took a long sip of juice and watched Jessica lean forward slightly to hear the rest of Meredith's sentence.

"But I have something to ask you."

"Anything," Jessica said.

Meredith knew Jessica would want to do whatever she could to make Meri feel comfortable. She also knew Jessica was all sweetness and very little sauciness, which had caused misunderstandings in their friendship when Meri had tried to tease Jess about something but Jess didn't get it.

The two women had met when Jessica sent a proposal for a series of children's books to Meri's publishing house. Meri had traveled to Glenbrooke to offer Jessica a book contract. However, little Travis decided to enter the world that very same day, and since then, Jessica had discovered she didn't have the time she thought she would to pursue her interest in writing. The project was on hold indefinitely. But the friendship between the two of them had continued to blossom.

Keeping her friend's tender spirit in mind, Meredith chose not to say, "Thank you, Jessica, for sending a man to my room this morning."

"This is really funny," Meredith began. "You're going to laugh when you hear what happened. Some guy thought my room was his room, and he came in and…well, I think I really scared him off."

"Was that you screaming?" Jessica asked. "Kyle told me he heard something upstairs a little while ago. Are you okay?"

"Oh, of course. Terrific. Fine. I'm okay. I think he may be

a little shocked because I had this stuff—"

Before Meredith could finish, Kyle came dashing into the kitchen, zooming one-and-a-half-year-old Travis around like an airplane and making all the appropriate noises. Blond-haired, red-cheeked, squealing Travis was enjoying every second of the ride.

"Hey, good morning," Kyle said when he noticed Meredith. "We're on our way out the door. I saw your parents leave a little while ago. Would you like to ride over with us?"

"Sure. Is there anyone else going with you?" Meredith asked coyly.

"I think everyone else is already there, aren't they?" Kyle looked at his wife and tucked Travis under his arm like a sack of potatoes. Meredith liked Kyle. Everyone liked Kyle. He was the nice master of the castle. A solidly built, dark-haired paramedic whose energy seemed to measure up to his abundance of projects, he was always building something or initiating some new vision. He and Jessica had a storybook look about them, the handsome prince and the fair damsel.

Meredith had once asked Kyle if he had any brothers. He had two, but they were both married. One of them, Kenton, lived in Glenbrooke with his wife, Lauren. He owned and ran the local newspaper, and Lauren had replaced Jessica as the English teacher at the small Glenbrooke High School.

"No one is still here at the house, then?" Meredith ventured.

Jessica and Kyle looked at each other.

"I think everyone has already gone," Jessica said.

Just then they heard water running in the pipes overhead, indicating that someone had turned on a faucet.

"Oh yeah," Kyle said, readjusting the squirming, fussing Travis onto his shoulders. Travis grabbed his daddy's dark hair with both fists and kicked at Kyle's arms with his little cowboy boots as if trying to persuade his "daddy horsie" to giddy up. "I forgot about our most honorable Mr. Wartman."

Meri's hopes plummeted. Not that she truly expected the mystery man to be Jacob Wilde, the actor. But how could she weave a successful fairy tale about someone named Mr. Wartman?

"Oh, did he get here this morning?" Jessica said. "I didn't hear him come in."

"He pulled in about eight-thirty. The poor guy is fried," Kyle said. "He was on a red-eye from New York, and his flight back to L.A. goes out of Eugene at something like four o'clock this afternoon."

"He must be exhausted," Jessica said.

"I told him to crash in the room at the end of the hall. I thought that would be the quietest room."

"At the right end of the hall or the left?" Jessica asked.

"Right, of course. Meri's in the Patchwork Room." Kyle began to bounce up and down slightly to keep Travis entertained. "Not so tight, buddy," he said, trying to loosen Travis's grip on his hair.

"I think he went into the wrong room," Jessica said, glancing over at Meredith and lifting her eyebrows slightly. "He must have thought you meant the room at the end of the hall on the left because Meri had a little visitor."

"Really?" Kyle said with a mischievous grin. "I thought Meri had a little lamb."

"You are such a comedian," Meri said. "But don't worry about it. I think Mr. Wartman nearly had a little cow, so that makes us even all around."

Kyle chuckled. "We better get out of here, then, before a barnyard brawl breaks out between all these sheep and cows."

"Moo," Travis piped up from his princely perch.

"That's right, honey," Jessica said with pride. "A cow says 'moo.'"

"We're out of here," Kyle said. "You ready, Jess?"

"Sure. Do you have the diaper bag?"

"You mean Trav's duffel bag? Yep, it's by the front door."

"Duffel bag," Jessica repeated, shaking her head and looking toward the ceiling. "Oh, Lord, please let this next baby be a girl so we don't have to name every piece of baby gear something masculine. Amen."

"Amen," Meri repeated, siding with Jess.

"It'll be a boy," Kyle said soundly. "Gordon and Teri had two boys. We have to keep up with the Allistars."

"It could be a girl," Jessica said calmly as she placed some fruit and muffins in a wicker picnic hamper. "I'll leave a quick note here on the counter and then meet you guys at the truck."

Meri followed Kyle out the back door and around the house to where Kyle's pickup was parked. She noticed a shiny black Mustang convertible parked on the side.

Mr. Wartman's, no doubt. Flashy sort of fellow. I wonder what he's doing here?

"There you go, big guy," Kyle said, strapping Travis into his car seat. Meri wondered if she should crawl into the after-cab now or wait until Jessica arrived. Travis fussed and arched his back as the seat belt came over his shoulders. "He hates this thing," Kyle said.

"It's okay, Travis," Meri said. She slipped onto the front seat next to him and left the door open. Picking up a squishy toy, Meredith said in a squeaky voice, "Let's have a puppet show. Say hi to Mr. Duck. Quack, quack, quack." Meredith made the bright yellow fellow dance for Travis.

"I forgot the duffel bag," Kyle said. "I'll be right back." He took off jogging to the house, and Meri assigned herself the task of keeping Travis entertained.

"One day Wally the star was floating in the sky so, so high…" Meredith pulled the soft star figurine up, and Travis followed it with his eyes. "And Wally said to himself, 'I'd like to go down there and see what it's like on earth.' So, do you know what Wally did?"

Travis didn't respond to the question, but he stopped whimpering.

"Wally tumbled down, down to the earth, and there he met Mr. Duck. 'Hello, Mr. Duck. I'm Wally. Do you want to play?'

"'Why, yes, I do. Quack quack,' said Mr. Duck."

Meredith had both the toys merrily dancing now. Travis was enthralled.

She sang a silly impromptu song in a little voice, and the corners of Travis's mouth began to curl up. "'Yay, yay, yay, we dance all day! We're the happy little friends, and we like to play. Yay, yay, yay, we play all day!'

"The two friends danced and danced all day long, and then do you know what happened?"

Travis looked away from her, out at the driveway. Meredith thought fast, trying to get his attention. "Then Wally the star and Mr. Duck got so hot from all their dancing, they decided to go for a swim. With a great big splash, they dove into the water." To demonstrate the dive, Meredith hopped off the seat and "dove" to the truck cab's floor. She had Travis's attention again.

"The water felt so good that Wally the star said, 'I think I would like to live here all the time. I'm going to stay here and never go back up to the sky.' He settled right into the sand all nice and comfy." Meri demonstrated by wiggling her backside into the cramped space.

"Mr. Duck was swimming away on top of the water, happy as can be, and he said, 'Where did Wally go? Where did Wally go?'"

Travis stuck the first two fingers of his left hand into his mouth and with his right finger pointed down to where Meri held the star on the floor. He jabbered some baby words as if he were telling Mr. Duck where to find his old friend Wally.

"Mr. Duck stuck his face in the water, and in a very wet and wobbly voice called out, 'W-a-l-l-y!'" Even Meri was surprised at how funny her underwater "Wally" cry sounded. She kept up the silly voice.

"'I'm here, Mr. Duck. I like it here. This is where I'll stay,' said Wally. 'I won't be a star anymore. I'll be a starfish at the bottom of the sea.' 'Then I will come and visit you every day,' said Mr. Duck." Meredith held the duck so that his nose was down in the "water" and his tail was straight up.

"And that is why whenever you see a duck sticking his head into the water, you know he's paying his daily visit to Wally the starfish." Meredith peeked at her audience from her cramped position. Travis wasn't looking at her. He was looking out the passenger door.

Meri followed his gaze, and there, by the open door, stood the mysterious, brown-eyed Mr. Wartman, with a half-grin on his handsome face.

Chapter Three

The uninvited guest slowly applauded Meredith's story. She struggled to unwedge herself from the floor of the cab.

"Only one problem," the man said. "Starfish live in salt water, and ducks swim in fresh water."

"It's only a story," Meredith protested, one arm grabbing the seat and the other one pushing against the underside of the dashboard. Her right leg had fallen asleep.

"Nevertheless, integrity of story is the crucial element in all quality fiction," he said.

Meredith raised her eyebrows and took a good look at this guy. "Gabriel Kalen," she said slowly. "Gabriel Kalen said that in his book, *The Art of Story.* I quote him all the time in my workshops."

Now Mr. Wartman's eyebrows arched with apparent interest.

Meredith was unstuck enough to pull her body out of the cramped space. She raised herself onto the seat without the slightest bit of grace and wondered if this man had figured out yet that she was the nightmarish, avocado-faced vision that had greeted him less than an hour earlier. If he did know, he wasn't letting on.

She calmly brushed back her hair and straightened herself with as much dignity as possible. Meredith handed Wally-the-star-turned-starfish to Travis. He held the soft figure to his cheek and sucked on his fingers.

"Have you met Gabe?" Mr. Wartman inquired.

"Gabe?" Meredith echoed.

"Gabriel Kalen."

"No," Meredith said. She wasn't sure where to look, at Travis or at this fine example of God's creation who was standing only a few feet away.

Kyle and Jessica came down the front steps of the house hand in hand. Jessica held a picnic basket, while Kyle had slung the duffel bag over his shoulder. Meredith knew her intriguing yet embarrassing encounter with this man was about to end.

"Have you?" she asked quickly, tucking her hair behind her ear and casting her ocean green glance at him. "Have you met Gabriel Kalen?"

"Yes," he said, resting his arm on the rim above the door and leaning forward out of the sunshine. He took in a full view of Meredith, and she was uncomfortably aware of how intensely he was studying her. Would he figure out who she was? Had he already?

"Everybody ready?" Kyle called out when he was a few feet away from the truck. "Did you two meet?"

"Daddy!" Travis cried out, pulling his fingers from his mouth. "Daddy!"

"I'm here, big guy," Kyle said, tossing the duffel bag, which looked exactly like a diaper bag, onto the backseat. "You ready to go?"

"I'm heading over to the conference center now, too," Mr. Wartman said. "Would one of you like to ride with me?"

"Why don't you take Meredith with you?" Jessica suggested. "I wanted to talk with Kyle on the way over."

"Meredith," he repeated slowly as if he had just figured out the missing word in a long crossword puzzle. "Would you like to ride with me, Meredith?"

Knowing she couldn't refuse, she slid out of the cab and silently followed him to his black convertible. Her heart was pounding but not too much. She felt foolish that he had seen her on the floor of the truck but not too foolish.

In the past, this would have been a Barbie dream come true, a perfect moment to launch into a flirting campaign. But her sister had drilled into her that flirting was not the best way to get a man's attention. Meredith had come to realize it wasn't the most forthright, honest way to get to know someone. Mentally, she agreed with all these concepts.

Still…all Meri's clever lines gathered in a row in her head and stood at attention. She reviewed the troops and selected the finest. If she were to flirt, she would employ these lines. They would slide in undetected, hit their mark, and not leave a trace of their presence behind. The poor, unsuspecting Mr. Wartman would never know what hit him. But she must not release any of those flirty missiles. She must not.

He opened the door for her, and she slid in gracefully. The sun had been baking the leather seat, and the instant Meredith's flesh touched it she let out an unplanned, "Yeouch!" She quickly pressed her lips together to silence them. That was definitely not one of the chosen phrases. Who let that renegade loose?

"You okay?"

"Hot seat," she said with a sheepish grin. She pulled her sunglasses from her shirt pocket and rolled up her white sleeves.

Elegant, that's the look you're after here. Grace Kelly in hiking boots. Pay no attention to the third-degree burns on the back side of your thighs. You are as calm and cool as a summer breeze.

Meredith reviewed what she knew about this man as he pulled a pair of sunglasses from the visor. How did he know about the playwright Gabriel Kalen? Kalen had created a screenplay based on one of the classics for which G. H. Terrison Publishing held the rights. That was before Meredith began working for them, but the video sales had hit four million copies in the first year and put G. H. Terrison on the map with their quality children's products.

She wanted to pepper this mysterious Mr. Wartman with questions but knew it was best to let him go first. No sense scaring him off. She would keep a poker face and let him play the first card.

He came to the end of the driveway, slowly easing over the bump and said, "The conference center is to the left, isn't it?"

"Yes," Meredith said. "Turn left here."

He eased onto the uncrowded main road. They drove under the lacy shadows of the great cedars and hemlocks that lined this stretch of country road.

"Sorry about the, ah, mix-up in your room this morning. My mistake."

"Oh," Meredith said, glancing at him with controlled calm. *So he knows. He's being awfully gallant about this.* "I'm sorry I frightened you."

He smiled, keeping his eyes straight ahead on the road.

Meredith couldn't contain herself anymore. Their absurd first encounter was just too funny. She tossed her head back and released her contagious laughter. It filled the silent space between them like a hundred iridescent soap bubbles, each one floating gleefully before popping with a fizz.

He laughed with her. "You're Shelly's sister, aren't you?" he asked after each of the invisible giggle bubbles had disappeared.

"Yes." She decided to play one of her cards. "And you are…?"

He didn't fill in the blank with a proper introduction. Instead, he glanced at her, then back at the road, then at her, and again at the road. "What do you know about me?" he asked.

"You sleep with your shoes on," she said quickly. "Like a horse."

He laughed again, unaided by her infectious giggle. "What else?"

"Kyle called you Mr. Wartman."

"Did he? Mr. Wartman, huh?"

"Yep. And that's it, Mr. Wartman. That's all I know. Oh, except you flew in from New York last night."

"And boy, are my arms tired," he quipped.

Now Meredith laughed on cue.

He looked at her, then back at the road, then back at her.

"What?" Meredith felt unnerved by his glances. She checked all her buttons.

With another glance he raised an eyebrow and said, "You really don't know who I am, do you?"

"Should I?"

"I'm your sister's old neighbor," he said smoothly.

"Ah, the little old neighbor from Pasadena," said Meri. She invisibly gave herself one "witty" point.

"I remember seeing pictures of you. But you seemed much younger."

"All Shelly had was our baby pictures, right?"

"There was one of you all in black," he said. "Your hair was different. You were holding a musical instrument, and you were sitting next to an older gentleman."

"That was taken about four years ago. The instrument was a flute."

"Do you still play?"

"Only for fun. That picture was taken at my last recital."

Then, because there was a pause, she added for flair, "The older gentleman in the picture was my first husband."

"Really?"

"No." Meredith laughed. *He's gullible. This is good.* "He was my high school band instructor. I don't know why Shelly likes that picture."

Meredith just realized she had laid down nearly all her cards and this mystery man sat there still holding almost a full hand. "You're not Brad, are you?" Meri asked. She remembered hearing about Shelly's neighbor Brad because he had married Shelly's former roommate, Alissa, a few months ago. Shelly was in the wedding.

"No, I'm not Brad."

"You're the other guy."

"I'm the other guy."

Meredith flew through her memory files trying to remember something, anything, about Shelly's old neighbors. Nothing came to mind. No names, no bits of information. He seemed to be able to read the "vacant" sign across her forehead.

"I can see Shelly had a lot to say about me."

An uncomfortable wave washed over Meredith. Had Shelly dated this guy, and had it been a bad experience? It would feel awfully strange to show up at Shelly's with one of her old boyfriends, especially if Meri didn't even know his name. Apparently, Meredith Jane Graham, the queen of cat-and-mouse games, had met her match.

"Turn left at the next road," Meri said, suddenly paying attention to where they were. "It's about a mile and a half from here."

He turned. The car hummed along. The wind blew through her hair. He smiled a straightforward, closed-lipped smile and said nothing.

Meredith knew they were almost there. She had to play the last of her cards since he was refusing to lay down any of his. "So, do you want me to go around calling you Mr. Wartman all day?"

He glanced at her again and said, "You can call me 'J.'"

"Jay," she repeated.

He nodded. "Is this the entrance? Nice sign."

Meredith was filing the info. *Jay Wartman. What a horrible name. If I were this guy, I would have changed it long ago.*

"Have you been to the waterfall here?" he asked.

"Several times," Meri said. "It's beautiful. Jonathan has transformed the whole area so the waterfall feeds into a small lake. They even have a few boats."

"Really? How's the lighting?"

"The lighting?"

"Yes. Is there a lot of open space over the lake, or does most of the sunlight come through the trees?"

Meri laughed. "I've never noticed."

He parked the car and unplugged the cell phone that had been recharging off the cigarette lighter.

Meredith didn't know if she should open her door and go her own way or wait around for Jay to say something. To her surprise he reached over and carefully removed something from her hair. He showed her the dead bug he had extracted from her tousled, silky locks.

"The disadvantage of riding in a convertible," Jay said.

"It was a greater disadvantage to that fellow than it was to me," Meredith said.

Jay smiled and let a low chuckle rumble from his broad chest. "Do you need to get up to the conference center right away?" he asked. "Or do you have time to show me the way to the waterfall?"

Now Meredith felt they were getting somewhere. "Sure. Let's go before my sister realizes I'm here and hands me one of her to-do lists."

"Does she still make people take off their shoes before they come into the house? She was fastidious about that in Pasadena."

"Not so much anymore," Meredith said. "She and Jonathan live in a log cabin here on the property, and it's impossible to keep out the dirt. Especially with Bob Two."

"Bob Two?" Jay asked, tucking his keys into his jeans pocket.

"He's their dog. A pathetic cocker spaniel."

"You don't like dogs?"

Meredith shook her head. "Too slobbery. Too hairy. Too hyper. Do you like them?"

Jay paused. "No, too eager."

Slow down, Meri! You're going to spook him with questions that appear to be fishing for common interests. Let him speak. Play it cool. Don't give out too much information. Whatever you do, don't act too eager.

Jay opened his door and popped up the trunk. Meredith opened her own door. She walked around to the back of his car and peered into the trunk. Several black luggage bags were neatly lodged in the space. Jay pulled out a smaller bag and slung it over his shoulder.

Just then Jessica and Kyle pulled up and parked the truck. Kyle walked around to open Jess's door and then unstrapped Travis.

Jessica came toward them with the wicker picnic basket slung over her arm. "Do you know how to get to the waterfall?" she asked Jay.

"Meredith has agreed to act as tour guide," he said.

"Why don't you guys take this with you?" Jessica said, handing them the basket. "It's just the leftover fruit and muffins from breakfast. I don't think either of you had time to eat. There are some great picnic spots near the waterfall."

"Thanks," Meri said, accepting the outstretched offering. "Tell Shelly I'll be up to the lodge in a bit."

Jessica smiled. The scar curled up on her top lip. "Take your time," she said. "Moments at the waterfall should not be rushed."

Chapter Four

*M*eredith and Jay took off down the wooded trail that led to the waterfall. He offered to carry the basket for her, but Meredith said it was no problem. He had his arms full with all his gear, and she could certainly manage a wicker basket.

"Are you planning to take pictures?" she asked as their shoes smashed down the damp carpet of the forest floor. She guessed he was carrying a camera bag.

"Yes," he said. He stopped at the fork in the trail and pulled a light sensor from his bag of tricks.

"The waterfall is to the right," Meredith said.

Jay looked up through the tall trees and seemed to be listening to the distant rumbling of the falls. He looked pleased, as if he were shopping for something special and had found it.

Meredith listened. A chorus of birds trilled their morning glories in the treetops. A chattering creature who was too fast for Meredith to track, darted through the foliage.

"It's pretty here," Meredith said.

"It's perfect," he murmured, still lost in his apparent lighting calculations. "How much does it rain in June?"

"In June? I don't know." Meredith laughed. Her sweet, cheery laughter floated easily through the forest air.

Jay turned to look at her. He smiled.

He likes my laugh. This is a good sign.

"You don't live here, do you?" he asked.

"No."

It was her turn to withhold information. If he wanted to know where she lived, he could ask. But he didn't.

"You say the waterfall is to the right?"

"Yes," Meri said. She noticed that the sun was shining through the branches and reflecting on his hair. He had gorgeous thick hair, a perfect warm shade of sunny golden blond. Maybe she would highlight her hair that way. Of course, she would have to break down and pay someone at a salon to do it if she wanted it to come out right.

Could I be serious about a man who goes to a salon to have his hair colored? Meredith shrugged as they headed down the trail. *I don't see why not. We could make appointments at the same time and go out to lunch afterward. I wonder if he goes to a tanning salon, too…. And what about the gym? He must work out. Look at those shoulders.*

They stopped again, and Jay pulled out his photographer's light sensor.

Man, between the gym, the hair salon, and the tanning booth, when would a guy like this have time to go out with anyone? I wonder if he is dating someone now.

"Is it much farther?" he asked.

"Not much."

They came to the end of the trail, and he stopped abruptly. Meredith had to admit it was a breathtaking scene. The waterfall was not much more than ten feet high, but it spilled into an idyllic small lake that was surrounded by huge ferns and dark rocks. The lake looked different than it had when Meri first saw it. Jonathan had engineered a major improvement by moving all the boulders out of the lake and expanding the sides so it was almost twice the size it had been originally. An old rowboat, tied to a stake near their feet, bobbed and swayed calmly in the sweet morning sun.

"Perfect," Jay muttered. He scrambled to pull his camera from the bag. Standing back, he took a long shot, then zoomed the lens in for a close-up of the waterfall.

Lost in his project, Jay began to walk around the lake as if Meri weren't even there.

She looked for a place to set down the wicker basket, and then, because the boat was so close, she decided to sit in it instead of on the muddy ground. With basket in tow, she stepped carefully into the boat and sat on the backseat.

An edge of the cloth was hanging from the basket. When Meredith peeked inside, she found it was a woven tablecloth. Jessica had packed grapes, strawberries, tangerines, and lemon poppy-seed muffins. Meredith pulled out the cloth, the plates, fruit, and two small bottles of cranberry juice. It was almost as if Jessica had packed this picnic with Meredith and Jay in mind. It made Meredith wonder.

She busily set up the breakfast feast inside the boat. With careful glances every so often, Meredith traced Jay's path around the lake. He seemed to be looking for a way to get behind the waterfall. Meredith knew it wasn't possible without getting soaked. Too many large rocks rested in the side of the lake's bank directly behind the waterfall. Jay seemed to figure this out without drenching himself.

I wonder what the fascination is with this waterfall. He doesn't look as much like a movie star as I first thought. The actor from Falcon Pointe *was taller.*

Then, as if he had taken his final measurement, Jay turned his attention to Meredith. From across the lake, he directed his camera toward her and held it still for a moment. She didn't know if he took her picture or not. The waterfall was too noisy to hear the sound of a shutter click. Nevertheless, she didn't move when he focused on her. She was a natural in front of the camera and felt at ease stretched out in the sun at the back of the boat.

Go ahead. Take a picture. It has to be better than the one you saw of me at Shelly's old apartment. What does this mean, Camera Man? Are you intrigued by me? You know I'm intrigued by you, don't you?

Jay hiked back to where she lounged in the docked boat. Tucking his camera into the bag, he made one last light check and then put away his gear. He swung the bag into the boat and followed in a lanky lurch.

"Whoa!" Meredith said, reaching for the precarious feast as it swayed. "Don't rock the boat, baby."

"What's for breakfast?" Jay asked, casually making himself comfortable across from Meredith in the swaying craft.

"Good stuff," she said, letting go of the plates she had been protecting.

Jay picked up a cluster of grapes and began to pop them into his mouth. "Alissa was right," he said. "This place is perfect."

"Perfect as in perfect for a morning picnic?" Meri ventured. "Or perfect as in the perfect location for the next meeting of the Photo Buffs of America Club?"

He smiled. Avoiding her question, Jay held a grape between his thumb and forefinger as if aiming for her mouth. "Can you catch?" he challenged.

Meredith laughed. He laughed. She opened her mouth and tilted her head back. The first grape hit her forehead.

"Can you throw?" she challenged right back.

"Best two out of three," he said.

With careful aim he shot, and the second one hit the side of her cheek.

"Work with me here," he said.

Meredith laughed. "If you would throw straight, we wouldn't be having a problem."

"Oh, is that what you think? Open up."

Meredith kept her head down and her lips firmly closed in an act of defiance. "Why should I?" she said through tight lips.

Jay popped the grape in his own mouth and seemed to be thinking. A smile spread up his tanned jawline. "Because if you don't open up, I'll tell all your friends what you look like first thing in the morning."

The vision of her green face and plastic-covered head came instantly to mind. Meredith opened her mouth without a word.

Taking careful aim, Jay launched the grape into the air. With a solid plop, it hit its intended target.

"Yes, score one for the Jakester," Jay said with a muscle-flexing raised fist.

"The Jakester, huh?" Meredith repeated.

Jay looked surprised.

"Are you sure that shouldn't be the jokester?"

A settling smile returned to Jay's face. "I suppose you want a chance to retaliate."

"No," Meredith said calmly, picking up a strawberry and eating it in two dainty bites. "I'm not much for throwing food."

With the challenge dissolved, Jay reached for a muffin and pulled back the paper liner.

"I wouldn't eat that if I were you," Meredith said.

"Why?"

"Did you smell it? They don't seem right."

Jay lifted the muffin to his nose and took a sniff.

Meredith seized the opportunity. In one smooth motion she leaned over and pushed his hand forward so that he smashed the muffin into his face.

Speechless, Jay searched her face for an explanation.

"I don't throw food because I'm much better at mashing it." Her contagious, shimmering laughter filled the air, competing with the rush of the waterfall.

Jay cracked up. There was no other way to explain it. He started to laugh so hard he couldn't even brush all the cakey muffin from his face and shirt.

"You have a little more on that cheek," Meredith said, motioning to the spot on her own right cheek. "And some of those tiny black seeds are still there on your chin. No, on the other side. There. You got it all." They lingered, contentedly chuckling in the afterglow of a prank well executed.

"Where do you live?" he suddenly asked.

Oh, so now he asks.

"Whidbey Island."

"Where's that?"

"Outside Seattle."

"Oh."

Meredith waited a breath and a half before asking, "Do you still live in Pasadena?"

"Yes. Same duplex for the past four years."

"What do you do?"

He took off his sunglasses and placed them on his leg. With his warm brown eyes he seemed to study her again. "Well, I used to be a waiter," he said without moving. "At a little place in Santa Monica called Chez Monique's."

"I've heard of it," Meredith said. She didn't want to mention that she knew of the restaurant because it was often listed in her favorite Hollywood gossip magazines as the hot spot for actors who wanted to be seen around town. "You used to be a waiter," Meredith repeated his words. "What do you do now?"

"A little bit of everything," he said vaguely. "I've had a lot of changes in my life the last six or seven months. I'm sort of between jobs right now."

Meredith nodded her false understanding. How can anyone his age be so nonchalant about his career? Why was it that all the good-looking ones were flakes?

She took her strong work ethic seriously. From the moment she discovered as a junior in high school that she had scored high in the field of publishing on a career test, Meredith had pursued that goal above all else. She went to summer school in college and sought out the most desirable positions in publishing. By the time she was twenty-three, she had landed her current position as an acquisitions editor. People patted her on the head and told her she was lucky. She knew she had earned every bit of that luck.

"I'm an acquisitions editor," Meredith volunteered. "For G. H. Terrison Publishing. I acquire children's products."

He seemed appropriately impressed, which was rewarding for her.

"I've been with them about a year and a half," she continued. "The best part is that I get to work at home and only go back to Chicago about six times a year."

Jay tilted his head. "May I make a comment here?"

"A comment?"

"Yeah, an observation."

"What?"

"You just said, 'I am an acquisitions editor.'"

Meredith nodded. "I am."

Jay shook his head. "An acquisitions editor is what you do. It's not who you are."

"Right," Meredith said quickly. "I know that."

Jay slipped his sunglasses back on. "Then you are a wiser person than I."

Chapter Five

*J*ay remained an enigma as their breakfast picnic continued. They talked about Shelly and the conference center. They
chatted about the bugs that swarmed around their food. They
even talked about the weather. But little personal information
about either of them was exchanged.

Jay seemed relaxed, though. He gave every indication that
he was charmed by Meredith and even offered her his hand as
she stepped out of the boat when they left. He let go as soon as
she was out, which she expected. This man she had just met
had no reason to hold her hand as they walked back through
the forest together. But Meredith was dying to know if he
wanted to hold her hand.

*What must he think of me? First the shrieking fit in the bed-
room, then the puppet show in the pickup, and then a smashed muffin in his face. Does all this amuse him? delight him? disgust him?
And why should it matter to me what he thinks?*

Because, you doof, her alter ego chimed in, *you're amused, delighted, and intrigued by him. When was the last time that happened? You want to see this guy again, and you can't remember when you felt this way after a first date, can you?*

No, I can't, she answered herself silently.

"Are you going back to L.A. today?" Meri asked as they hiked together through the woods.

"Yes," he said. "Do you ever come to L.A.?"

She was surprised by the way her heart did a little hopscotch around his words. *So he is interested. A little.*

"As a matter of fact, I have a trip to L.A. next month for a writers conference. It's in Anaheim, I think."

"Is it the Stories and More Conference?" he asked, looking a little surprised.

"Yes, I think that's the name of it."

"What a coincidence. I'll be at that conference, too."

"Really?" *Don't get too jazzed and scare him off, Meri!* "How about that?" she said calmly. "Nice coincidence. We'll have to get together then. I'll buy you a muffin."

"A muffin?"

"To make up for the one you didn't get this morning."

"Okay," he agreed. "I'll let you buy me a muffin."

It appeared to Meredith that he wanted to say something else. He looked worried. Maybe not worried but hesitant.

She decided to remain quiet and calm. If he wanted to open up a little more to her, he could do that. If this wasn't the time for him to say anything more personal than he had already said, then she could accept that, too. The comfortable silence emanating from her was meant to be an invitation. He didn't R.S.V.P.

They left the woods without further conversation and entered the parking lot, where dozens of cars now lined up in tidy rows. Lots of people from Glenbrooke and the surrounding area were showing up right on time. For a small community, this was a big event. Jonathan and Shelly had said they expected close to a thousand people.

"Looks like the festivities are about to begin," Meredith said, glancing at her watch. "Are you leaving now, or are you planning to come up to the lodge?"

Jay checked his watch. "I'd better get going. Hey, before you come to the conference…"

"Yes?"

The cell phone in his shoulder bag rang before he could finish his sentence. He mumbled an apology and took the call, turning his back to her. A stream of cars pulled into the gravel parking area. Jay had to plug his ear to hear the person on the other end.

Noticing that he had dropped the phone cover onto the gravel, Meredith picked it up for him just as he was saying he would call the person back. The pouch was soft black leather and felt smooth to the touch. Meredith looked down at the case and noticed a name engraved in gold letters across its side. She looked closely in the glare of the midday sun, trying to make sure she had read the name correctly. There was no mistake. The name on the phone case was Jacob Wilde. Jay turned back to her, and Meredith looked up at him with new eyes.

"Jacob?" she questioned. "You're Jacob Wilde?"

Some of the shimmer fell from his eyes. He didn't answer right away. A group of four women who had exited a car parked behind where they stood slowed down when they overheard Meredith.

"You are, aren't you?" Meredith began to feel a rush of excitement. Her face turned bright red. This is what she had dreamed of her entire life, meeting a movie star face-to-face. And here he was, only a few feet away.

Unable to control her amazement, Meri let out a scream and then pressed her hand against her mouth in an effort to stifle her sudden reaction. "I thought it was you this morning! I even told my mom. I said, 'Mom, I just saw a guy who looks like Jacob Wilde.'" Meredith's voice was at a raised pitch. The four women stopped and looked at Jacob. They began to whisper.

"My mom thought I was crazy, but that's okay. She always thinks I'm crazy. But I knew it was you, or at least I thought it was you. Why didn't you tell me? Why did you say your name was Jay?"

Jacob began to look nervous. The four women stepped closer. One of them held a pen in hand and quickly scrounged in her purse.

"What I said was that you could call me J." He made the letter *J* in the air with his finger.

"Oh! *J*, not Jay. I see. But where did the Wartman come from?"

Jacob appeared to be blushing. He looked down and adjusted his sunglasses.

Before he could answer, the woman came closer with a scrap of paper and held out the pen. "Would you mind giving me your autograph? I loved you in *Falcon Pointe*. Do you have any more movies coming out soon?"

"No," Jacob said as he quickly scrawled his name on the back of the woman's grocery list. He smiled pleasantly at her and said, "Thanks."

"Oh no! Thank you," she said.

Her friend stepped forward and wedged herself between Meri and Jacob. "Would you mind if we took a quick photo?"

Before Jacob could answer, the camera had clicked, and the woman was already saying thank you.

"It's Jacob Wilde!" the woman in glasses announced to the

teenage girls heading toward the lodge. With a whoosh, five, six, then nine more women were gathered around Jacob.

Meredith felt overwhelmed. Where had all these people come from? Why were they pushing their way between Jacob and her? Couldn't they see that she was with him? She was, wasn't she?

So much was happening so fast. One of the women excitedly asked Jacob to sign the back of her checkbook. Two more people got out of their cars and came over to see what all the commotion was about. Meredith was being pushed farther and farther to the side as the curious crowd pelted Jacob with questions.

As Meredith watched, Jacob patiently answered everyone's questions. He posed for two more photos and signed more autographs. When he glanced at his watch again, Meredith knew he was leaving. Jacob turned and looked at her through the cluster of fans. His expression was completely different from the way he had looked during their time at the waterfall. A sadness hung over his smile. Or was he angry? Could it be that he was mad at Meredith for blowing his cover? At the moment, she couldn't blame him.

"I have to go," Jacob said to the crowd while still looking at Meredith. "Nice meeting all of you."

She didn't try to move closer to him as he got into the car. Other women followed him. One of them looped her arms around his neck and before he could get into the car, planted a big kiss on his cheek. Jacob took it all good-naturedly, but Meri couldn't help noticing he wasn't eating up the attention. It seemed to embarrass and frustrate him.

She felt bad. Everything had been so dreamy until she drew attention to who he was. His comment at the waterfall suddenly made sense. This movie-star role wasn't who he was; it was what he did. Apparently he had struggled with that and was now finding ways not to flash his name all over the place. That is, until Meredith made this flock of admirers appear. They had cut her off from him. And she had invited them to do it.

What were you thinking? she scolded herself. *Why did you have to act like that? It's bad enough that you revert to being a child around your mother, but why, oh, why, did you act like that around him? Why couldn't you have just ignored the phone case? He didn't want to be found out. That's why he was so secretive about his name. You've ruined everything, you know.*

Jacob started the engine and gave Meredith a slight wave and a hollow smile. The smile was vastly different from the ones he had showered on her an hour ago. This smile was forced and not at all joyful.

She returned a smile, which she imagined must have looked about the same as his. "Bye," she called out, lifting her hand to wave. There she stood, one of the many starstruck admirers, smiling and waving as the actor left Glenbrooke in his shiny black convertible.

"Is he gorgeous or what?" one of the women said as Jacob's car rumbled over the gravel and out of the conference center's entrance.

"Did you see his eyes? What color were they? He had those sunglasses on, and I couldn't tell."

"Brown," Meredith muttered to herself. "Brown like warm cocoa." She knew it was futile to muse over this guy. She would never look into those cocoa brown eyes again. When he saw her next month in California, he would run and hide. She was sure of it.

The crowd made its way to the conference center, looking like one big wave of chattering, laughing excitement ready to hit the reception and douse all those in attendance with the great news.

Meredith remained fixed in the parking lot, not wanting to go into the conference center. She knew her mother would be there, ready to scold her for not showing up early to help out. All those fans would be raving to everyone that they had seen *the* Jacob Wilde. The one who had kissed him would have the grandest tale to tell. Meredith wanted to go home to her safe little Tulip Cottage on Whidbey Island and skip the rest of this day.

Snap out of it! This isn't about you. It's Jonathan and Shelly's day. You came for them. Go in there and be happy for them.

Putting one boot in front of the other, Meredith made her way to the lodge with several dozen others who had just arrived. It was an impressive lodge. Grand in size and design, it had been made from logs at Kyle's insistence and fronted with a wide porch at Jessica's insistence. All the details inside had been Shelly's selections. A large, river-rock fireplace was circled by forest green couches, and two long, cushioned window seats ran along the room's back side with a fabulous view of the unspoiled meadow. Shelly had designed built-in nooks for coffee and tea service in the main lounge. She had grouped chairs and end tables in cozy half circles to invite quiet conversations. The adjoining dining area seated eight hundred at round tables.

Meredith had seen it all before. She had spent hours listening to Shelly's plans and giving her input. She had even helped Shelly pick out the curtain fabric for the dining room.

And now the grand opening had come at last. Meredith tried hard to pull herself together the last few steps up to the lodge. She couldn't spoil this day for her sister. She wouldn't.

Chapter Six

"Are you all right?" Mom said, sweeping across the crowded room and coming to Meredith's side the moment she walked in the door. People were everywhere, standing, sitting, sipping glasses of pink lemonade.

"I'm fine," Meredith said, forcing a smile and trying to lower her voice so it wouldn't sound juvenile. "Sorry I didn't make it in time to help."

"There wasn't much to do. You know your sister; she had everything organized and under control before we even got here." Mom smiled over the top of Meri's head at a couple walking in the door. "Jessica said you went to the waterfall with somebody named Jake."

Meredith nodded, still keeping her pleasant look intact.

"Did you have a nice time?"

"Yes. It's beautiful at the waterfall. Have you and Dad seen it since Jonathan pulled out all the boulders and widened the lake?"

"No. Speaking of Jonathan, here he is."

Jonathan Renfield, the man with the nonstop smile, stepped over and kissed Meredith on the cheek. "Hey, I wondered when you were going to show up." Jonathan had grown up next door to the Grahams and was as much of a brother to Meredith as he was a brother-in-law.

"I was just telling Mom how great the lake at the waterfall looks. You did an incredible job of transforming that place."

"You think so?"

"It's beautiful," Meredith said.

Jonathan's gray eyes lit with appreciation for her praise.

"Maybe it's beautiful enough to be a setting for a movie." An unshaved man with long brown hair stepped into their conversation uninvited. "What do you think?"

Meredith thought the guy was rude but in a charming sort of way. He looked vaguely familiar.

"Have you met Brad Phillips?" Jonathan asked, slipping his arm around Brad's shoulder in a quick, friendly squeeze. That was Jonathan's way of inviting Brad into the conversation. "Brad, this is Shelly's sister Meredith and their mom, Ellen Graham."

"We've met," Ellen said. "Excuse me. I'm going to find Perry."

Meredith knew that was her mom's polite way of saying, "I've met this person, and I don't deem him worthy of my attention, so I'm going to leave."

"Brad was Shelly's neighbor in Pasadena," Jonathan said to Meredith after her mom left.

"Oh!" The lightbulb went on in Meredith's attic. "Jacob's roommate. It was sure nice of you to come up for this."

"It was my wife's idea," Brad said.

"Have you met Alissa yet?" Jonathan asked.

"I don't think so."

"She'll be hard to miss," Brad said, glancing around the room. He took a sip of his lemonade and said matter-of-factly, "She's the most gorgeous woman here."

Meredith let out a glimmering laugh.

"She is," Brad said without batting an eye. He took another long, cool sip of his lemonade. "If I'd known married life could be this awesome, we would have married long ago."

"I remember Shelly going to Los Angeles for your wedding," Meredith said. "Wasn't it just last month?"

Brad shook his wild hair. "Tomorrow it will be exactly two months."

"Congratulations," Meredith said. Her mouth was delivering proper, polite conversation, but her mind was reeling with the image of Jacob Wilde's being a roommate of this earthy man who now stood before her in a flannel shirt and shorts. The two guys were opposites. Or were they? She didn't know enough about Jacob to determine whether he and Brad had more in common than met the eye. She was dying to know more about Jacob.

"Thanks," Brad said. "You should have come to the wedding with Shelly. We had it at Descanso Gardens. The day was perfect."

"It was a really nice wedding," Jonathan agreed. "They had it in a rose garden, and the flowers were beautiful."

Meredith wondered if Jonathan was a little envious. He and Shelly had wanted to marry outside, but Mom had insisted the weather was too unpredictable in Seattle in May. The wedding was held inside the church where Meri and Shelly's dad had served as the minister for more than thirty years. Then, as if God were using the opportunity to validate their mother, it rained hard that day.

But Meredith was wondering what Jacob looked like in a tux. Was he the best man? Maybe Shelly had a picture somewhere.

Then something perplexing dawned on her. How could all these people know Jacob and not be impressed with his fame on the silver screen? Shelly had never once mentioned that she knew a movie star or that her next-door neighbor was an actor.

Why didn't she ever tell me? Was she afraid I'd run right down there and make a fool of myself? She knew her sister might have had a point there.

Then, because her curiosity was killing her, Meredith asked Brad, "What was it you were saying about a movie being filmed at the waterfall?"

"Look out," Jonathan said, giving Brad a playful punch in the arm before taking off to greet some other guests. "My sis-in-law here is a movie-star addict. Don't tell her about you-know-who."

"Who?" Meredith challenged as Jonathan began to walk away. "Jacob?"

Jonathan looked back over his shoulder.

"I already met your dear Mr. Wartman, and I didn't faint or anything."

Jonathan gave her a chin-up smile and kept going, blending into the crowd.

Brad's face took on a fixed grimace. "You called him Mr. Wartman, and he didn't slug you?"

"I didn't call him that. Kyle did."

"Well," Brad tipped up his glass and sipped the remains. "I guess potential investors can call potential producers anything they want."

"That's not his real name?"

"Yes, it's his real name. Jacob Frederick Wartman. He hates it. His agent changed it to Jake Wilde when he started doing commercials a couple of years ago. Then they changed it to the more sophisticated Jacob Wilde when he did *Falcon Pointe*. But don't divulge that info to the rags. Kyle thinks it's funny, and he can probably get away with it, but Jake hates to have people throw the 'Wartman' in front of him."

"I can understand that," Meredith said. "But it is his name. I mean, family and heritage aren't something to cast off just like that."

"He has a goofed-up family. But then," Brad added, "in this day and in our society, who doesn't? His grandparents raised him, and he was an only kid. They weren't even his grandparents. They were a kindly old couple who adopted him when they were in their fifties. They're both gone now, so he doesn't feel a real strong obligation to carry on the Wartman name."

"I see," Meredith said. She found all this inside information about Jacob amazing. No wonder Shelly and his other friends didn't idolize Jacob. To them, he was just an ordinary guy— their friend. Oh, how Meri wished she could turn back the clock and just be Jacob's friend.

"How do you know Jake? Through Shelly?"

"Actually, I met him this morning at Kyle and Jessica's."

"He's here?" Brad looked surprised. It was the first hint of emotion. "I thought he was in New York until next week."

"I guess he flew in this morning, but he left about half an hour ago. I think he's going back to L.A."

"I didn't tell him Alissa and I were coming up. He'll be surprised to find out we were here," Brad said.

Meredith's curiosity was insatiable. "I have to ask you something. Is Jacob, or Jake, as you call him, thinking of making a movie here? You said something about the waterfall and Kyle investing."

Brad nodded. "Last I heard, Jake and Kyle were in the final negotiations. It's a script Jake's been working on for as long as

I've known him. Some kind of fantasy tale or something. He met this guy Kalen, and he's been helping Jake with the screen-play."

"Gabriel Kalen? Jake has been working with Gabriel Kalen?"

"Yes, you know him?"

"Only by his reputation. I work for a publishing house that distributes Gabriel Kalen's video for children."

"Then you should have talked shop with Jake. He's going after this project big time."

Meredith's mind was whirling with thoughts of Jake and his screenplay. Was that why he was going to be at the Stories and More Conference? They were sort of in the same line of work. Why hadn't Jake said anything?

"Excuse me," Brad said. "I'm going back to the watering hole. Be sure to introduce yourself to Alissa. She'll be glad to meet you."

"I will. Nice meeting you, too."

Meredith stood alone in a room packed with hundreds of people. She couldn't stop accusing herself of the way she had turned into a crazed fan around Jacob and spoiled the beginnings of a normal friendship.

Making her way through the crowd, Meredith moved to the kitchen. She knew she could find some solitude there and maybe something salty to eat. Whenever she felt depressed, she wanted potato chips. Before she made it to the kitchen, Shelly intercepted her and grabbed her arm.

"Where have you been?" Shelly's words didn't sound accusatory the way Mom's had. Her full lips lit up her bright smile. "Jessica said you and Jake went to the falls. Well? How did it go?" She had on a navy blue jumper with a soft pink, short-sleeved T-shirt underneath. Her long silky brown hair fell softly over her shoulders, and her brown eyes sparked with curiosity.

Meredith had long envied Shelly's natural looks. Whenever she complimented Shelly on her welcoming appearance, Shelly groaned and said she wished she had inherited the finer features Meredith had—the narrow chin, the thin nose, and the dainty lips. They shared some common features, though. Their eyes were similar in shape although different in color. Meredith's green eyes were enhanced by her tinted contacts. Both Meredith and Shelly had well-defined, arched eyebrows. Shelly had taught Meredith how to pluck sparingly and coax the dramatic brows into obedience. Meredith had taught Shelly, the tomboy, how to shave around the ankles without nicking the ankle bone.

"There's nothing to tell," Meredith said. "He's a nice guy. I'm surprised you didn't tell me about him before."

"I told you about him lots of times. You were never interested. He's a sweetheart, isn't he?"

"Were you and Jessica in on this together? Were you trying to set us up or something?"

"No!" Shelly looked shocked that her sister would suspect such a thing. It was definitely the kind of thing Meredith would do, but Shelly didn't go in for matchmaking.

"Why did you want to know how it went? How was it supposed to go?"

Shelly pulled Meredith out of the noisy room and onto the back deck. The sun had warmed the deck, and the Adirondack chairs that faced the meadow were all empty. Shelly sat down on the edge of the first chair and motioned for Meredith to sit next to her. Shelly had worked as a flight attendant for five years and had a smooth way about her when she wanted people to cooperate with her arrangements. Meredith sat in the hot chair.

"Yeouch!" she said, pulling down her shorts to cover the back side of her legs. "Second time in one day. It's been far too long since I've worn shorts and far too long since I've been in the sun on a hot day."

"I know. The weather is perfect, isn't it? I love it here!" Shelly leaned forward. "Don't feel pressured about Jake. I don't mean to sound pushy. It's just that it looks as if he's going to bring a film crew here in a couple months, and everyone's excited about it. You might want to come down again when they start production."

"I heard about the film," Meredith said. "It sounds like it will be a lot of fun for you guys."

"You're going to think I'm crazy," Shelly said, "and maybe I am. This is so unlike me, but when Jessica told me you had taken off for a walk with Jake, I thought, Of course! Meri and Jake. They're perfect for each other."

"You thought that, huh? Just like that? Out of the blue?"

Shelly smiled. "I told you before, didn't I, that I went out once with Jake?"

Meredith felt uncomfortable. She had suspected something like this.

"What a disaster!" Shelly said with a shake of her head. "He likes classical music, like you do, so we went to this summer concert in the park. They played all your Vivaldi music, and we sat on these low beach chairs on the grass. It was a gorgeous, warm evening, and Jake leaned his chair back and fell asleep. Talk about a scintillating first date. He had been working long hours at the restaurant and as a gaffer at a studio just to get some film-industry experience. The poor guy was fried. That was our first and last date."

Meredith didn't know how to tell her sister about her first and last date with the same man. It seemed pointless, even in light of Shelly's ravings about how well they would get along.

"I don't think there's much chance of Jacob's being interested in seeing me again," Meredith said softly. "He seems like a really nice guy, like you said, but I kind of hit three strikes with him all in a row. I think I'm out." She decided not to list the three strikes and was glad Shelly didn't ask for details. It was humiliating enough to remember how she had stood green faced before the innocent man as he slumbered and how she had screamed at him to get out. Then there was the puppet show. The muffin in the face, which might or might not have been a bad thing. But it didn't really matter. The king strike was the way she had turned into a raving ditz when she found out who he was. She was outta there.

"Oh," Shelly said softly. She placed her hands over her stomach and said, "It was just a thought. Don't feel like I'm pressuring you into anything."

"That's okay. I know you're just being a sis, and I appreciate it."

"It's funny," Shelly said. "I always think of you as the matchmaker. Now I see why it's kind of fun to be in that position."

Yeah, well, now I know it's a lot more fun to be the matchmaker than the one being matched up. Meredith looked out at the meadow. The powerful midday sun was causing the tall wildflowers to slump over. Soon their brilliant color would be dried up, and Jonathan would whack them all down with his power mower. She felt just like those wildflowers. Her brief, shining moment with Jacob had come and gone at the waterfall this morning. Inside she felt slumped over, too.

"I wanted to tell you something else," Shelly said, catching Meredith's gaze and bringing her back to the deck and into the small circle of confidence that embraced the two sisters.

"Yes?"

"I'm six days late."

Chapter Seven

ate for what?" Meredith said absentmindedly.

"You know." Shelly giggled. "I'm six days late." She paused. "I think I might be pregnant."

Meredith brightened and grabbed Shelly's hands. "Really? Do you think you are?"

"I don't know. I've never been this late before."

"Did you tell Jonathan?"

Shelly shook her head. "No, he's been so swamped with all the details here at camp that I didn't want to put anything on him until after this was over. I was dying to tell somebody, and I'm dying to find out! Don't say anything, okay?"

Meredith nodded.

"You promise?"

"Yes, of course!" Meredith put out her little finger, and Shelly automatically linked it the way they used to do as kids when they sealed promises.

"Now, I have a huge favor to ask you. Actually, this is why

I wanted you to come over early this morning."

"Sorry I wasn't here."

"No, don't worry about it. It's okay. But what I wanted to ask is if you could run to the drugstore in town to buy a home pregnancy test for me. Everyone in town knows me, and if I go, it'll be gossiped all around before I even have the results from the test. I would have gone into Eugene to buy one, but I couldn't get away the last two days. If it's positive, I want to be able to tell Mom and Dad before they leave."

"You'd better tell Jonathan first."

"Oh, I will. I just need to get a pregnancy test."

"Point me to the nearest drugstore. I'm your silent partner," Meredith said.

"Oh, good. You can take my car. It's parked over by our cabin. You know the drugstore on Main Street, don't you?"

Meredith nodded.

"Here's some money." Shelly pulled some cash from the pocket of her jumper. "When you get back, leave the test in the bathroom at our house and then come tell me."

"Got it," Meredith said. She loved the thrill of an adventure. "Where are your car keys?"

"Inside the house in the basket on the counter. Don't let Bob Two out. He knows something is going on around here today, and he knows he can't have the run of the campground. We're trying to get him to calm down."

"I'll be back in a flash," Meredith said, grabbing the cash from Shelly and taking the deck stairs with a light step. "Mum's the word," she said over her shoulder. "Or should I say, Mommy's the word?"

"Shhh," Shelly said, placing her finger to her lips.

Meredith made a grimace. "Sorry! I'll be right back." She was sure no one had heard her. Too much noise was coming from inside the lodge. Meredith made a beeline for the small, charming log cabin Jonathan had built for Shelly and himself. It consisted of two bedrooms, one bathroom, a kitchen, and a living room. According to Jonathan, that was all anyone needed.

Bob Two, the caramel-colored cocker spaniel, started to bark before Meredith even reached the front door. "It's only me," she called out. "I'm coming in to get the keys, so don't bite me, you mongrel."

It flashed through her mind that Jake didn't like dogs either. The thought made her laugh aloud. Maybe they did have a lot in common, as Shelly had suggested.

Maybe Jake can overlook my "strikes." Maybe he'll call me. He knows I live on Whidbey. Maybe he'll look up my number. Or call and get it from Shelly. And we can have a second chance. We'll start a phone friendship, or better yet, an e-mail romance!

Meredith paused before opening the front screen door. *Naw, that would never happen.*

"Back off, flea bait," she said to Bob Two. Actually, for a dog, he was okay. Not too much slobber; just a little overeager. "I'm coming in."

Bob Two didn't seem to realize that Meri thought he was okay. He gave every indication that he didn't like her. Backing himself into the corner of the kitchen, he barked, and his ears flopped. Meri grabbed the keys and blew a sarcastic kiss to the pooch. "See ya!"

Making sure the screen door was closed tightly behind her, Meredith headed for Shelly and Jonathan's Jeep. Bob Two was still barking.

The engine's roar drowned out his protests, and she took off down the gravel drive and headed toward town. Once she was on the smooth main road, Meri tilted the rearview mirror toward herself and checked her appearance. The top of her nose appeared sunburned as well as the high arch of her cheeks.

"Ah, summer sun. How I've missed you." She noticed that her hair was unusually cooperative and still looked good despite the ride in the convertible, the hike to the falls, and the jog to Shelly's cabin.

What did Jake think of me? Am I plain compared to the glamorous movie stars he hangs out with? Would he think less of me if he knew my hair was really as brown as Shelly's? No, I don't think he would. I think he likes blonds. I think he liked my hair. He noticed it. I know he did. And he took a picture of me. I wonder what he's going to do with that picture....

Meredith stopped her train of thought. *Wait a minute. This is pointless. Why am I still thinking about him? Let him go, Meri.*

She rolled into town and slowed the Jeep way down to the posted 25 m.p.h. speed limit. The town looked cleaned out. Few cars were parked along the street at the little shops. Meri knew why. They were all at the conference center.

She parked the Jeep and hopped out, anxious to buy the pregnancy test and get it back to Shelly. She was as eager to know the results as her sister was. Well, maybe not as eager, but she felt special knowing that Shelly had confided in her before telling anyone else. She liked sharing in these significant moments with her sister and was glad to do what she could to participate.

A bell chimed over the door as Meredith entered the small pharmacy. It looked as if nothing had changed in this store since the fifties.

That's what Shelly had said she liked about Glenbrooke. It seemed to be the town that time forgot. Many of the people lived by the values of a half-century ago. Everyone knew everyone. Some of the people who lived here had never been outside of a fifty-mile radius of their gentle town. It helped explain a little better the wild reaction when the women saw Jacob earlier. Movie stars just didn't come to Glenbrooke.

Meredith stopped in the pregnancy-tests aisle and quickly scanned the boxes. She had three choices. All she knew to do was check for an expiration date on the boxes. They were all current. They were all about the same price. She did an eenie-meenie-minie-mo and picked the larger white box. Grabbing a pack of spearmint gum and a Milky Way candy bar, Meredith hurried to the counter. She remembered from their childhood that Jonathan liked Milky Way candy bars. If this test was positive, a Milky Way might help the news go down. Maybe she should buy a Milky Way for Shelly, too. And for their parents.

Why not? she thought and scooped up the whole box of a dozen or more candy bars. She plopped the box down on the counter in front of the white coated elderly gentleman and nonchalantly placed the pregnancy test next to the mound of candy bars. The pharmacist eyed her purchase suspiciously and said, "Will that be all for you today, miss?"

She smiled at him. "Yes, thank you."

The bell over the door chimed again. Meredith hoped the guy would hurry up and finish. He was ringing up each candy bar separately. For the first time she realized how embarrassing it was to buy a pregnancy test and understood why Shelly didn't want to come in here to make the purchase herself. Even though no one in Glenbrooke knew Meredith and she knew she had nothing to apologize for or be embarrassed about, she still felt her cheeks beginning to heat up with more than the tinge of sunburn that graced them.

Come on, come on! Hurry up!

"This doesn't have a price on it," the man said, holding up the pregnancy test and looking on the underside and all around the box.

Meredith was aware that whoever had entered the drug-store a moment ago was now standing behind her in line.

Put down the box, mister! The price is right there on the top. Can't you see it?

Before Meredith could point it out, the pharmacist found the sticker and punched the numbers into the cash register. The total appeared in the register's window. Meredith suddenly realized she didn't have enough money.

"I'm fifteen cents short," she said, aware that she was holding up the person in line behind her. "Could you please take off one of the candy bars? Or wait, just take off this pack of gum."

The pharmacist gave her a blank look, as if she had just asked him to recite the Declaration of Independence backwards.

"Here's fifteen cents," said the calm male voice behind her.

She knew that voice. Meredith bit her lower lip and turned around slowly. "Hi," she said to the reluctant movie star behind her.

"Hi," Jacob replied.

Meredith remembered that Shelly had made her promise not to tell a soul about the pregnancy test. So she just turned back to the pharmacist. He was stuffing the goods into a paper bag. Certainly Jacob had seen the pregnancy-test kit.

"It's not for me," she said quickly, looking at Jake again.

His expression didn't change.

"And the candy bars aren't for me, either."

Neither the pharmacist nor Jake said a word.

Then, because she didn't know what else to do, she bolted toward the door.

"Meredith!" Jake called out.

On impulse, she turned around and said, "I'm sorry about what happened in the parking lot."

Jacob headed toward her, the bottle of aspirin he was about to purchase still in his hand. "It's okay," he said calmly.

She felt nervous. This was Jacob Wilde talking to her. He was looking at her with those warm brown eyes. What was he thinking? She hadn't felt nervous like this when he was Mr. Wartman.

"Don't worry about it," he said, glancing at the bag and back at Meredith.

He's changed his opinion of me, too. I can tell. He's standing here, trying to be polite, but he's not intrigued or charmed anymore. The tiny bit of electricity that sparked this morning is gone.

"I had a good time at the waterfall," Meredith said, nudging herself forward. "I'm sorry I reacted the way I did and drew so much attention to you."

"It's okay," Jake said. "I probably should have said something to you earlier, but, to be honest," he paused and his voice softened, "I was enjoying being Jay for awhile."

Meredith nodded her understanding.

"I would have gone up to the lodge with you, but sometimes it can get a little crazy in a crowd. I went back to Kyle and Jessica's to make some phone calls, and—"

"Hey," Meredith cut in, "I wasn't trying to say that I thought you should have stuck around. I understand completely."

"Good," Jacob said.

An awkward pause hung between them. It felt to Meredith that the contents of her bag were burning a hole in her arm. She wanted to say something to him—anything. Did he think she was pregnant? All her thoughts wadded up like a ball of gum and stuck to the roof of her brain, making it impossible to think. He looked as if the same malady had struck him as well.

The door opened, and a teenage boy walked in. He stopped and stared at Jake. "It *is* you! My sister said you were

here. She said you were driving a black Mustang, and I was
going home, and there was your car, and—oh, man, I can't
believe it! Here you are!" He excitedly spilled his words all over
Meredith and Jacob.

Once again Meredith knew what it was like to be cut off
from Jake. And right when things had the potential of being
patched up, too.

"Man, oh, man! Can you wait here one second? I have to
get Russell. He's never going to believe this. Don't go, okay?
Just one more minute. Stay right there." The boy burst out the
door and took off running down Main Street.

"I'm sorry," Meredith said.

Jake put on a smile as if the camera had just turned on him
and it was time to play the closing scene. "Don't give it another
thought. This is how it goes sometimes." His voice lowered,
and he tilted his head to the right. "None of this is your fault
or your responsibility."

Before Meredith could add her closing thought, the door
burst open, and seven teens came rushing in with the young
guy who had left a few moments earlier.

"See, I told you it was him!"

"Can we have your autograph?"

"Are you going to make any more movies?"

"How come you're in Glenbrooke?"

"Here, sign my arm. I don't have any paper."

"This is the coolest thing that's ever happened in my whole
life!"

"You're the first movie star I've ever seen!"

Meredith was once again brushed aside as Jake was
ambushed by the young fan club. He looked over at Meredith
and smiled.

"I owe you fifteen cents," she said.

"You don't owe me anything," he said, signing a pad of

paper. His words seemed like the closing line.

You don't owe me anything.

"Well, bye, then," she said, carelessly tossing her words into the huddle of admiring teenagers.

Jake glanced up. A boy was pulling up his T-shirt sleeve and begging Jake to write on the back of his arm with a permanent marker.

"Good-bye, Meredith." His voice carried a bittersweet echo as she left the drugstore and stepped into the Jeep. Jake's rental car was parked four spaces down from hers.

Good-bye, Meredith. Did he mean that as in good-bye forever or good-bye until our paths cross again?

Slowly backing up the Jeep, Meredith cranked the wheel and headed to the conference center with the pharmacy bag on the seat next to her.

Chapter Eight

"Do you want me to come in?" Meredith asked Shelly half an hour later as she stood outside the door of Shelly's bathroom.

"Sure," Shelly said, opening the door. She held a white plastic stick in her hand. The box for the pregnancy test rested on the sink's corner.

"Now what?" Meredith asked.

"It says here to wait three to five minutes. If one line shows up on this stick, it means I'm not pregnant. If two lines show, then I am."

"Three to five minutes, huh?"

"Yes," Shelly said, glancing at her watch. "This is going to be the longest five minutes of my life."

"I'll tell you a little story to pass the time," Meredith offered.

Shelly gave her a mildly irritated look. Stories were not Shelly's way of getting her mind off life.

"I think you'll like this story. It's about a loving sister who goes to the drugstore in a small town and buys her precious sis a home pregnancy kit. Then the customer in line behind her turns out to be a friend of the potentially pregnant woman. But he, of course, thinks the pregnancy test belongs to the loving sister."

"Who was it? Kenton?"

"No," Meredith said slowly.

"That's right," Shelly said. "Kenton and Lauren are gone this week. Who was it? Everyone else was at the conference center."

"Almost everyone else."

Shelly definitely looked irritated now. "Who was it, Meredith?"

"Try a certain Vivaldi-loving man with gorgeous hair and a trail of crazed fans following him all over Glenbrooke."

"Jake was at the drugstore?"

"He came in after I did, but I didn't see him until I was at the register."

"You didn't tell him the pregnancy test was for me, did you?"

"No, I told him it was for me," Meredith said sarcastically. She could see her sister beginning to perspire.

"If you told him," Shelly said, her face turning red, "and he tells Brad, this will be on the six o'clock news before I have a chance to talk to Jonathan."

"Don't worry. He didn't ask, and I didn't tell. Can you imagine how I felt with him standing there looking at me with a pregnancy test in my hand? Just what we needed to make sure there was never any possible, slightly hopeful chance of a relationship developing between us."

"Oh, Meri, I'm so sorry." Shelly calmed down and glanced at her watch.

"It's okay. Really. I thought you should know so you can give your crazy matchmaking plans a rest."

"I won't say anything about it again. I'm sorry you were stuck in that embarrassing situation because of me."

"I'll remember that the next time I want a favor out of you," Meredith said.

Shelly quickly glanced at the stick. She didn't say anything. Meredith came closer. The two sisters stood with their heads touching, staring at the plastic stick, willing the second line to appear. A full minute and a half passed.

"It's only one line," Shelly said.

"How long has it been?" Meredith asked.

Shelly looked at her watch and then placed the test stick on top of the box. "Seven minutes."

"Are you sure?" Meri said, trying to offer hope.

"Yeah. Seven minutes," Shelly said with a sad sigh. "There's definitely only one line."

They were quiet for a moment. Shelly gathered up the instructions and put all the pieces back into the box.

"It's probably all the stress you've been under lately," Meredith suggested. "You've had a lot of strain on you getting ready for this grand opening."

"You're right. I'm sure that's it. Besides, we really aren't ready to have a baby. We talked about trying in a year or so. We have a lot going on right now, you know, with the opening of the conference center and everything."

Meredith spotted a solitary tear on the rim of Shelly's eyelid.

"Don't be so brave. You were almost pregnant, and you have every right to be emotional about that." Meredith opened her arms, and Shelly received her comforting hug.

"And who knows," Meredith said as Shelly pulled away

and wiped her tears. "You still could be pregnant, but you're just not pregnant enough for it to show up on the test."

"That's true. Except I don't think I can stand the suspense of doing another home test. If I haven't started by the end of next week, I'm seeing a doctor."

"Good idea. Are you going to tell Jonathan?"

"Yes, of course. I eventually tell him everything. Do me a favor and don't say anything to Mom, though, okay?"

"I won't," Meri promised. "Do you want to get back to your lodge full of guests now?"

"I suppose I should. There aren't that many people left, I don't think." Shelly tossed the remains of the home test into the bathroom trash can. "I'm sorry you missed the dedication ceremony while you were at the drugstore. It was really wonderful. Dad prayed, Kyle said some very nice things about Jonathan, and I cut the ribbon. Wish you could have been there. But I appreciate your going to the pharmacy for me, even though it ended up embarrassing you."

"That's okay. I was glad to do it for you."

Shelly opened the bathroom door. Bob Two was sitting there, panting and waiting for them. Scooping up the little fur ball, Shelly said, "For now you'll be our baby."

He licked her cheek, and Meredith cringed. "How can you stand to have dog saliva on you?"

"Haven't you ever heard how clean a dog's tongue is?"

"You have to be kidding. No offense, Bowser, but I saw you licking around the kitchen trash earlier. You're a big ole slimeball, you know that?"

"Don't talk to my baby that way!" Shelly said, putting Bob Two down. "You stay here, Bob Two. We'll be back later tonight. I can't let you out because too many sweet old ladies are around here, and you might scare them to death."

"Yeah, right," Meredith muttered.

Bob Two barked as they slipped out the screen door.

"He doesn't like you," Shelly said.

"Of course he doesn't. He's a male. Tell him to get in line," Meri said.

"You know, I was thinking. Why don't you call Jake?" Shelly suggested as they walked back to the central lodge.

"Why? And I thought you weren't going to mention him again."

"Well, I changed my mind. I think you should call him to tell him the pregnancy test was for me and you promised not to say anything. It doesn't matter now because I'm not pregnant."

"You don't think you're pregnant."

"Same thing at this point."

"I don't think my calling him would change anything," Meri said. "It wasn't just the questionable appearance of my buying a pregnancy kit. I terrorized the guy all day long. He doesn't want to hear from me again; I can guarantee that."

"Terrorized? What did you do?"

Meredith cautiously described the early morning encounter with the avocado face and blue bonnet. Shelly burst out laughing.

"There's more," Meri said and proceeded to share the part about the puppet show, the smashed muffin, and the immature outburst in the parking lot.

"You know," Shelly said after she managed to control her laughter, "if nothing else, you made a lasting impression on the guy."

"That's what I'm afraid of," Meri muttered.

They stopped just outside the lodge and beyond the hearing of the dozen or so people sitting on the front porch visiting. "You know what I think?" Shelly said. "I think your picnic must have been a refreshing experience for Jake after battling the attention he's gotten ever since *Falcon Pointe* came out. No one expected that movie to become such a big hit. He was a no-name, out of nowhere, and now he's suddenly famous and being assaulted in parking lots and drugstores. It must be frustrating. I can see why he didn't want you to know who he was for as long as possible."

"I wish I could turn back the clock and start this day over."

"No, you don't. This is life. This is your crazy, amazing life, and nothing happened to you today that didn't pass through God's fingers before it came to you."

Meri smiled. She used to be the one who was quick to offer spiritual insights and encouragement to her sister. Now Shelly was the one counseling her.

"If God is really in control, then I think he must be in a very strange mood today," Meri said.

Shelly looked serious. "Do you really think God has moods?"

"I'm kidding," Meri retorted. "Let's go inside. Do you suppose any food is left?" Then she remembered the candy bars. "Oh, I bought all those Milky Way bars. Where did I put them?"

"You left them on the counter in the kitchen. They'll be fine there. Jonathan will thank you profusely. You've brought him a two-week supply, you know."

"Just so your mutt doesn't get to them."

"Don't worry. Bob Two hasn't figured out how to climb up onto counters yet."

"When he does, you're in big trouble."

They walked up the front steps together, and Shelly warmly greeted all the people on the benches and in the rocking chairs.

"Your mother was looking for you, Meredith," one of the older women said.

"I bet she was," Meri muttered under her breath. Then she

smiled and said, "Thank you." Something inside of her started to shrink down to junior high size all over again. She knew the minute she saw her mom she would be lectured about missing the dedication ceremony. And what would she tell her mother? "I was at the pharmacy, but I can't tell you why"?

Fortunately, Mom was busy in the kitchen and didn't pay much attention to Meredith until the long day came to a close, and Meredith and her mom and dad drove back to Kyle and Jessica's after nine. Mom nonchalantly said, "I didn't see you at the ceremony, Meredith. Where were you standing?"

She took a deep breath. "I had to run an errand in town. I didn't get back in time."

"What kind of errand?" Mom wanted to know.

"Whose car did you take?" Dad asked.

"I took Shelly's Jeep, and it was nothing. A quick errand to help out Shelly. That's why we came down, isn't it? To help out? Well, I was helping out."

Mom turned around and gave Meredith a disapproving look. "I only asked a simple question," she said. "You don't need to be so defensive."

Meredith thought about that line as she washed her face and prepared to crawl into her comfy bed in the Patchwork Room. *But I do need to be defensive with you, Mom. How can I tell you that? Don't you see how much you've changed in the last few weeks? You're trying to tell me what to do all the time, and you're not treating me like an adult.*

Meredith placed the warm washcloth over her face and drew in the steamy water with a deep breath. *Maybe she's treating me like a child because I let her. I turn into a little girl whenever I'm around her. Why am I doing that? I didn't used to.*

Slipping into her nightshirt and heading for bed, Meredith noticed something on her pillow. She had taken out her contacts and couldn't make out what it was. Greenish in color, it definitely wasn't a mint. Was it a bug? She picked up the closest weapon, which was a book of poetry on the night stand. Cautiously she approached the intruder with the book in position, ready to smash at any moment. Meri squinted her eyes. Was it? It was!

"A grape," she said aloud. "How did one lonely grape get in here?" A smile spread across her face. She picked up the green grape and laughed. Even Meredith felt better when she heard her own laughter. Jake must have put it there when he came back to the house to make his phone calls.

Crawling under the covers, she held the lone grape between her thumb and forefinger, rolling it back and forth. She smiled contentedly to herself. *So, the man has imagination.*

Chapter Nine

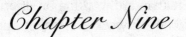

A week later, Meredith was sitting at her cluttered desk in her home office when the phone rang. She jumped before picking it up on the second ring. The phone's ringing in the middle of the day shouldn't have surprised her. It rang all the time. But at the moment she was lost in a dream.

"This is Meredith," she said after she pushed the button on the speaker phone.

"It's me," Shelly said. "You busy?"

"Not really. What's up?"

"I started," Shelly said.

It took Meredith a moment to catch her meaning. "Oh. Are you okay?"

"Sure. I'm fine. A little bloated, but you know how that goes. I think you were right. I got all messed up because of the crazy schedule and the stress. Things should even out now."

"Good. I hope they do," Meri said. "What's happening with you guys?"

"Kyle and Jonathan are working on clearing the meadow today. It's been so hot all week everything dried up, and Kyle thinks it could be a fire hazard. I hated to see all the wild-flowers go."

"I can imagine," Meredith agreed. "It's a beautiful meadow." She picked up a pen and began to doodle on her desk mat's corner. Only a week ago she had compared herself to the wildflowers in that field: fresh and charming one day and plowed under the next. Her own prophecy had come true for herself. She had waited all week, but Jacob never called. He didn't e-mail, and he didn't write. All hope had dried up, drooped, and withered. Certainly any man with enough imagi-nation to leave a grape on her pillow was capable of contacting her within a week's time if he wanted to.

"I talked to Jake last night." Shelly said.

Meredith didn't respond.

"I told him about the pregnancy test. I told him it was for me."

"I'm sure he was vastly relieved," Meri said.

"That sounded pretty sarcastic."

"Why did you feel the need to tell him?"

"I wanted him to get a more accurate opinion of you."

"Oh, well, thank you very much, Shelly, but I think it's too late for that. My brief encounter with that unsuspecting man was so much larger than life, you know? If he and I had met under other circumstances, in another lifetime, on another planet, there may have been some hope for your endeavors."

"He said he enjoyed meeting you," Shelly divulged.

"Are you sure he didn't say it was 'memorable'? If I were he, I would use other words than 'enjoyed.'"

"He said enjoyed."

"How gracious of him."

"Meri, don't you even want to know what else he said?"

"I don't think so."

There was a pause. "I'm going to tell you anyway. Jake said he enjoyed meeting you because you're so original."

"Original!" Meredith hooted. "Oh, that's good. That's terrific. I'm original. That ranks right up there with 'She has a great personality.'" Meri shook her head and scribbled out the sunflower she had been doodling. "How sad. He thinks I'm 'original.'"

"Meri, you're so funny when it comes to men. I never have understood you. You have all these guys clamoring to go out with you, but you never act interested in them."

"So?"

"So now here's one you're interested in, and you won't admit it."

Meredith felt frustrated with her perceptive sister. This was not Shelly's usual role, which made the situation even more uncomfortable. Shelly had never pushed her to a higher opinion of a guy before, except when they were in high school and Dennis Trammel asked her out to a Christmas banquet at his church. Meri turned him down because she thought he was a loser. Shelly had scolded her and told her it wasn't nice to write him off so quickly. She had told Meri she should be willing to date a few guys she wasn't entirely interested in because, if nothing else, she could practice her dating manners. Then, when Prince Charming came along, she would be all practiced up.

Meri went to the Christmas banquet, had a terrible time, and then Dennis tried to kiss her when he walked her to the front door. She pushed him away, slammed the door in his face, and marched upstairs to her room, where she announced to Shelly that she would never again "practice her dating manners."

The sad part was, during the years that followed, very few potential Prince Charmings came along, but a long line of guys to practice manners on did. Meredith used to joke that she was a "jerk magnet." Every walking jerk in Seattle seemed to be drawn to her.

"Okay, so I'm interested in Jacob Wilde. There, I admitted it. Now I can get in line with half the women in America. We'll form a line of 'original' women interested in Jake. Does that make you happy?"

"What's with you? You sure are snippy today," Shelly stated.

"Sorry. It's just that I'm not used to taking direction from you, of all people, on my love life. I thought you weren't going to do this."

"I changed my mind. Why shouldn't I be allowed to help Cupid fling a few arrows in your direction?" Shelly asked. "You sure went all out when it came to Jonathan and me getting back together. Can I help it if I think you and Jake would be good for each other?"

"No, you can't help it. That's your sisterly opinion, and I'll take it graciously. Thank you. Now let it go. It's not enough for you to think we're good for each other. Jake has to think that, too. If he didn't feel compelled to contact me within a week of our first meeting, then there's no interest on his part. That's the law of relationship development."

"Oh, really?" Shelly said. "You have this law written down somewhere?"

"Not yet," Meredith said, lightening up. "I'm thinking of writing a book on the subject, and then it will be written down."

Shelly laughed. "I want a copy when that book comes out because I'd love to be able to quote back to you all the sage advice you poured out to me not so long ago."

"I have another call," Meredith said when the call-waiting tone sounded in her ear. "I do love you; you know that, don't you?"

"Yes, I know that. And I love you, too. Talk to you later."

Meredith pushed the button on the phone and took the next call. "Hello, this is Meredith." One of the art designers from her publishing house needed to discuss the layout for a picture book they had been working on.

Fifteen minutes later, Meredith hung up and checked the clock. 3:27. Time for a break. She hadn't had any lunch yet and was hungry, but she didn't know what she was hungry for. Trekking downstairs to the kitchen in her quiet cottage, Meredith rummaged through the refrigerator looking for something interesting. She settled on a carton of boysenberry yogurt and went out onto the front porch to eat it.

The spring afternoon was alive with the colors, scents, and sounds of the living forest where the Tulip Cottage sat near a small lake. Drawing in a deep breath of the fresh air, Meredith perched on the porch's railing and looked out on her small garden. She had fenced it off, but somehow the wild rabbits were still nibbling off the carrot tops and the lettuce. Everything was in the budding stage, and she was afraid it would all be eaten by the forest wildlife before her garden had even begun to show what it could do.

An itchy-nose pollen smell in the air prompted Meredith to start sneezing. So much for fresh air and organic gardening. *Everything in life has a flip side, doesn't it? I guess my life has a flip side, too. I love working at home, but here I am, isolated from the rest of the world.*

Meredith wasn't used to feeling sorry for herself. She usually had so much going on that time to reflect on what was happening inside her heart was severely limited. *The truth is, I'm crushed. I thought he would call. I can understand why he didn't, but I had hoped. And hope deferred makes the heart sick. Where does the Bible say that?*

Curiosity compelled her to pick up her Bible from the

kitchen table. Flipping to the concordance in the back, she scanned the verses with the word *hope* in them until she found the one she had spontaneously quoted.

She found it in Proverbs 13:12, "Hope deferred makes the heart sick, but a longing fulfilled is a tree of life." She underlined the verse and leaned against the side of the counter.

"So, what's my longing that's not being fulfilled? Is it that I want to get married because all my friends are? Or is it because two are better than one since they have a good return for their labor?"

Meredith realized that was another verse. Being the daughter of a minister had filled her mind with random verses over the years, much the same way being an acquisitions editor had filled her mind with a colorful variety of stories. Back to the concordance she went and found the "two are better than one" verse in Ecclesiastes 4:9. She read the verse before it. "There was a man all alone; he had neither son nor brother. There was no end to his toil, yet his eyes were not content with his wealth. 'For whom am I toiling,' he asked, 'and why am I depriving myself of enjoyment?' This too is meaningless—a miserable business!"

Meredith went to the refrigerator for something else to eat. She wondered about Jake. Brad had said he was raised by an elderly couple who were now gone. Did Jacob feel like a man all alone who was working hard in the entertainment industry yet feeling discontented with his wealth? Did he ever wonder why he was depriving himself of enjoyment?

A smile played across Meredith's lips as she remembered the way Jacob had relaxed with her at the waterfall, how he had tossed the grapes and laughed deeply when she smashed the muffin in his face. Moving the mayonnaise jar aside, Meredith pulled out a tiny glass jar from the back of the refrigerator and held it up to the light. It had been a maraschino-cherries jar, but now it held only one pale green orb floating in a sea of white vinegar. The lone sailor was not a maraschino cherry but the grape Jake had left on her pillow.

She smiled. It seemed to be preserving itself nicely. One week in its watery captivity hadn't done much damage to the memorialized fruit. Back in the far corner of the fridge went the jar, leaving Meredith feeling contented, like a kid who was succeeding at a science experiment.

Now, if only I could preserve a relationship the way I pickle grapes. Then I'd have something to write a book about!

Content to settle for an apple as the final course of her lunch, Meredith took a hike to the mailbox at the end of her long driveway. The weather had been unseasonably warm in her corner of the world, and all the spindly wildflowers were bent over the edge of the road. Pretty little maids in waiting dipped their blue bonnets, surrendering their final bit of color to the occasional passerby. Meri felt sorry for them. And in feeling sorry for the doomed wildflowers, she felt sorry for herself again.

Maybe he wrote me a letter. Maybe a passionately romantic letter waits for me this very second at the end of the road in that big silver box. I'll stand here in the sunshine and carefully slit open the envelope with my thumbnail. A butterfly will flutter over to see what's so interesting. I'll let her sit on my shoulder and share my secrets. Together we'll read each tender line,

"*My dearest,*
    You have been in my thoughts every night and every day. When I sleep, it is your face I see in every dream. Every morning the sun pours into my room, and there you are, riding on every sunbeam, your laughter spilling over me like a refreshing spring shower. You are in my heart. I won't even try to banish you from my deepest thoughts. You are here. And here you will stay. Forever. Jacob."

❦

Meredith put her hand to the rusted metal latch, and the silver cave groaned its discomfort as she opened the door and peered into the darkness.

Chapter Ten

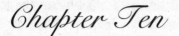

he mailbox was stuffed. This was a good sign. It meant the odds were greater that a letter from Jake was part of the pack. Meredith pulled out the two large manila envelopes first. They were both from an agent she worked with frequently. Two new manuscripts and proposals for her to review. She extracted the other mail carefully. Two magazines, four catalogs, one advertisement for a new pizza place, and four envelopes.

The first envelope was her phone bill. That was always depressing. She would open that one last. The next two were bank statements, one from checking and one from savings. The last letter was from a credit-card company announcing all over the front of the envelope that she was being rewarded for her excellent credit.

Meredith checked inside the hollowed-out mailbox one more time. It was empty. She stood still just a moment, listening to the chickadees in the glen across the road. No butterflies came anywhere near, let alone perched on her shoulder.

With a kick at the nearest pebble in the road, she headed back home. She had so much work to do. Maybe it was a good thing she hadn't received any kind of interesting mail. It would have sidetracked her, and she would have spent the rest of the day in La La Land.

And what would be so bad about that? I work too hard. I always have. What was that verse? "For whom am I toiling…and why am I depriving myself of enjoyment?"

She couldn't answer that question. Even her sassy alter ego had no comment to make.

"I need some enjoyment," Meredith said later that night as she was talking to her old college roommate on the phone. "Any chance you can leave that possessive husband of yours for a weekend so we can get together?"

"When?" Karlee asked.

"I don't know. Whenever you can get away. We promised each other we would still do our wacky weekends even though you're married, remember? I think it's time to plan some fun. We haven't done anything crazy for more than a year."

"Sounds fun," Karlee said. "How about the second weekend in August?"

"August? This is May, Karlee. I don't want to wait until August!"

"Blake has summer school starting in two weeks, and the weekends are the only time we'll see each other since we're both working full-time. What's wrong with August? We'll get some of the other wild women together and have a blast."

"We can do that," Meri said flatly. "It'll be fun. Let me know what's best for you, and we'll make our plans from there."

They chatted a few more minutes, but Meredith was feeling a surge of depression coming over her again. It didn't help that apparently Blake had begun to tickle Karlee, and Meri could hear Karlee putting her hand over the phone and saying, "Stop it, Blake! I mean it!"

Meredith was no love doctor, but she knew what was going on. "I'll let you go," she said. "Call me sometime."

"Okay," Karlee said, stifling a giggle. "I will. Bye."

Before Meredith hung up, she heard Karlee letting loose with a burst of hilarity. "You asked for it!" Karlee said playfully, and then the line went dead.

Meredith sat for a long time and wondered what to do with her longings. It would be nice to have a companion, a pal, a person who tickled her while she was on the phone, someone who loved her and whom she could love. In short, she wanted a husband.

Her thoughts reminded her of the prayer she had prayed consistently since she was fourteen years old. That summer her camp counselor, right here at Camp Autumn Brook, had told her to start praying for her future husband. And so Meredith, sitting in her Tulip Cottage, prayed once again, "Father God, please protect my future husband wherever he is, whoever he is, and direct him on a straight path. Bring him to yourself if he's not already a follower of you. Prepare me in my heart and life for him so that when we do come together we can be well suited to serve you together. Amen."

The prayer was familiar but not canned. She meant every word, even though she had prayed it hundreds of times over the past ten years.

Ten years, Meredith thought. *I've been praying for the same thing for ten years. Either God has forgotten about me or he's been working extra hard and long on a hero for me who will surpass my expectations.*

An image of Jacob Wilde materialized in her thoughts.

Yeah, right, she chided herself. Before her imagination

could make up any tantalizing stories, Meredith stood and warned herself, *Don't go there, Meri Jane. Fantasy is a wonderful thing but not when it comes to true matters of the heart. Stay level-headed. God is preparing someone just right for you.*

Her long-held image of that someone came to mind. He would be short and balding with thick, horn-rimmed glasses. And he would be eminently practical in all the areas of life where Meredith was a klutz. He would raise their children with a firm hand and teach them to respect their elders and eat their lima beans. He would never take money from the retirement account to buy a car, and he would smile warmly at Meredith whenever she entered the room.

"Ha!" Meredith declared aloud. "Ha, ha, and double ha!" It dawned on her that all these years her image of God's pick for her husband had been a duplicate of her father.

How scary is that? I have to rethink this longing-of-my-heart business.

She stared at the kitchen cupboards. As she did, her mind was diverted from thinking about marriage. She had never noticed before, but the cupboard on the end had the profile of a face in the dark wood grain. Amazing. If she tilted her head to the left just so, it kind of looked like Elvis. Elvis in the early years.

"I think I need a goldfish," she suddenly declared to the silhouette in the cupboard. The idea came out of the blue, where her best and most imaginative thoughts came from. And she thought it was a good one.

On Monday morning, Meredith got up early, showered, drove into town, and entered the only pet shop on the island promptly at nine A.M., just as the doors opened. There wasn't much selection.

"Are these your best goldfish?" she asked the shopkeeper.

"Everything in my shop is the best," he answered in a burly voice.

"I'd like that one right there." She pointed to a pudgy gold-fish with an iridescent stripe along the side of his gills. The salesman plunged a small net on a metal wand into the tank.

"Not that one," Meredith said. "This one over here. Oops, there he goes. Over there. See him? That one with the stripe. Can you get him?"

The man turned and looked at Meredith. "They're all the same, really."

"No, they're not. They're all different. I want the fat one with the shiny stripe on the side. Right there. That one."

The man tried to oblige her, but Meredith's pick was a crafty fellow and slipped out of the net before it was drawn from the water.

"Good for you, Elvis," Meri said. "I like a guy with imagi-nation."

The salesman slowly turned to look her over again.

"Don't give up," she urged, unaffected by the owner's stares. "Here he comes. I'll do it. Give me the net. I'll catch him."

Meredith took the net from the man before he had a chance to protest. In one quick snatch she captured her favored fishy. "That wasn't so hard," she said, slipping Elvis into the plastic bag half filled with water.

"Now, I need a bowl and some food, and do you have any of those little deep-sea divers with the ceramic treasure chests?" Meredith smiled at the man, who was far from amused by her childlike enthusiasm over this new pet.

"Last aisle on the right," he said. Then he turned and went to the cash register as if it were more important to guard the till from this customer than to help her find what she was after.

Meredith located a bowl, some colored rocks for the bot-tom, plastic green foliage, a small cardboard canister of fish food, and a sea-horse decal, but no miniature divers with a treasure chest.

"You seem to be out of divers and treasure chests," she said when she had brought all her goodies to the cash register.

"Oh, are we now?" the man said.

"Do you think you'll be getting any more in?"

"It's unlikely."

Meredith realized this was a small pet store on an island with limited resources. Seattle was only a ferry ride away, but still she thought the man would want to special order for customers to keep them happy.

Meri paid for Elvis and his accessories. Then, before she left the shop, she turned and asked, "How do you tell if it's a boy?"

"He's a boy," the man said. "Trust me. He's a boy."

Meri shrugged and trotted off to her Explorer. "Ready to go to your new home, Elvis?" Then, to make sure his journey involved the least amount of discomfort, Meri held the sloshing plastic bag in her right hand and drove with her left. She was halfway home when her cell phone rang.

"Okay, hang on, Elvis. You sit right here on the seat but try not to wet anything, okay? Not that it would be your fault if you leaked."

"Hello? This is Meredith."

"Hi," a familiar female voice said on the other end. "Glad I caught you. Did you get the manuscripts I sent the other day?"

"Helen!" Meredith greeted the literary agent who had also become her good buddy. "How are you? Guess what? I got a fish!"

"Congratulations," Helen said. "How big is it?"

Meredith glanced over at the jostling Elvis. "About an inch and a half, I'd guess."

There was a pause before Helen said in a dry tone, "Have you considered changing your bait?"

Meredith laughed and turned the steering wheel, maneuvering the Explorer onto the road that led home. "I bought him, you goof! At the pet store. His name is Elvis. Hey, Elvis, say hi to Helen." Meredith put the phone next to the bouncing bubble for a half-second and then put the phone back to her ear. "He's kind of shy," she explained to Helen.

There was another pause, and then Helen said, "Are you taking those herbal uppers, Meri?"

"No, of course not," she answered with a laugh. "I've actually been kind of depressed, so I thought a little goldfish would cheer me up."

"You're not going to swallow it or anything, are you?"

"No." Meredith laughed. "Of course not."

"Okay, well then I'd say as a pet, it seems the goldfish is working to cure your depression. Remind me to recommend your goldfish therapy to all my depressed editors. Now, back to business, or are you taking the day off?"

"Nope," Meredith said, slowly pulling into her bumpy driveway. "I'm on my way to the office right now."

"Do you want me to call you back?" Helen asked.

"No, I received the manuscripts, but I haven't looked at them yet. They're in the stack, and you know how fair I am about taking my stack in order."

"Listen, if you ever wanted to score some points with the powers that be, this would be the time to shuffle the stack and move my client's manuscript out of that envelope and onto your desk."

"Why?" Meredith said, slowly bringing the car to a stop in front of her cottage and turning off the engine.

"It's a honey," Helen said simply.

Helen had different levels for the projects she pitched to Meredith, and Meri had learned her code. A "honey" was the top-of-the-list, highest-awards kind of manuscript, at least in Helen's opinion. Next down the list was a "player." That meant

the proposed project could hold its own at any reputable publishing house, but Meri was honored to be one of the chosen
few to have a first look. The third grade of project was a
"keeper." Helen never had bad manuscripts or projects, but
the keepers were the ones that might not quite fit in the front
lineup.

"Good. It's been a few months since you sent me any honeys," Meredith said, unbuckling her seat belt. "I must say, it's
about time."

"Speaking of my sending you honeys…" Helen said.

The cell phone began to break up its transmission, and
Meredith realized the battery needed to be recharged. "Say that
again," Meredith said.

"I said I'm coming through Seattle with a client on Friday.
You want to meet us in town, or should we come out to see
you?"

As much as Meredith liked Helen, she did not like making
special trips into Seattle to meet Helen and her clients. The last
time they had tried to meet, Helen's plane had been delayed,
which meant Meredith had missed a whole afternoon of work
just waiting around at the airport. When Helen did arrive, she
had only twenty minutes before her next flight, and her client
was so shy she barely said two words.

"If you have time, come see me. I'll feed you and introduce
you to Elvis."

"Can't wait," Helen said. "Expect us around dinnertime,
then."

"See you," Meredith said. The transmission cut out before
she heard Helen say good-bye. She cautiously lifted Elvis's bag,
picked up all the other goodies, and headed into the house.

"You're going to like it here, Elvis. Just you and me and the
crickets outside my window. You have a preference which side
of the kitchen counter you live on? Or do you want to hang out

in my office? Yeah, that's where you belong. Up in the office loft with me. It's kind of a mess, but it's cozy."

Meri unlocked her door and happily went about setting up Elvis in his new fish bowl. Once he was released and swimming free, Meri rested her head on her hands and watched her new friend make himself at home.

"Sorry I couldn't get you a little diver and sea chest. But keep it on your birthday wish list, and we'll see what happens."

Meredith suddenly stood up straight. "Birthday!" she said aloud. With a glance over at the wall calendar, she double checked. Sure enough, Friday was her birthday. "Oh, great. I get to spend my birthday with Helen and one of her clients. Not that I mind spending the evening with Helen, but now it's going to be business."

A sweeping wind of depression came over her. She was going to be twenty-five in four days. A quarter of a century should be marked by a big blowout, but who would plan such an event for her? Shelly would send her a present, and her other two sisters would send cards a few days late with notes hastily scrawled inside saying how one of the kids had chicken pox or the water heater had broken or some other legitimate reason they were late in their birthday wishes.

Meredith knew her parents would made a concerted effort to do something for her. They would probably invite her over to their house for dinner, and Mom would have one of those slick round cakes from the grocery store with number candles stuck in the top of the waxy white frosting. They would give her a gift certificate to J.C. Penney. That's what they always gave the four Graham girls for their birthdays.

With a sigh, Meredith picked up Elvis's bowl and slowly made her way up the stairs to her loft office. In a way, she was glad now that Helen was coming Friday. It meant she didn't have to go to her parents' and eat grocery-store cake with waxy white frosting and be humbled by the fact that, at twenty-five (as the bold candles affixed in the center of the cake would proclaim), she was very much alone in this world with no one to celebrate with her.

"I'll just have to tell my mom we already have plans, won't I, Elvis?" Meredith pushed some papers away from the corner of her desk and placed the fish bowl on top of an old memo from her publishing house. "So, how do you like the view?"

Elvis swished his tail. Meredith leaned closer and imitated his open-lipped kissing motions. Elvis didn't seem to notice.

"This is good for me. A male who is oblivious to my charms, even when I try to offer him kisses."

The phone rang before she could slump into a ditch of depression. It was a conference call with her publisher. She had forgotten about it.

"Yes," Meredith said, switching to her professional tone and pretending she was wearing a designer suit with a silk blouse instead of overalls and a bandanna. "How are all of you this morning?"

The conference call lasted almost an hour. She watched Elvis the whole time and doodled on her blotter. This was not a meeting that she needed to "attend," and it was hard to appear interested long distance. It was also torture to sit there with mounds of work stacked up around her. Meredith had learned the hard way that it didn't pay to try to do paperwork while on one of these conference calls. Her phone didn't have a mute button, and those on the other end could hear every piece of paper rattling over the speaker phone. They could probably hear the scratching of her automatic pencil as she doodled. But they couldn't hear Elvis, which was another reason he was such a wonderful addition to her life.

Chapter Eleven

*M*eredith bought some balloons in town on Friday afternoon when she went to pick up groceries for her birthday dinner. She tied them to her mailbox just to make herself feel happier. If Helen had forgotten it was Meri's birthday, the balloons might spark a memory when she drove in tonight.

After Meredith tied the balloons onto the mailbox's rusty latch, she checked inside the box. Nothing yet. And there might not be anything at all. Certainly the possibility of a letter from Jake was almost nonexistent. It had been close to two weeks. She would see him in twelve more days at the conference in Anaheim, but then, who was counting?

Shelly had already sent her birthday present. It arrived on Thursday and was a gorgeous, way-too-expensive leather briefcase that Meredith had been eyeing in an in-flight catalog for almost two years now. She would never buy it for herself because it seemed like such an extravagant shoulder bag. Shelly was famous for her inconsistency in giving gifts. She wouldn't buy anything unless it had meaning or was really nice. Some birthdays all Meri received from her was a phone call because Shelly's philosophy was not to buy a trinket just to say she had purchased a gift. If she was going to give a present, she would wait until she found something fantastic.

Meredith certainly thought the briefcase was fantastic. When she called Shelly last night to thank her, Meri reached the answering machine. She had teased Shelly and said, "I love the leather pouch, Shel! The only thing is, I know I'll be in my early thirties before I ever get another present from you."

Meredith hoped Shelly had managed to obtain some kind of discount, because the briefcase was offered in an airline magazine and Shelly had worked for that airline for five years before marrying Jonathan. It wasn't likely, but it was possible the company gave discounts to airline personnel.

At any rate, it was the nicest present she could have asked for, and she would put it to good use for many years.

Pulling up to the front of the cottage, Meri noticed a large box on her front porch, which UPS must have left while she was in town. *Who else would send me anything? I don't think Mom and Dad would switch from gift certificates to actual merchandise-type gifts this late in the game. All my other friends are married and broke or single and forgetful. Who could have sent something?*

For one childish moment, she thought Jake had finally made his move. The large box was a giant fruit basket. That's what it was!

She left the groceries in the car and dashed to see who the box was from. The instant Meredith saw the return address, her heart sank. It was from Aunt Jane. Aunt Jane, the quirky spinster who fit the description of every strange and wonderfully kooky relative who ever lived. The gift would be something completely useless, wildly impractical, and valuable only when one needed an outrageous white-elephant gift.

Two years ago at Christmas—or was it three?—Aunt Jane had given Meredith two matching umbrella hats. These were not hats to be worn in the rain but rather sun umbrella hats. They fit snugly on the head and sported a colorful striped umbrella that fanned out like a psychedelic mushroom. They were great for laughs, and Meri actually wore one of them while working in the garden. It served its purpose well. But then, nobody saw her wearing it.

Meredith tore at the packing tape with her car keys and wondered what catalog her aunt had found this hummer in. It was double wrapped and was posing a problem on the front porch. Meredith kicked the big box into the house and scooted it over to the living-room floor. She would wrestle the beast later, after she brought the perishable groceries inside.

Since it was her birthday dinner, Meredith had selected all her favorites. She had bought fresh pasta, her all-time favorite food. An Italian restaurant near the ferry terminal sold fresh pasta by the pound. Meri picked up fettuccine and herb-and-garlic linguine. She bought some of their fresh marinara dip and mozzarella sticks for an appetizer. She would make the Alfredo sauce herself right before Helen arrived.

The item she was most concerned about in the grocery bags was the raspberry cheesecake from a little restaurant called Rondi's, which was located on the other side of the island. She brought that box in and refrigerated it right away. No number candles would perch on the top of this cheesecake, and no waxy frosting would stick to the roof of her mouth. This might not be such a bad birthday after all.

Once Meri had put away all the groceries and checked her voice mail, she returned to the living room ready to see what

Aunt Jane had sent. Slicing the tape carefully with a kitchen knife, Meredith peeled back the first layer and found a big card from Aunt Jane taped with duct tape to the gift-wrapped box.

"Happy Birthday, Meredith Jane," it said on the outside envelope. Aunt Jane liked to remind Meredith that she had inherited *Jane* as her middle name. When Meredith was younger, the family would tease her after she had pulled one of her wacky stunts and tell her she was just like Aunt Jane. It bothered Meri so much that they finally stopped. A twinge of fright mixed with anger came to her with the memory. Here she was, twenty-five years old and single. She lived alone in the woods and talked to goldfish. Maybe she was turning out to be just like her Aunt Jane after all.

No, Aunt Jane was wealthy yet lived like a pauper. Meri would never be like that. If Meri ever inherited a large sum of money from a strange piano teacher, she was certain she would find wonderful ways to pad her life with beautiful excess. The only excess Aunt Jane had indulged in was a tiny cabin on the Oregon coast where she spent her summer months.

Ripping back the yellow rose gift wrap, Meredith could see the label on the box. She immediately convinced herself that the words on the box did not have any bearing on what was inside the box.

Aunt Jane would not send me something like that!

Meredith pulled open the top of the box, which was sealed with wide copper staples. She slowly pulled the long, plastic contents from the box. The instructions came with it.

Still in shock, Meri read the instructions. "Meet Guard Man! The only bodyguard you'll ever need. Guard Man is life-like and poseable. Dress him in casual clothes when he sits in the chair by your front window or in formal attire when he accompanies you to a night on the town. You'll always feel safe when Guard Man is near!"

Meredith stared at the deflated rubber dummy her crazy aunt had sent her. *I can't believe this. Aunt Jane sent me a blow-up man!*

She started to laugh, and the whole cottage reverberated with the mixture of her shock and hilarity. Ripping open the duct-taped envelope of the birthday card, she found a card and a flattened "patch kit." The card was actually a piece of yellow-lined paper that read, "I got to thinking about your living there all alone, and I thought you should have your very own Guard Man. I've had mine for two years now, and I haven't been robbed once. My Guard Man goes to town with me, too, and I feel safe as can be. Enjoy! And be safe. Your Aunt Jane. Love."

She always signed that way: her name first and then her closing sentiment. Meredith skimmed the card a second time and pictured her sixty-eight-year-old auntie scooting around town with Guard Man in the passenger seat of her 1979 Volvo.

"This is unbelievable!" Meredith went for the portable phone on the kitchen wall. She punched number three, and the phone speed dialed Shelly's number.

Shelly answered on the second ring.

"You're not going to believe this," Meri said. "Guess what I got for my birthday?"

"Do you like it?" Shelly asked.

"Like it? Oh! You mean the leather case. Yes, I love it. Didn't you get my message? Thank you so, so, so, so much, Shelly. It's way too expensive, and you shouldn't have, but I love it completely and will use it constantly. Thanks."

"You're welcome," Shelly said.

Meredith took a little breath and looked over at the massive blob on the floor. "Now guess what else I received for my birthday."

"Let me see. A gift certificate to Penney's?"

"You have no imagination at all, Shelly. Come on. Try to guess."

"At least give me a clue. Who's it from?"

Meredith knew her sister had little patience for guessing games. "It's from Aunt Jane, and it came in a big box and is slumped on the floor in the living room right now. It comes with instructions."

"From Aunt Jane? I can't even begin to guess."

"Shelly, she sent me a blow-up man."

"A what?"

"A blow-up man. One of those life-sized plastic man-nequins. Guard Man. I'm supposed to dress him up casual for afternoons around the house and formal for those snappy evenings out on the town. Can you believe this?"

Shelly was laughing so hard that Bob Two started to bark in the background. It took a minute before she could respond to Meredith. "That has to be the best gag gift ever!"

"She didn't mean it as a gag gift." Meredith moaned.

"Don't you dare try to white elephant Mr. Guard Man! I want him there, in shorts, on the front porch the next time I come up for a visit."

"In shorts?" Meredith repeated. "I can accommodate you there. That's all Mr. Guard Man is wearing. White, painted-on boxer shorts."

Shelly burst out laughing again. "Thank goodness for that! At least he's modest."

"What am I going to do with this guy?"

"Same thing you've always done with your boyfriends: Hide him when Mom and Dad come over."

"Very funny."

"They are coming over tonight, aren't they?"

"No. I told them I had plans. Helen is coming into town with a client, and I'm fixing dinner for them."

"You could play a hilarious joke on Helen," Shelly said. "Get Guard Boy all dressed up and put him in the pantry. Then send Helen to the pantry for something, and he'll scare her silly."

Meredith liked the idea. Helen had a good sense of humor. She would like the joke. Of course, Meredith had no clue if the client would be a stuffy old coot or a timid young thing.

"You're a genius," Meri said. "When did you get so creative? One Guard Man in the pantry coming right up."

"Call me tomorrow and tell me what happens," Shelly said. "Oh, and by the way, you'll never guess who's going to have dinner with us tomorrow night."

"I give up." Meredith was too busy trying to figure out what clothes she had around for Mr. Guard Man to guess.

"The one and only Jacob Wilde," Shelly said proudly.

Meredith's heart and plans stopped.

"They have clearance to film his new movie here at the waterfall, and he's coming to make the final arrangements with Jonathan. Is there anything you want me to tell him?"

"When does your matchmaking license expire?" Meri said. "You have to let this obsession go, Shelly."

"I'll tell him you say hi and you're interested in hearing more about the film."

That part was actually true. "What's it about?" Meri asked.

"Kyle said it's a children's film that's a remake of *Pilgrim's Progress* with a Narnian twist, if that makes sense. Kyle is a big fan of *Pilgrim's Progress* and has started a collection of the older volumes of the book. He read the screenplay a while ago, but I guess it needed some work. They hired some well-known guy to rewrite it, and now they're working on filming it."

"It sounds like a great project," Meredith said calmly.

"Kyle's behind the film a thousand percent. You really should come down this weekend, Meri. Not just to bump into

Jake again; this is going to be fun. Come join in the adventure. We're all pretty excited. Come down tonight. Can you call Helen and reschedule?"

"I don't think I can do that. She'll be here in two or three hours. Besides, I have the best trick in the world to play on her. I'm not going to let this one slip by."

"Come tomorrow morning," Shelly urged.

"I have too much work. I've been playing all day and haven't done anything."

"Well," Shelly said slowly, "is there anything you want me to say to Jake? Any messages I can pass along?"

"No, thanks. I'm going to see him in a couple of weeks at a conference in Anaheim. I'd rather wait and try to start all over with him. I think the less said till then the better."

"Okay. I'll honor that."

"You better."

"I will."

"Thanks again for the beautiful birthday present. It's my second-favorite present so far."

"What's your favorite? Mr. Guard Man?"

"No, the gift certificate from J.C. Penney. Now I have money to outfit my new permanent houseguest."

Chapter Twelve

"Y ou need what?" Jack, the director of Camp Autumn Brook, asked Meri. The camp bordered the property on which the Tulip Cottage sat, and every month Meredith paid her rent directly to the camp because the owner had recently deeded the cottage over to the conference center. Meredith had grown up at this camp, attending family camp and summer and winter conferences. She had helped Jack out more than once, and now it was his turn to do her a favor.

"Old clothes," Meredith repeated her request. "Any old lost-and-found men's clothes."

"What are you doing? Making a scarecrow?" he asked.

"Yes," Meri said with a giggle, "that's exactly what I'm making. A scarecrow-man-thing."

"Fine with me if you help yourself. You know where we keep all the lost and found, don't you?"

"The shed behind the pool?" Meredith guessed.

Jack nodded. "It's open; so go on in and help yourself. If

anyone tries to stop you, tell him I said it was okay."

Meredith didn't see any other camp staff as she made her way to the shed behind the pool. Mounds of forgotten clothes and goods were heaped along the south side of the shed. It took her less than five minutes to find a complete outfit for Guard Man, including shoes, socks, and a New York Giants baseball cap. She had brought a Nordstroms shopping bag with her and had to control her giggles as she stole across the conference-center grounds back to her house, her posh shopping bag loaded with smelly camp clothes. Once inside and feeling "safe" again, Meredith set to work washing the soiled clothes, starting the salad for dinner, jumping into the shower, and then inflating Guard Man and outfitting him for the grand event. This was turning out to be a pretty fun birthday party after all. Then, because she didn't want Elvis to feel left out, she went upstairs and brought her goldfish down to the coffee table, where he could be in the center of everything.

Elvis and Guard Man seemed to ignore each other. "At least I know you're not the jealous type," she said. "Either of you. We might be able to work out an agreeable arrangement here. You don't snore, do you, Guard Man?"

The brunette mannequin with the backward baseball cap responded with a fixed gaze. Meredith reached over and made him shake his head.

"I didn't think you did. What about chores? Can you sit over in that chair all day and keep it weighed down so it won't slide across the floor in case of an earthquake?"

Guard Man nodded his head, with a little help.

"Okay. Then as long as you never leave your toenail clippings on the carpet, it looks like we have a deal."

Meredith took Guard Man's hand and shook it.

"I am utterly, completely losing my mind," she muttered.

"It was bad enough when I talked to a pudgy-lipped fish all day, no offense, Elvis, but now look at me! I'm making deals with a certifiable airhead!" Meredith leaned over and took a closer look at her fish. "You don't really have lips, do you? I take that pudgy-lips comment back."

Meredith glanced at the clock on the kitchen wall. "Yikes! Time to dress. You stay here and read the paper or something." She positioned Guard Man in the easy chair and crossed his legs. Adjusting his shoulders so he didn't look so stiff, Meredith placed the newspaper in his hands.

Curiosity tortured her until, despite her robe-and-slippers wardrobe, she ran outside and looked in the window from the driveway. "Amazing," she murmured, in awe of Aunt Jane's gift. "He does look real."

Slipping back inside the cottage and rifling through her closet, Meredith settled on a slim black dress. It was basic but much more formal than Mr. Guard Man's attire. Still, it was her birthday, and she could wear whatever she wanted. After weeks of shorts, jeans, and overalls as her daily career apparel, she wanted to wear a dress.

Helen always dressed nicely. She would most likely show up in a pants suit with a long jacket covering her ample backside. Helen's cropped hair would be moussed in place, and she would wear big earrings. Her heels would be too high and impractical for the gravel driveway and the uneven boards on Meri's front porch. But that didn't matter. Helen would take off her shoes within ten minutes of her arrival, complaining about having walked too much that day. Then she would rub her soles on the carpet like a cat on a scratching post. That was Helen. The only feature open for speculation would be her hair. She changed hair color as often as she changed shoes.

Meredith hurried with her makeup and smoothed her hair

to the side. She patted the flyaway ends into place as she gave her hair a quick spray and then shook her head to make the hair settle naturally.

Another look in the mirror prompted Meredith to examine herself more closely. She smiled, and fine lines scrunched around her eyes. "I'm getting wrinkles. Did you hear that, Guard Man? I'm getting wrinkles. I'm old today. Twenty-five. How old are you?"

He didn't respond.

"Ah, the strong, silent type. I can respect that." She scrutinized her outfit. "Boring. It needs something. A necklace? A scarf? What do I have?"

Meredith rarely wore earrings. Her ears weren't pierced, and since she spent so much time on the phone, she was likely to leave one clip-on earring on her desk and then take off to the grocery store looking like a pirate.

The gold chain, the string of fake pearls, and the silk scarf she tried with the outfit made it look too formal. She settled on a long string of wooden beads and a thick wooden carved bracelet that toned down the sleeveless black dress and gave her more of an earthy look than a formal one.

Don't want to outdress my Guard Man after all.

"How are you two doing in here?" Meredith asked, coming back into the living room, where Elvis and Guard Man remained exactly where she had left them. "Everybody happy? What do you think of the outfit?" She turned around. "No complaints? Good. Time to get some dinner going."

Meri put on an apron and set to work, filling a big pot with water and placing it on the stove. She rinsed two bunches of fresh broccoli and prepared them for steaming. The linguine and fettuccine were ready to be cooked, and the mozzarella sticks were neatly lined up on a cookie sheet to pop into the oven at the last minute.

Meredith looked at the clock. It was 6:37, but there was no sign of Helen. Meri didn't want to start anything until Helen arrived so it would all be fresh and hot. There was plenty of time to set a fancy table, or so it seemed. Meredith pulled her three place settings of good china from the top shelf of her cupboard. Three settings was all she had, but that's all she needed. One for her, one for Helen, one for Helen's client. Guard Man wouldn't be eating with them tonight.

Guard Man! I almost forgot!

Meredith dashed into the living room and grabbed the dummy from the easy chair. She stuffed him into the tiny pantry and squeezed the door shut.

"There. Now take shallow breaths, and you won't use up all the air. When Helen opens the door, you say, 'Boo!'"

Meredith finished setting the table and even found a candle for the center. She pulled the small table out from the wall and angled it to the side so there was more room all around. It looked nice. All she needed were some flowers. No problem. The woods around her house were loaded. At least they had been a month ago. It might be harder to find them among the now-drooping grasses. But she knew some spots near the house were shaded by the great evergreens that filled the island. The sun probably hadn't seared those spring beauties yet.

Venturing into the cool of the evening, Meredith picked up the hem of her apron and began to gather violets, lupine, and wild pansies. The air smelled warm and musky. It would probably rain tonight. A closing-in-of-the-clouds feeling settled on her like a shawl as she walked. Dirt stuck to the bottom of her clogs, and dried stalks of field flowers, now faded, brushed against her bare legs.

Overhead a phoebe bird wailed her evening cry, "Fee-bee, fee-bee." It sounded to Meredith like the cry of a lonely soul, looking for its mate. "Fee-bee, fee-bee," it cried with what Meri thought of as a frantic wail. The dusk ushered in the close of the day.

"Fee-bee," Meredith whispered back. She sat down on an uneven, moldy stump and looked up at the sky streaked with pale, gray clouds. The sun wouldn't set until almost nine. It would be a perfect night for a walk around the lake before the gathering clouds rained on her parade.

All was quiet.

Meredith drew in the scent of the rich earth around her and released her own "fee-bee" cry to God. "I know you're here, Father. I know you love me deeply and intimately, but it's not the same as being loved by another human. You know what I mean, don't you? Of course you do. You know everything."

A sudden flapping of wings sounded as a group of feathered friends took off out of the tree behind Meredith and headed for the lake. "I know I'm supposed to delight myself in you and you will give me the desires of my heart. And I do love you, God. I do. I'm learning how to delight myself in you. It's just that I have this longing. What was that verse? 'A longing fulfilled is a tree of life.'"

She lifted her chin and studied the trees surrounding her. A tree of life. What does that mean? It struck her that all around her was life. The trees were full of it. She spotted a woodpecker busily digging out his dinner. Two bushy-tailed squirrels chased each other across the limbs. Baby birds chirped persistently somewhere to the left of where she sat. These trees were full of life.

"I love my job; I love my house; I love everything you've done for me," Meredith continued her prayer. "But I guess I want my days to be more full of life, you know? I want to share my days with someone who loves you and who loves me. I want my little 'tree' to be more full of life. Real life. Not just silent goldfish and posed inner tubes wearing camp clothes."

Contentedly waiting for her whispers to be carried off on the evening breeze, Meredith sat still, gazing at the bouquet of wild flowers gathered in her lap.

She had underlined and pondered many verses over the years as she thought of them relating to her future spouse. She had even made a list of them and kept it in the back of her Bible. One of them was Proverbs 14:22, "Those who plan what is good find love and faithfulness." Another was Psalm 84:11, "No good thing does he withhold from those whose walk is blameless." Then the ever-popular Proverbs 3:5–6, "Trust in the LORD with all your heart and lean not on your own understanding; in all your ways acknowledge him, and he will make your paths straight."

These and other bits of Scripture like Matthew 6:33, "Seek first the kingdom of God and His righteousness, and all these things shall be added to you," had formed her foundational philosophy of husband hunting while she was in college. It was easy to hold up her virtuous creed because she attended a small Christian college and most of the students at least gave lip service to the same philosophy. They all said they believed God was the one who brought two people together. Each person's part was to wait on him and to do what Scripture told him or her to do.

Meredith still believed those core principles. But it was harder the older she became to remain convinced that this plan actually worked. She had talked about it once with Helen, who called herself "a nonpracticing Protestant who married a Jewish lawyer because I believe in the power of love." Helen had merely laughed when Meredith told her she felt she was getting old.

"Herb and I were in our late thirties when we met," Helen

spouted. "It was the first time for love and marriage for both of us, and it's been absolutely marvelous. You're barely halfway there, girl! So cut out the old-maid bit and live your life merrily while you can still wear Spandex in public."

Meredith meandered her way back to the front of the cottage. She still saw no sign of her dinner guests. Instead of going in, she did a quick check on the flower bed along the side of the house. There, waiting for her, were two late-blooming tulips, both a soft purple shade and only about six inches high. The daffodils were long gone. She had "dead headed" them a week ago, snapping off their dried-up blossoms and leaving the tall green stalks to wither on their own before she trimmed them away. That's what Mom always did to her daffodils; so Meredith followed suit, even though she didn't know why she was doing it.

What other things do I do in my life that are merely imitations of what I've watched someone else do? Is this theory of waiting for God's best some kind of mindless mimicking of my peers who are now all happily married? Or is this mine? Do I really believe God has one perfect man for me?

Meredith was surprised that some deep blue, burgundy, and yellow primroses were beginning their second bloom of the season in the side garden. A few pink hyacinths clustered in the far corner, and a clump of white candy tuft was spilling over the rock border in the front. The little spring bulb garden had been neglected this year since Shelly was the one who liked flower gardening. Meredith was more drawn to the vegetable garden. There was something poetic about a blooming pea vine as it climbed up a trellis or the way carrot tops fanned out like green lace when they were full grown. She picked the hyacinth and promised herself she would work on the patch next week.

Overhead five or so cheeping birds swooped in unison and

darted into the woods. The patient phoebe cried out again in the pleasant coolness of the evening, "Fee-bee, fee-bee."

I could wait, God. I could wait another twenty years as long as I knew there really was someone for me. Someone who, right now, in his corner of the world is also talking to you like this about me. Someone who wants a soul mate as dearly as I want one. Someone who also thinks that two are better than one because they have a good reward for their labor. You are working on this, aren't you? I mean, you haven't forgotten about me, have you?

Chapter Thirteen

$\mathcal{M}$eredith gathered the flowers in her apron and went back inside to finish decorating the table. It was 7:40 now, and still no sign of Helen. The error on Meredith's part, she realized, was that she hadn't asked specific questions. Helen had merely said "dinnertime." That could mean a variety of things to Helen. Then there was the ferry factor. If Helen hadn't managed to crowd onto one of the ferries during the five o'clock rush hour, she could end up waiting in line for an hour or more.

It would have been easier if Meri had gone into Seattle to meet Helen, Meri now realized. She would have been going against traffic, and she could have gone early and spent the afternoon shopping.

Too late now to change plans. She arranged her flowers and waited. There was no hurry to eat. The pasta would be delicious whenever she made it, even if it was at midnight.

Meredith washed a stalk of celery and sat down to nibble

on it while she watched TV. Nothing that interested her was on. She was about to turn off the television when she surfed across a cable program that caught her eye. It was a ballroom-dance competition.

Watching and snapping her celery stalk, Meredith heard a mocking voice inside her head. *Look at you. It's your birthday, and you're alone, eating celery and watching people with glued-on smiles do the tango.*

Meredith ignored the voice. Ever since Elvis and Guard Man had come into her life, she had developed a soft spot in her heart for those who lived with pasted-on smiles. Neither the mannequin nor the fish could help it that he never changed his expression. The thought of the two of them made her decide to check on Guard Man to make sure he hadn't sprung a leak in the pantry. Aunt Jane had sent the patch kit for a reason, Meri figured.

Guard Man was fine. He popped out appropriately when Meri opened the door. She knew he would send Helen through the roof. Whenever she arrived, that is. Until then, Meri felt a little sorry for Guard Man. The music on the TV changed to the cha-cha.

Taking Guard Man by the hand, Meri asked, "Would you like to dance?" With his hand on her shoulder and her right hand holding his right hand waist high, Meri and Guard Man trotted across the kitchen floor and into the dining room.

"No, like this," she instructed her silent partner. "One, two, cha-cha-cha. That's it. One, two. You've got it."

She reached over and turned up the TV's volume so they could feel the rhythm of the music. "You're pretty good," she shouted into her blow-up man's ear. "Matter of fact, you're very good. I think I have the perfect name for you: Fred. You like it? There are a lot of very cool Freds, you know. There's Fred

Astaire, the dancer. Fred Flintstone, the caveman, and Fred Mertz—you know, Ricky Ricardo's best friend. They're all very cool, just like you."

Meredith attempted a spin. Facing her Fred once more, she giggled and said, "What's that? You think I watch too much late-night television? You could be right."

The music stopped. The TV audience applauded, and the next couple whirled out onto the floor. The commentator announced their dance style, and Meredith said, "I don't know this one. Do you?"

She watched the TV over her shoulder and attempted to imitate their dramatic moves while keeping Fred in tow. Forward, back, side, side. It was a quick, staccato dance, and Meredith laughed at how silly it felt to move her shoulders and hips the way she did, imitating the professional woman in the twirling purple skirt.

Her laughter continued as the big finish arrived. Meri caught the cue of the music and leaned way back as if Fred were dipping her like the guy on TV was dipping his partner.

Meri's beaded necklace flew up in her face as the top of her head nearly touched the top of the coffee table. She froze.

There, less than five feet away, stood Helen, who had opened the door to let herself in. Next to Helen stood her client.

Even though Meredith was upside down, she knew that face. The tanned face with the startled expression could only belong to one man: Jacob Wilde.

Meri stayed frozen. She didn't know how to explain herself out of this one. Helen and Jake were frozen, too, their eyebrows raised in bemusement.

Slowly straightening, Meredith led Fred over to the easy chair and put the newspaper back in his hands. She calmly adjusted her dress and hair, and then, clearing her throat, she turned to face her company.

Helen's eyes were still wide behind her round glasses. Her mouth was open. Jake's lips were pressed tightly together. He looked as if he was about to crack up the way he had at the waterfall when she smashed the muffin in his face. To help him along, Meredith broke into a smile, then a giggle, then a laugh, then a gut-splitting roar of hilarity.

Helen and Jacob quickly followed. None of them moved from where they stood. They just looked at each other and laughed. Helen pointed to Fred, and they laughed. The TV blasted the music from the ballroom-dance competition, and Meredith laughed until the tears slid down her cheeks. She wiped away the tears, her shoulders still shaking.

When Helen finally found her voice, she wiped her own tears and said, "Meredith Graham, I'd like you to meet Jake Wilde."

As soon as she made the introduction, Jake and Meri burst out laughing again.

"We've met," Jake finally managed to say.

"Under even more embarrassing circumstances than this, if you can believe it," Meredith said as she turned off the television.

"I believe it, girlfriend!" Helen said, slipping off her shoes and heading for the nearest chair. "Never in my life…You are the funniest…. If only I had a camera." Helen plopped down on the chair and drew in a deep breath. Her hair was deep red this week. The same shade as her flushed face.

"I didn't know you were Helen's client," Meri said to Jake, trying to salvage any shred of professionalism she might have left. "Helen never mentioned your name."

Jacob smiled at Meredith and took a seat on the couch. "I asked her not to."

"But I didn't know you two knew each other," Helen said. "I thought the incognito plan was because of all the movie-star attention you always complain about."

This changes everything. Jacob knew he was coming to see me. Isn't he the sly one? Did he arrange this with Helen after I told him I worked for G. H. Terrison?

"Now we know what the balloons were for," Jake said to Helen. "A party is going on."

"It's my birthday," Meredith announced. She figured she had nothing to hide and nothing to lose with these two. If Jake already thought she was "original," she would take the opportunity to prove it to the tenth power. He must like original women. Why else would he be here? "Fred and I were just doing a little celebrating."

"Fred!" Helen burst out in another fit of laughter. "Where did you get him?"

"My aunt Jane sent him today. He's a Guard Man. Guaranteed to protect me out here in the boonies."

"We thought a party was in full swing when we pulled up and the music was so loud. You couldn't hear us knock. We could see you through the window," Helen said. "It looked as if you were dancing with a real man."

Meredith was still standing in the middle of the living-room floor. "Let the party continue!" she said. "I'm sure it'll be lots more fun with guests who talk back. No offense, Fred. Why don't you two just relax a minute, and I'll start dinner. I bet you both would like something to drink. I have juice, diet soda, and iced tea."

"Do you have any white wine?" Helen asked. Then she answered her own question. "No, you don't, do you. I should have brought you a bottle. For your birthday. I should have remembered. Happy birthday, Meri. Sorry I didn't bring you anything."

A mischievous little voice inside Meredith's head said, *Are you kidding? You brought Jacob Wilde to my front door!*

"I'll have an iced tea as long as it's not sweetened," Helen said.

"May I get anything for you, Jacob?"

"What's with the 'Jacob'?" Helen asked. "I thought you said you knew him. Call him Jake."

"Would you like anything to drink—" she paused—"Jake?"

He looked a little embarrassed. "Iced tea is fine."

Meredith filled two tall glasses with tea from the pitcher in the refrigerator and reached for some ice cubes in the tray in the freezer. Helen and Jake couldn't see her. Something inside her wanted to kiss the ice cube she was about to drop into the glass for Jake. She didn't. It was a silly, girlish thing she would have done when she was twelve. Ah, to kiss the ice cube that would touch the lips of her favorite star.

But Jake wasn't really a star anymore in her mind. He was …well, a lot of things. A movie star was the least of his qualifications. Tonight he was her guest, and she was a champ when it came to hospitality. He was also Helen's client, and Meredith could be sure Helen had an agenda. Most important, he was a man who intrigued her despite all the awkward circumstances. Hadn't Meredith just been praying about and pondering God's choice for her future husband? And here was Jake, sitting in her living room. He was smiling. He wanted to be here. This was too good to be true.

"Here you go," Meredith said, serving the iced tea.

"Can we send your Fred to another room?" Helen said, rubbing her stocking feet on the rug. "He's looking at me funny."

"I was going to stuff him in the pantry," Meredith said. "It was Shelly's idea, actually. Then I planned to send you to the pantry, Helen, and see what happened when you opened the door and he lurched at you."

"I would have jumped out of my skin! Good thing we crashed your party before you had a chance to play your wicked prank on poor, unsuspecting me." Helen pushed up her glasses. "Where did you get the clothes for him?"

"From the lost and found over at camp." Meredith picked Fred up by the arms and carried him into the guest room. Since Shelly had moved out a year ago, all Meri had in the room was a bookshelf and a chair. She kept an inflatable mattress in the closet for guests who stayed over. Now her inflatable man could join her inflatable guest bed in the closet. She didn't have the heart to let out Fred's air, so he went into hiding full figured.

"Great tea," Helen said when Meredith stepped back into the living room. "You want some help with dinner?"

"It's no trouble. I have pasta, so it won't take long to fix."

"Of course you have pasta," Helen said. "You live on pasta. I don't know how you do it." She got up from the chair and followed Meri into the kitchen. "Come on, let us help. It's your birthday. The least we can do is assist the chef."

Suddenly Jake was standing in her kitchen, smiling down at her. "What kind of pasta?" he asked.

"Fettuccine and linguine." She told him about the place down by the ferry landing. "I haven't made the sauce yet; I could do that while you guys do the broccoli and pasta. I have some appetizers, too."

"How about your letting me make the Alfredo sauce? I picked up a few tips at Chez Monique's," Jake said.

"Monique who?" Helen asked, finishing off the last sip of iced tea.

"Chez Monique's," Meri answered for Jake. "It's a restaurant in Santa Monica where Jake used to work."

"Oh yes. I remember," Helen said. "Now tell me again how you two know each other. Here I thought I was going to have the surprise of a lifetime for you, Meri. Is there more tea in the fridge?"

"Sure. Help yourself." Meredith waited to see if Jake would explain how they met.

Neither of them had to because Helen let out a squeal and extracted something from the refrigerator. It was a small maraschino-cherry jar. "What in the world is this, girl? Looks like my husband's appendix. He demanded that the surgeon keep all the parts, just like the mechanic when he fixes the car."

Meredith felt her cheeks turning red. "It's nothing," she said quickly, helping Helen return it to the back of the shelf. "Here's the tea."

"I'm telling you," Helen said, pouring her tea, "I won't let Herb keep stuff like that around anymore. No more pickled polyps! That's what I told him."

Meredith was relieved to see that Jake hadn't noticed the discovery of the sentimental grape. He was busy making himself at home with the pots and pans.

"You plan to use this one for the pasta?" he asked, pointing to the largest pot, which was filled with water and waiting on the back burner.

"Yes. But if you need it, go ahead."

"No, this pot will be fine." He turned toward Meredith. They were only inches away from each other in the tight-squeeze kitchen. It was the closest she had ever been to him. A subtle, cocoa-butter smell seemed to float from his skin. "Do you have an apron to spare?" he asked, warming her with his deep brown eyes.

Meredith forced herself to look away. "Right behind you on the hook. Sorry, but I don't have any particularly manly ones."

She had two aprons hanging on the peg on the wall. One of them she had worn earlier when gathering the flowers. It was white with thin yellow ribbons woven through the eyelet along the top, across the bottom, and through the straps that tied around the neck. The other apron didn't have any lace. It was a smattering of bright yellow lemons on a royal blue background. Jake chose that one.

"I have a feeling I'm going to be in the way here," Helen said, wedging out of the kitchen. She made herself comfortable at the elegantly set table and faced the two cooks, both of whom had donned aprons. Helen smiled her blessing on them. "This could be interesting," she said. "Two of my favorite people creating dinner together." Lifting her glass, she added, "Go ahead. Amaze me."

Chapter Fourteen

When they sat down together at the table half an hour later, Meri lit the candle and turned off the lights in the kitchen.

"Smells marvelous," Helen said, tucking the last bite of her appetizer into her cheek.

"Are we ready?" Jake asked.

"Looks like it," Meri said, quickly scanning the table. She had tossed the dressing in the salad. The Parmesan cheese was in a glass dish with a spoon, and all the glasses were filled with water and a lemon wedge. The table looked perfect.

Jake cleared his throat and said, "I'd like to give thanks before we eat."

Meri's heart melted just a little. She knew Jake was a Christian; Shelly had made that clear in one of her many pitches to get Meri interested in him. But Meri had known many Christian men who didn't initiate prayer at meals, especially at a business meal with an agent who wasn't particularly open to spiritual things.

"Do you hold hands when you pray?" Helen asked. "Herb has a born-again client who insists we hold hands and pray before we eat. Even in restaurants. I've gotten used to it. You want to hold hands?"

Without a word, Meri offered her open hand to Helen on her right and Jake on her left. Helen placed her cool hand in Meri's, but Jake hesitated.

Meredith peeked at Jake from her bowed-head position.

"I don't hold hands when I pray," he said.

"Suit yourself," Helen said, letting go of Meri's hand. "Just get the prayer over. It's a sin to keep this hot food waiting."

Jake prayed, "Father, thanks for this food that you have provided. Thanks for the opportunity we have to meet together and discuss potential business arrangements. Please direct our conversation and our time together. We pray this in the name of Christ, amen."

"Amen," Helen said, reaching for the bowl of fettuccine. "This smells heavenly."

Why didn't he want to hold hands? Was it me? Is this all business to him so he doesn't want to act too friendly? He offered me his hand at the waterfall. Was that different because I was trying to get out of the rowboat?

"Before we start talking business," Helen said, "I have to ask you, Jake, only because you got my curiosity going: is holding hands with women when you pray un-Christian?"

"Possibly," he said with a straight face.

"Possibly?" Helen repeated. "What? You shouldn't mix spiritual with physical?"

"They're already mixed," Jake said, offering to pour the sauce over the fettuccine on Helen's plate. "We're whole people. The physical and spiritual are already mixed. I just don't like to confuse the two parts."

"You lost me there," Helen said. She twirled the pasta on her fork and eagerly took a bite. Then, closing her eyes and letting out a low, happy hum, she said, "I am amazed. This is bliss!"

Meri eagerly tried her first bite. Helen was right. It was wonderful. "This is delicious, Jake. I hate to admit it, but your sauce is better than mine. My compliments to Monique and to you."

He followed their example and took a bite. "Now that's fresh pasta," he said. "Does this place accept mail orders? How's the linguine?" He helped himself to a scoop of the steaming noodles.

"I like the fettuccine the best of the two," Jake said a moment later.

"I love it all," Helen said. She twirled another hearty forkful before returning to her questions for Jake. "So give me your philosophy, Jake. You don't believe in holding hands with women when you pray. I didn't know this. What else don't I know?"

Jake ate quietly, thinking before he responded. Meredith noticed that his hair looked lighter than it had a few weeks ago. He had a faint birthmark on the right side of his face. The small, brownish patch, about the size of a dime, was located on his jawline by his ear. She realized she was staring and looked back at her plate.

It was no good. Instead of seeing pasta and salad, she saw the image of Jake in her kitchen wearing her blue lemon apron over his dark green knit shirt and jeans. He was invading her consciousness. He was sitting right next to her. His cocoa-butter scent was still close enough for her to draw in if she turned just right.

Meredith was startled. She didn't remember ever feeling so

overwhelmed by a man's presence. Without warning, her heart began to beat faster, and she suddenly felt thirsty.

"My philosophy of life or of love?" Jake asked Helen.

"Love, of course."

"Love is a choice that involves commitment. You can marry anyone and make the marriage work if you're both committed to it. The emotion of love is not the foundation for a marriage relationship. Commitment is."

"Don't tell my Herb that," Helen responded. "He says it's our love that keeps us together. We're going on two years now."

"That's longer than the average," Jake said.

"Average what?" Meredith asked, slightly annoyed at his unfeeling approach to things as sacred as love and marriage.

"The average couple stays in love eighteen months. All kinds of studies prove it. Falling in love, as we call it, is little more than a chemical reaction. Once it wears off, all that's left is commitment. That's why it's a choice. To choose to marry means you're looking far beyond the immediate chemical reaction your brain is experiencing when you fall in love. You're choosing to make a commitment for life, even after the chemical reaction is gone."

Helen plopped down her fork with a fwap. "That has to be the most ridiculous bunch of hogwash I have ever heard! People don't make logical value assessments like that when it comes to love and marriage. They fall in love and get married. That's all there is to it. It's magical and wonderful and overpowering. Not a chemical reaction! Where did you get all this nonsense?"

Jake appeared unmoved by her strong response. "My roommate Brad. He did his thesis on it. 'The Fallacy of Falling in Love and Why Americans Spend Their Lives Trying to Recreate the Sensation.' It's a fascinating paper."

Meredith remembered how blunt Brad had been when she

had met him at the conference center. She also remembered that he was married and had made a comment about how he would have married sooner if he had known how great it was.

"Brad seems to be awfully happy as a married man," Meri said.

"Sure, he's happy," Jake said. "It's been all of what? Three months. He knows the thrill will rub off. That's what his paper is about. Most people don't expect the feelings to go away, so when they do, people think something is wrong with them or their mate, and they go searching for whatever it is that will restore those feelings. That's why Americans, more than individuals in any other culture, make poor choices when it comes to meeting their emotional needs. They'll forget commitments, logic, and virtue in the quest for feeling that chemical reaction of love once more."

"You have a point," Helen said. "I have a friend who just walked out on a fifteen-year marriage because she said her husband repulses her physically. I've seen her husband, and I can tell you there's nothing repulsive about him. It's that her feelings have changed toward him."

Meredith couldn't disagree with Jake either. She had heard her dad talk over the years about how stunned he always was when a couple came into the church office and announced they were divorcing. Many times the reason they gave was that they weren't in love anymore. Her father had preached grand sermons on making love last. He had written a paper for their denomination on teaching young people to enter marriage with a view to selflessly serve the other for a lifetime.

Meredith, the most compliant of the four Graham daughters, had listened intently to her father's teachings when she was nearing the end of high school and trying to figure out her up-and-down emotions. As a result, she corralled her heart well. Many men over the years confessed to her that she lit a flame within their hearts. She silenced them all with her truthful admission that she didn't feel the same about them and asked them just to be friends.

"I think you're right in some ways, Jake," she said. "But when you look at people like Brad and Alissa or my sister and Jonathan, don't you see something more than a logical choice to get married? I think Shelly and Jonathan are definitely in love emotionally, and they've known each other their whole lives, which is way past your eighteen-month limit."

"That's because they have chosen to be in love, and they are experiencing the chemical reaction that comes with that choice. The feelings will wear off, and then where will they be?"

When Helen and Meri didn't answer immediately, Jake gave them his clinical answer. "They'll be in commitment. Not necessarily in love. And the commitment is what lasts for a lifetime."

"I take it," Helen said, sloshing her last bit of linguine in the puddle of white sauce on her china plate, "that you have never been in love."

"I've been in love lots of times, starting when I was about twelve," he said with a grin. "I've never been in commitment, though. And I don't plan to be for quite some time."

"Should we assume that's why you don't allow yourself to hold hands with women when you pray?" Helen said. "The slightest touch might lead to a chemical reaction, and there you'd be, having to make a choice about lifetime commitment."

Jake didn't answer. His facial expression told them Helen was close to the truth, but he wouldn't admit it because her wording sounded so stern.

Meri felt ripped off. What good was it to guard her heart

all these years only to find that when, for the first time, she was experiencing a chemical reaction and was eager to consider the possibility of lifetime commitment, the other party was shut down like a fireworks stand on the fifth of July?

"You know," Helen said, wagging her empty fork at Jake, "you make great food but lousy table conversation, Jacob. Only men do this. They analyze all the romance out of romance."

"What is romance?" Jake challenged.

"I don't want to hear your opinion," Helen said good-naturedly. "I'm a big fan of romance, and I won't let you spoil it for me. Let's talk business. It has to be more enjoyable than this."

"I'll make coffee," Meredith said, excusing herself and leaving her plate half full of pasta. She had lost her appetite when she lost all hope that Jake might be interested in her. It seemed so unfair. First her emotions had soared, a birthday high, as she worked side by side with Jake, making her favorite foods. Then the image of Jake in her lemon apron and the discovery of the birthmark below his right ear had warmed her heart. So what? He had all but put in writing that he wasn't interested in her. What good were hopes when you had hit a quarter of a century and had lost all interest in eating your own birthday cake?

"You did read Jake's manuscript, didn't you?" Helen called after Meredith as she left the table.

She hadn't even opened the manila envelopes Helen had sent her. If she had known one of them was Jake's, would she have moved it to the top of her pile?

"No, not yet."

"Meredith!" Helen spouted. She sounded upset. "How are we supposed to have a business discussion if you haven't even looked over the material yet?"

Meredith wanted to turn around and yell at Helen the way

Meri and her sisters used to fight by saying, "You didn't tell me I was supposed to read it before tonight. You didn't tell me Jacob Wilde was the client you were bringing. Why is this my fault? It's my birthday, and everyone is supposed to be nice to me, not yell at me and dash my hopes!"

But she said in her professional voice, "Why don't you both give me a summary? I'd love to hear it directly from you."

"It's a deal for the book rights to accompany the film Jake is producing," Helen said. "For goodness' sake, Meri, how hard would it have been to open the envelope and have a quick scan? I told you this one was a honey."

"Yes, you did," Meredith said, scooping the ground coffee into the bleached white filter and filling the water up to the ten-cup level. "Tell me more."

Jake turned around and watched her for a moment before giving his input. "It's a series for kids," he said, his tone a notch softer than when he had been spouting his love philosophy. "I call it Young Heart. The hero is a ten-year-old boy who is on a journey, like in *Pilgrim's Progress*. You know, the classic by John Bunyan."

"Yes, I know it well," Meri said.

"It could actually be classified as a fantasy. Sort of *Pilgrim's Progress* with a Narnia twist, if you will. We're looking at six videos and the companion books to go with them. There's potential for more books. We only have funding for the first six videos; however I'd like ultimately to do twelve."

"I heard from my sister that you're planning to do some filming at the Heather Creek waterfall," Meri said.

"Yes, it's really perfect for several forest scenes. I meet with Kyle and Jonathan tomorrow, and if all goes well, we should begin to shoot in a month."

Meredith cleared the plates as they waited for the coffee to brew.

"The beauty of this project," Helen said, "is that the books are nearly written, and if Terrison Publishing jumps right on it, the books could hit the racks the same time as the videos. We could do a strong cross promotion to launch the series and develop some ancillary products right out of the gate. I was thinking of action figures and pens and pencils in the shape of a sword, like the sword Young Heart carries." Helen's face lit up with her enthusiasm. "We'd want Terrison to front the money for the ancillary products and agree to a working franchise with the film production company."

"Whoa," Meredith said. "You're going to have to negotiate all that with Dan in the legal department. I don't have much say when it comes to that side of the deals."

Helen leaned forward and cut to the chase. "I'd like a six-book contract for my client here, with an option for six more and an escalating royalty scale. Release of the books must coincide with the release of the videos, or we'll take it elsewhere." Helen sat back in her chair and eyed Meredith like someone who had just thrown down her gauntlet. When Helen talked business, she talked business.

"You know I can't give you an answer right now," Meri said. "But it sounds very intriguing." She caught herself. *Intriguing? Why did I use that word? That was my word for Jake. Am I going to be able to separate the man from the project? I guess I'm going to have to.*

"I have one question," Meri said, looking at Helen and then at Jake. "You said the books were almost written. What exactly does that mean?"

Chapter Fifteen

he coffeemaker dripped the last drop, and Meredith served the coffee while Helen and Jake came up with an answer to her question.

Jake spoke first. "I've slanted the manuscript to a screen-play format. The stories are all right there; they just need to be lifted out and restructured into twelve books."

Meredith tried not to laugh as she placed the cup of coffee before Jake. "That's a boatload of work," she said.

"Is it?" he asked innocently.

"We would need to hire a ghostwriter," Helen stated. "Jake's time is booked from here on with the videos. Don't you have access to ghostwriters?"

"Of course I do." Meredith handed Helen a cup of coffee and returned to the refrigerator for cream. She grabbed the sugar bowl from the cupboard and placed the white ceramic set on the table. "I work with ghostwriters all the time. It helps if they have access to the author, of course, while the project is in its beginning stages."

"We could work something out," Helen said. "I want the best writer."

"Of course," Meredith said, sipping her coffee. "Can you tell me a little more about the stories? What age group are you targeting? What's the length of each book? Is it written in third person or first person?"

Helen and Jake looked at each other and then returned twin blank stares at her.

Meredith dropped her gaze into her cup of cream-infused coffee. *They have no clue. This is going to be so much work!* Looking up and gathering her courage, Meredith started with the first question. After all, this was her area of expertise. She shouldn't be intimidated by anyone, not Helen and certainly not the pragmatic Jacob Wilde.

"What's your target group? What age?"

"I guess kids," Jake said blankly.

"Kids, meaning two-year-olds to five-year-olds? Five to seven? Eight to twelve? Twelve to sixteen?"

"All ages, I think." Jake took a sip of coffee. "This is good. What kind is it?"

Meredith shrugged. "You're in Seattle. All coffee in Seattle is great."

"Are you talking about the age group for the videos or the books?" Helen asked.

"The books, of course," Meredith said. "Picture a kid sprawled out on his bed reading one of these books. How old is that kid? Can he read it himself, or is his mom reading it to him?"

"He can read it," Jake said. "He's about nine years old."

"Will his five-year-old sister like the story as much as he

does, if he reads it to her?" Meri asked.

"She might. His eleven-year-old sister would like it better." Jake leaned back, and a calm grin eased across his tanned face. "Helen said you were good. Now I see why. I hadn't even thought of this angle. We have to know our audience before the curtain goes up."

"Exactly," Meredith said.

"I'm offering six books minimum with a contract option for six more," Helen said firmly.

"I understand," Meredith said. "But you're on a close time frame with the videos going into production. You want these to be released with the videos, but they're not written yet."

"They're nearly written," Helen corrected her.

Meredith smiled. "You know exactly what we're talking about timewise, Helen. It's nine months minimum before we could get a job like this on the shelves."

"Nine months is good," Jake said.

Meredith held up her hand. "You realize everything I just said was hypothetical. We don't even have a verbal agreement here. I'm only talking in generalities to let you know how the process works. I have to look over the proposal first. I'll do that tomorrow and let Helen know what I think."

Jake looked startled. Was this man so unaccustomed to being told no? Did it surprise him that Meredith didn't swoon at his feet and beg for the opportunity to publish his stories?

What Jake probably didn't know, but what Helen should have known by now, was that Meredith had earned the reputation of being good at what she did because she was cautious and used integrity in all her business deals. Helen should have known that Meri would treat a movie star's book proposal with the same interest she used to consider the handwritten manuscript from the unknown grandma in Mississippi who had sent in the only story she had ever written. All manuscripts were judged on their quality and how well they fit into the marketing plan of G. H. Terrison Publishing.

"I don't suppose it would be of any value to talk advance money now, would it?" Helen said dryly.

"Talk all you want. My hands are tied until I take the proposal to committee and the budget is set. Then we can talk. More coffee?"

Meredith reached for the pot to fill their cups. A quietness hung over them. If Jake had managed to dash her hopes with his practical approach to love and commitment, she had just dashed his hopes of being published overnight. His earlier speech had nothing to do with the way she handled her end of this business conversation. This is what she did, and she wouldn't turn soft for anyone. Not even a movie star.

"Cheesecake is on the menu, if either of you has room," Meredith said, returning to the kitchen and pulling the box labeled "Rondi's" from the lower shelf. "Raspberry cheesecake."

"Sounds like a must," Helen said. "Mind if we retire to the living room?"

"Good idea," Meredith said. "I know these chairs aren't the most comfortable."

Helen headed for the couch with her coffee cup in hand. "Is this real?" Helen asked, nodding to Elvis in his bowl.

"Of course he's real. Don't you remember when I introduced you two on the phone? That's Elvis."

"Hello, Elvis," Helen said, cocking her head to the side and gazing into the bowl. Then she called back over her shoulder, "Honestly, Meri, I don't know why you don't get a little poodle like normal people."

"She doesn't like dogs," Jake stated. Before Meredith could stick her head back into the living room and acknowledge that he remembered something personal about her, Jake asked,

"Mind if we put on a little music?"

"Go ahead. The CD player's remote is on the coffee table," Meri said. She lifted the cheesecake out of the box. For one fleeting moment she wished she had some silly old numbered candles to stick on the top.

An instant later, the first CD began to play. It was *The Four Seasons* by Antonio Vivaldi. Meri turned her head to see Jake's reaction. She hadn't planned this; it was just the next CD in line.

Jake was sitting in the easy chair where Fred had been. He turned toward the kitchen and looked at Meredith, a glimmer of pleasant surprise on his face. She knew she couldn't say anything about knowing he liked Vivaldi or his falling asleep on his only date with her sister. Men who don't believe in love but who choose to make a commitment shouldn't care about such things as common tastes in music, should they? And they also shouldn't remember whether or not a woman likes dogs, unless they're interested in that woman.

Meredith looked away and set about cutting her birthday cake. Before she cut the first slice, she silently sang, *Happy birthday to you, happy birthday to you, happy birthday, dear Meredith, happy birthday to you.*

She stood for a moment, wondering what she would wish for if she did, in fact, have candles to blow out. But there were no candles, and she had no wishes. Only guests waiting in the living room for their dessert.

"You know what surprises me," Helen said, as her fork slid into the cheesecake, "is that you haven't said one word about Jake's movie career. You're the only one I know who seems to be able to ignore that side of his life."

Meredith sat next to Helen and answered without looking at Jake. "Someone once told me that what you do is simply what you do; it's not who you are."

Jake caught her eye as she looked down at her plate. Once again he seemed pleasantly surprised.

"Turned into a philosopher on me now, have you?" Helen said.

Meredith kept her thoughts to herself and took a bite of birthday cheesecake.

"This is very good," Jake said. "Another island specialty?"

"Yes," Meredith answered without looking up.

"It's marvelous," Helen agreed. "Now let me do my job as Jacob Wilde's literary agent and brag on him some. Jake's success with *Falcon Pointe* didn't come out of thin air as many of the critics want you to believe. He's been working steadily in Hollywood for the past five years, but his break came a number of years ago with a pain-reliever commercial that ran longer than any other for that product."

Helen took a breath, ready to go on with her praises of her client, when Jake cut her off. "It's all in the bio. I'm sure Meredith can read it over when she has a look at the manuscript proposal." He kept working on his cheesecake without looking up.

Meredith sensed tension in the air. And it wasn't necessarily between the client and the agent. Was Jake embarrassed that Helen had gone over his résumé with Meri? Or didn't he want to divulge anything that could be considered personal to her? Either way, she felt slighted. She could understand his desire to keep his career separate from who he was, and after seeing how he was mobbed in Glenbrooke, Meri honored that. But what good was such a division of life and career when he also chose to keep his life off-limits to others?

"One other tiny, interesting fact isn't listed in Jake's bio." Helen went on bragging about her client the way an overly protective mother brags about her only son at his first piano recital. "Jake plays the bongos. Isn't that fun? Have you ever known anyone who plays the bongo drums?"

"No, I don't suppose I have."

Jake seemed to light up with renewed interest in the conversation. "Did Shelly ever tell you about the bongo fests Brad and I used to have in Pasadena?"

"No, I don't think she did." Meredith had casually met Jake's gaze when he looked up, and now she was having a hard time releasing it. Sitting in the easy chair, he was the antithesis of Guard Man Fred. They were about the same size and filled the chair more or less the same way. But Fred only stared into oblivion. Jake's eyes were warm, full of life, and, oh, so intriguing. It made her mad.

Why do I feel this way when I look at him? He might as well be a big inflatable dummy for all the heart he seems to have. Why, oh, why am I so attracted to him? It's not because he's an actor, is it? No, I was intrigued by him before I knew who he was. I'm just drawn to him. Or, as Jake would say, I'm experiencing a chemical reaction. According to him, I should be able to choose to turn it off right now. So why can't I?

Jake spoke lightheartedly of the evenings in the backyard when he and Brad donned French berets and spontaneously beat their drums under the California night sky.

It really isn't fair that I should be struggling with this chemical reaction while he isn't having one. He's more excited about playing bongo drums than about me. Is it me? Am I that unappealing?

Meredith knew that wasn't the case. Dozens of men over the years had testified to her appeal and would have done anything to have her return their affection. She suddenly felt sorry for those men. Now she understood what it was like to be the one having the chemical reaction while the intended recipient of that interest, attention, and affectionate feeling was shut down, dormant, and unresponsive.

She considered for a brief moment sending a letter to each

of those men, apologizing for her lack of response when he had opened his heart to her. She would let them know that her aloofness was coming back on her tenfold at this very moment while she sat here with Jacob Wilde, knowing that, to him, she was nothing.

Chapter Sixteen

*H*elen and Jake left in a flurry when they realized they had to scramble to catch the last ferry off the island. Jake had reservations at a hotel near the airport. He planned to fly down to Eugene at six o'clock in the morning and then drive to Glenbrooke for his early morning meeting with Jonathan and Kyle. Helen had reservations on a red-eye back to New York and left in a panic that she wouldn't make her plane.

Their hasty good-byes consisted of a kiss on the cheek from Helen, a warm smile and happy-birthday wish from Jake, and a promise from Meri that she would look over the proposal first thing in the morning.

Helen's rental car peeled out of the driveway, tossing gravel and sounding much louder than anything Meri was used to in her quiet corner of the world. With a sigh, she stood on the porch, watching the moon play peek-a-boo with her through the thin layer of pale clouds. The rain that had threatened to fall earlier was either holding off or had blown over. So the phantom storm left the fainting spring flowers begging for one last drink.

Meredith knew exactly how they felt. It's one thing not to have rain. You accept that. But when the scent of rain is in the wind and the air is heavy with the promise of moisture, hopes rise. Thirsty souls become expectant. Then the rain never falls.

Meredith had experienced disappointment tonight, too. The hint of romance had come billowing into her life, heavily spicing the air with intrigue. Then it all had blown out the door.

As she stared at the moon, Meredith thought again of the verse she had underlined a few days ago. "Hope deferred makes the heart sick," she recited aloud. "And, boy, do I know that is true."

Maybe it wouldn't seem so overwhelming if I hadn't just prayed again tonight for God to prepare and send a man into my life. I'm not trying to be selfish about this, Father God. It's so that we can do what my dad preached all those years—work together for your kingdom. You said two are better than one. Did you really mean that? Is there really someone out there for me, or am I best suited to be single?

She thought she knew the answer already. To her, single meant Aunt Jane. That wasn't the kind of person she wanted to become or the kind of life she wanted to lead.

All I have to say, God, is if Jacob Wilde isn't the man for me, I dare you to find someone better.

Meredith's hand flew to her mouth and covered it tightly. One shouldn't go around daring God to do anything, should one?

"I'm sorry," she whispered into the cool night air. "I didn't mean that. I just don't understand. Why did you wire us frail humans to have all these emotions and deep longings if they're nothing more than a stupid chemical reaction? You made me this way. Now what am I supposed to do with all this passion and hope?"

Frustrated, Meredith turned on her heels and marched inside, slamming the door behind her. She glanced at the stack of dirty dishes on the kitchen counter and knew she was not going to spend the last hour of her birthday cleaning the kitchen. Instead, she headed for the bathroom, where she took out her contacts, washed her face, pulled back her hair with a wide stretchy headband, and crawled into her favorite pajamas. She stomped back into the kitchen, found herself a diet soda, and made a bag of microwave popcorn. Flopping onto the couch, she switched off the music and turned on the TV. The volume was so loud that poor Elvis nearly jumped from his bowl.

Switching channels until she found an old John Wayne movie, Meredith smiled contentedly to herself and settled in with a fistful of popcorn. Nothing like the Duke's swagger to take a woman's mind off her woes. She fell asleep on the couch and didn't wake up until three-fifteen when a loud commercial roused her. Turning off the noise box, she snuggled under the soft throw comforter and spent the rest of the night on the couch.

Meredith woke at seven-fifteen, stiff and with an aching stomach. She felt awful and wanted to go to bed, this time her own bed. Stumbling out of the living room and into her bedroom, Meredith crawled between the sheets and tried for more than an hour to fall back to sleep. It was useless. She might as well get up and enjoy the sunshine that was pouring through the windows.

A shower helped. The fresh breeze from her open bedroom window helped. A look at the mess in the kitchen didn't help.

Meredith decided to take herself out to breakfast. This

trick had helped her more than once feel as if she had a life when the home office became stifling. After all, it was Saturday. She didn't have to work. She had promised Helen she would look at Jake's manuscript, but she could do that later, after she felt a little better.

Grabbing her purse and heading out the front door, she saw a car turning into her long driveway. It was a Buick, a familiar, steady old Buick with her dad at the wheel. Mom was right beside him.

Meri waited in the warm sunshine on the front deck until he stopped the car. Mom waved pleasantly.

Unsure how she felt about her parents' arrival, Meredith casually waved back. She loved her parents and enjoyed their company, but couldn't they have called ahead? Just this once. The trip from their house to hers was nearly an hour. Meredith could have spent that hour cleaning up the kitchen.

"Hi, what are you two up to?" Meredith asked, shading her eyes from the sun as they came toward the house.

"I didn't get your card in the mail," Mom said holding out a card-sized envelope. "We had to come over here to camp anyhow to drop off the steaming trays we borrowed last week for the men's breakfast. It was such a nice day we thought we would combine the two errands."

"Were you about to leave?" Dad asked, noticing the purse slung over Meredith's shoulder.

"I was going to take myself out to breakfast," she said. "You want to join me?"

"Breakfast!" Mom said with surprise, checking her watch. "Perhaps a late brunch or early lunch. Were you up late last night with your guests?"

"Not too late," Meri said. Everything inside her had gone on alert. She refused to melt down into a child in front of her mother.

"Did you have a happy birthday?" Mom asked.

"Yes, I did."

"I'm interested in going out to eat with you, Meri. But I was hoping for a little walk along the lake." Dad had on his casual clothes and what looked like a new pair of tennis shoes. "What do you say we walk first and then go out for a bite?"

"I'm not up for a walk today," Mom said. "You two go ahead, and I'll wait here. Do you have any coffee on, dear?"

Meredith clenched her teeth and tried to understand why this was upsetting her so. She had been all set to take herself out to her favorite little coffee shop, Brewed Awakenings. There, she would have indulged in a full morning of French roast with lots of sugar and cream and at least one, and maybe two, wonderfully decadent pastries. Her mind would have leisurely wandered through all the information she had gathered about Jake, and she could have sorted it into neat piles the way she stacked the abundance of manuscripts in her office.

Now she was under her parents' rule. How could she not walk along the lake with her dad? When was the last time he had wanted to do that? Never in the almost two years she had lived here.

And how could she let her mom see the disastrous kitchen? Meri suddenly understood why one sister had moved to Brazil, another to the east coast, and why Shelly had gone to Los Angeles right after she graduated from high school.

Her parents stood there, waiting and looking pathetic in their eagerness.

"Okay." Meredith relented. "A walk and then food, but you're paying."

"Of course," her father said, not giving any indication that he understood she was joking.

"We'll be back in a little while," Meredith said to her mom, who was heading up the front steps as Meri was going down.

"And no, I don't have any coffee on; yes, I know my kitchen is a mess; and no, I don't want you to clean it for me."

They were only a few yards away from the house when Mom said, "Meri, the door is locked."

Meredith walked back, handed the keys to her mom and said again in fair warning, "Brace yourself. The kitchen is a disaster area."

Mom gave her a funny look. "We didn't expect you to clean things up for us."

"How could I?" Meredith said. "I didn't know you were coming." She said the words nicely without changing the sweetness of her tone.

Dad read meaning into her words and brought them back for examination the minute they hit the trail. "Did it bother you that your mother and I didn't call before coming over this morning?"

"It's okay. You're both welcome, of course, anytime. I probably shouldn't have said that."

Dad continued to walk at a brisk pace. "It's beautiful here," he said. "Just beautiful. Fresh air, sunshine, and look at that water. Might be a fish or two waiting to be caught in there. What do you think?"

"Maybe."

"Have you ever fished the lake?" Dad asked.

"No." It seemed a funny question to Meri.

"Then let's go fishing next time I'm up. Just you and me. Can we rent a boat from the camp?"

"I suppose so," Meredith said. She had the feeling her dad was trying to make up for lost time from her childhood or something. Some hobbies he had never managed to transfer to his four daughters. His love for fishing was one of them. They had all gone with him a few times during their formative years, but none of the Graham girls took a liking to the sport. So Dad had kept all his hooks and lures to himself.

"Perfect day for fishing," he said, looking up at the clear sky. "Wish I would have brought some gear with me. Didn't even think of it."

They walked on, Meri trying to keep up with her dad's quick strides.

"Look. Over there." He pointed to the flat surface of the water near the shore. "Did you see it jump?"

Meredith looked but didn't see anything.

"Come over here," Dad urged, heading for some smooth, gray boulders near the shoreline. He sat down in the shade and kept a steady eye on the water. "This would make a nice fishing spot," he said.

"Yes," Meredith agreed. She didn't feel connected to his thought processes at all. Why was fishing so important all of a sudden?

Dad turned and looked at her. A pleased smile spread across his face. "We're proud of you," he said suddenly. "You know that, don't you?"

Meri smiled.

"Your mother and I are proud of all you girls. No matter what, we can always point to the four of you and feel confident that we did something right."

"You've done a lot of things right," Meredith said.

Dad looked down. He sighed and said, "Not according to the board."

Meredith felt a catch in her throat. Her whole life the worst nights at the dinner table were those right before or right after a meeting of the church's board of elders. They were the ones who made the decisions as to how things were run at the church, even if their choices were completely opposite to her dad's ideas of how things should be done. The board was to her what the boogeyman was to other children. It wasn't that her dad ranted and raved about specific people or specific issues. It was the way his demeanor changed when he was about to defend himself to the board or when he came home defeated after a board meeting.

"What happened?" Meredith asked. She knew her dad wouldn't share specifics. He never did. It was obvious, though, that he was disturbed about something.

"They voted last week for me to take early retirement and for a new, younger minister to take my place."

"You're kidding!"

Dad shook his head. "We've known about if for some time, but your mother and I kept hoping that when the vote was taken the motion wouldn't pass. We wanted to stay on for another three or four years. But there's concern about my not attracting young families. They'll hire a man right out of seminary."

"Daddy, this is awful."

"It's not so awful. It's just a change, and changes are hard the older you get. We believe God is working out his plan, and we don't question him." He sighed again. "It's been the hardest on your mother. She's held it in for several weeks now. I don't know if you've noticed how it's worn on her. It's been, well…" He looked out at the water. "It's been hard on her."

"What are you going to do?"

Dad squared his shoulders and said, "Since the vote is final, I'll have to make the announcement from the pulpit tomorrow. We'll be at the church another month or two until the new minister and his family can move here. Next week a gentleman from the district office is coming to meet with us. It's a new program the denomination has to assist pastoral staff and their families as they cycle out of ministry."

"Cycle out of ministry?" Meredith repeated, folding her arms across her chest. "How do you cycle out of ministry?

That's all you've done your whole life—and at the same church. What are you supposed to do now?" It angered her that anyone would try to patronize her parents. Didn't the denomination recognize that her parents had both given their lives to this church? This was their home. How could they be cycled out of their home?

"We aren't quite sure what the next step is. We're praying about it and, of course, talking a lot about different options. That's why we decided to drive out here this morning. We thought it would give us some good thinking and talking time."

"I'm so sorry to hear all this, Dad. It seems so unfair."

"I suppose it seems that way. Your mother and I are trusting that this is God's timing, and we're trusting him for the next step."

It seems like pretty lousy timing to me.

As if her father had read her thoughts, he said, "Of course we know that God's timing isn't always the same as our timing." He rubbed his hands together and said, "His ways aren't our ways. His thoughts aren't our thoughts."

Meri remembered memorizing that verse long ago. The verse after it said, "As the heavens are higher than the earth, so are my ways higher than your ways and my thoughts than your thoughts." She tilted her head toward the silent sky. Not even a wisp of a cloud flawed the seamless blue.

What are you doing up there? Have you forgotten about us down here?

"Is there anything I can do for you and Mom?" Meredith asked as they started back to the cottage.

"Pray," Dad said. "Just pray for us."

Chapter Seventeen

$\mathcal{M}$eredith hadn't prayed a lot for her parents over the years. That seemed to be their job—to keep the church running and to pray for everyone, especially their four daughters. Mom was a capable woman. The only time she had hinted at needing prayer was when she had had a hysterectomy during Meredith's second year of college. Megan had come home for a week to help around the house, and Meredith had helped for a long weekend. Aside from that, her parents had never "needed" prayer for anything she could remember. They never needed anything.

"Would you like me to be there tomorrow when you make the announcement at church?" Meri asked.

Dad thought a minute. "Yes, I think that would mean a lot to your mother."

As Meredith shuffled through the pebbles along the lake trail, her head down, her heart heavy, she thought of how irritated she had been with her mom these past few weeks. It made sense now. Mom had been under an unusual amount of stress. Her natural response would be to try to fix or control the few areas of her life where she felt she still had some power. Meri, as the youngest and only unmarried daughter, probably seemed the logical choice of someone who needed "fixing."

Now that Meredith realized how much tension her mom must have been feeling, she understood why she had been so overbearing. After all, how do you go about everyday life knowing that with a show of hands "the board" has altered your life forever? Why couldn't they have let Mom and Dad stay a few more years as her parents had planned? They could have retired joyfully, with a big party and their future goals set. Now the church would be transitioning out of the old, and the big party would be to welcome the new pastor and his fresh, young family.

"I will be praying for you, Daddy," Meredith said when they reached the Tulip Cottage and started up the steps. "If I can do anything else, anything at all, you let me know, okay?"

"Thanks, Meri," her father said warmly. He reached over and took her hand in his to give it a squeeze. It startled her to feel the crooked roughness of his aging fingers and the thinness of his wrinkled skin. When was the last time she had felt her hand in his?

She squeezed his hand and gave him her biggest, most comforting smile. "I love you," she said softly.

For half a second he looked as if he might shed a tear at her words. But he composed himself and said, "I love you, too."

They entered the house. Meredith looked around, feeling like a girl in a fairy tale who had stepped into the wrong cottage. The place was clean.

"Mom?" Meri called out, noticing that the counters were cleared and wiped off and the dishwasher was making its happy, whirling sound. Even the table had been returned to its usual position.

"In here," Mom called from the back of the house. "I'm looking for a—" Her words were sliced through with a piercing scream.

Dad took off running toward the back guest room. "Ellen, what is it? Are you okay?"

Meri heard a loud thump. She dashed back and entered the guest room right after her father. Mom was flat on the floor with her eyes closed. Sprawled across her was Guard Man Fred, who had fallen out of the closet.

"Hey!" Meri's dad yelled in alarm. He grabbed Fred by the shoulder and belted him one, right on the ol' kisser.

Fred's baseball cap flew across the room, and Fred flopped to the floor, his pleasant expression unchanged. Ellen Graham's startled eyes opened and darted to and fro across the room.

Meredith's dad stood his ground, fist drawn, face red. When the mannequin didn't move, he leaned in for a closer look and said, "What? Who? How?"

"Meredith Jane Graham!" her mother spouted, pulling herself up. "Of all the… !"

"He's not real?" Dad surmised.

"What are you doing with that *thing* lurking in your closet?"

"Where did you get such an absurd, ridiculous…" Her father's voice trailed off.

"From your sister," Meredith said, swallowing her laughter.

"Jane sent you that?" Dad's face was still beet red.

"For my birthday," Meri answered. "She says she takes her Guard Man all around town with her for protection, which is what she thought I needed since I live alone here in the tules."

Mom and Dad looked at each other. Neither of them was willing to place blame on anyone now that the truth had come out and it pointed to Aunt Jane—that subject no one wanted to discuss.

"I named him Fred," Meredith said, a silliness bubble gurgling up inside her. "What do you think? He's a pretty good dancer and not real opinionated about stuff. The strong, silent type."

Mom smoothed back her hair. "Honestly," she muttered.

"What were you doing in here, Ellen?" Dad said, still sounding gruff.

"Looking for a mop. I looked everywhere else. Don't you own a mop, Meredith?"

"No, I don't."

"How in the world do you clean your floor?"

"With Windex and paper towels."

Mom looked at her incredulously.

"It's not a very big kitchen floor, Mother!"

Completely unraveled, Mom excused herself and went back out to the kitchen where her comforting cup of java waited for her on the counter. Meredith stuffed Fred back in the closet and, still swallowing her laughter, joined her mom and dad.

"Thanks for cleaning up, Mom," Meri said. "You didn't have to." She understood after her talk with dad how necessary it was for her mom to have something to order, sort, and organize. Surprisingly enough, it didn't bother her that Mom had cleaned up the remains of her birthday party. "I really appreciate it."

"I couldn't save much of the food," Mom said with a cluck of her tongue. "And such a pity. You left it out all night, and I didn't feel it was safe to keep."

Meredith nodded. She hoped Mom wouldn't launch into a lecture about how when she was a girl they had to eat everything on their plates because food might not be available tomorrow.

"Anyone else starving?" Meri asked, hoping to change the subject and get them out of the house—and get herself off the hot seat. But the minute she said it, she realized the timing and subject were bad.

"We could have had lunch here with the leftovers I had to throw out," Mom said, shaking her head.

"Come on." Dad tenderly led his wife by the elbow. "I'd like to take you both to lunch."

Meredith sat in the backseat and looked out the window. Somehow this position felt strange. When she was really little she had been the one who sat in the front between Mom and Dad while her three sisters ruled the backseat. Meri had secretly longed to be old enough or at least big enough to be relegated to the backseat, where her sisters pushed each other and whispered and always had fun things to read. Now she had the backseat all to herself and found it a lonely place.

"I told Meri about the board's decision," Dad said to Mom as they drove into town. "She asked if we would like her to come to the service tomorrow morning."

"What did you tell her?" Mom asked.

"I told her I thought that would be nice."

Meri felt strange sitting in the backseat of Dad's Buick, being talked about as if she weren't there. Was this what criminals felt like in the back of a squad car?

"Okay," Mom said. Dad had been waiting for Mom's stamp of approval before the invitation would be official.

He glanced at Meri in the rearview mirror. "We'll look for you, then, a little before ten. Now, tell us, where's the best place for lunch around here?"

Meredith suggested several places, and Mom made the final decision. Their time together was comfortable. The conversation revolved around the usual catching up on what was happening with family and friends. None of them brought up the impending crisis of Dad's forced retirement.

Later that evening, Meredith thought perhaps it had been better that way. Dad had told her what he wanted her to know. They didn't have any other details yet. To hash it all out would have been painful for her parents.

But Meredith was of the opinion that difficult situations should be talked through. People should examine their hearts and their minds to decide the next step. She had pushed her ever practical sister to reconsider her relationship with Jonathan during a time when Shelly couldn't admit she still felt something for him. Meredith liked to think that had been a good thing, especially since Jonathan and Shelly ended up together.

With her parents, though, she never pushed. They had their own set way of dealing with problems, and Meredith didn't see it as her place to instruct them in new methods of conflict resolution.

Taking the cordless phone out onto the front deck and perching on the railing, Meredith pressed three on her speed dial. Shelly answered, and Meredith could hear laughter in the background.

"Hi, did I catch you in the middle of a party?"

"Meri!" Shelly squealed. "We were just talking about you. It's Meri, you guys!"

"Who is 'we'?"

"Kyle and Jess, Lauren and Kenton, Jake, Jonathan, and me. Remember? I told you Jake was coming. He was just telling us about your Mr. Guard Man and the tango or what-ever it was you were dancing when he got there last night."

Meredith leaned her head against the porch's wooden frame. With the disruption of her parents' visit, she had for-gotten Jake was going down to Shelly's.

"Don't believe a word he says," Meri pleaded.

"I think it's hilarious!" Shelly said. Another round of laughter echoed in the phone.

Meredith found it disturbing to be the life of the party when she wasn't even there. "I just wanted to let you know something that's going on with Mom and Dad. I don't know if Mom was planning to call you or not."

The reverberation of Bob Two's bark broke up her words as Shelly said, "Just a minute."

Meri waited, and a moment later she heard a door closing, and the noise greatly diminished. "There," Shelly said. "I'm in the bedroom now. What did you say about Mom and Dad?"

Meri told her sister about Dad's announcement. Shelly had the same angered reaction Meri had.

"I'm going to the ten o'clock service tomorrow," Meri said. "I wanted to show them my support, but it seemed hard for them to accept it."

"Do you think Jonathan and I should come?"

"I don't know. It's a long drive for you guys to get there by ten o'clock. You would have to leave at around three in the morning, wouldn't you?"

"Maybe we could fly up," Shelly suggested. "I think there's a seven-fifty out of Eugene we could catch. I'll ask Jonathan what he thinks. I agree with you. Mom and Dad would never ask for our support, but this is one time when I think they would really appreciate it. Have you told Molly?"

"No. I think Mom wants to tell them after it's official. If you guys need a ride from the airport, let me know."

"No, I'm sure we'll rent a car if we come up. It'll be quicker. Thanks so much for calling. I wish Mom and Dad would have told us what was going on."

"I know. I think it's their generation or something. They feel more comfortable keeping woes to themselves."

"Maybe so," Shelly agreed.

"I'd better let you get back to your party."

"By the way," Shelly said, "the meeting went great today with Jake, Kyle, and Jonathan. It looks as if they're going to start filming here in about a month. You have to come down. It's going to be great fun. Jake offered our kitchen staff a contract to cater all the food for the crew. We're going to be busy! Our first group of campers for the summer arrives three weeks from tomorrow."

"You will be busy," Meri agreed.

"Oh, hey," Shelly said, "I heard about your goldfish. Jake said you named him Elvis. Was he another birthday present from Aunt Jane?"

"No," Meri said, offended by her sister's insinuation that Elvis was a strange sort of pet. "I bought him myself. He's adorable."

Shelly laughed. "I'm sure he is. I'd better go. I'll let you know what Jonathan and I decide about tomorrow. *Ciao*, baby."

"*Ciao*, baby?" Meredith repeated. Shelly didn't hear; she had already hung up. Was that movie-star talk or something?

Meredith sat on the railing and watched the sky turn pink in the west. That afternoon she had weeded and watered her garden. Now the rich scent of earth mixed with the evening breeze as the day cooled her heels, ready to hand off the baton to the night.

On an impulse, Meredith went into the house and pulled something from her hall closet that she hadn't looked at in months. She returned to the deck and opened the case. Lifting out the mouthpiece, Meri put the three parts of the silver stock together. With an agile fluttering of her fingers, the keys of her long-dormant instrument flexed their soft pads over the holes.

After blowing warm air into the chilly flute, Meri took a deep breath. It all came back to her. "Nocturne of the Flower Fairies." The first six bars rumbled low and mellow, sounding like the deep-chested humming of a miner coming up from the belly of the earth. Then it tumbled into the next measure like runaway dandelions racing across a meadow. Sweet, high, trilling notes echoed through the cedars. The playful refrain repeated as she played the end of the song without error.

Taking a breath that came from the hollow of her very soul, Meredith kissed the last note a tender farewell and let it breeze through her flute. That final note, an A-flat, released itself into the splendid night air, dancing and twirling as if it held in its arms an invisible flower fairy.

Meredith laid the flute in her lap and pressed her lips together. The only sound to be heard in the forest was the haunting call of the lonely bird in the tall trees. "Fee-bee, fee-bee," it cried.

Chapter Eighteen

*A*ll the enchantment of Meri's Saturday night concert was gone with the morning sun. She rose early to another warm, sunny day and hurriedly dressed in her most conservative beige suit. She caught the ferry just as she had hoped and arrived at church at twenty to ten.

Shelly and Jonathan had decided to fly up and arrived in their rental car about ten minutes after Meri. The three of them sat in the front row next to Mom, who was wearing an old dress. She had a dark look around the eyes but kept her thoughts to herself.

Dad stood in the pulpit, looking like a pillar of strength and virtue, as always. His sermon was on Gideon and how, when the angel of God appeared to Gideon, the angel called Gideon a "mighty man of valor." Dad preached on how we are all called to be strong and courageous when God asks us to do his work, especially when we don't feel strong or courageous.

Shelly and Meredith gave each other little pokes during the sermon. When they were little they used to nonchalantly pinch each other on the thigh to tease and torment during the long sermons. Now their pokes expressed love and a sharing in their knowledge of Dad's deeper message behind his sermon.

Mom sat tall and straight and kept her eyes forward.

At the end of the sermon, Dad made his announcement. His voice quavered a little at the end. The congregation gave a strange response. Some whispered in surprise. Some rustled in their seats. Overall, there was a startled hush.

Meri had noticed when they entered the church that the majority of the congregation were people over fifty. Many of them she had known her whole life, and they had greeted her with hugs and smeared lipstick kisses on her cheeks. The congregation was warm and loving and had been generous to the Graham family over the years.

However, very few young couples or singles Meri's age attended the service. And no teenagers, offering hope for a next generation of believers, sat in the pews. In a way, Meri could see why the board felt compelled to make a change in their pastoral staff. Everyone knows that the most money in tithes comes from the young families, especially the double-income households. Only the occasional retired parishioner who is well off will make a large contribution.

Meri felt angry with herself for allowing her thoughts to go that direction. Even though she knew it could be true, she didn't want to think that perhaps the board had made its decision to let Dad go based on finances. This was a large church facility on prime downtown real estate. Even with the weeknight activities, the building wasn't being used to its potential and hadn't been for a number of years.

It was all very sad. Being there, in the front row, and looking at her balding father as he held up his wrinkled hands in a benediction over the congregation brought Meri to tears.

They all went to her parents' home after church. As she had always done in their youth, Mom had stuck a pot roast in the oven before church. The house smelled warm and inviting. It was a glad, familiar fragrance.

Meredith automatically went to the china cabinet and took out the Sunday best to set the table, just as she had done every Sunday when she had lived at home. The three Graham women completed their tasks in a well-choreographed fashion, even though they hadn't played out this Sunday-after-church scene for more than six years. Shelly poured water into the crystal goblets and placed folded cloth napkins next to each fork. Mom carried in the platter of beef, carrots, and potatoes and set it in front of Dad's place at the head of the table. Meredith brought in the red Jell-O salad, wiggling on the plate. Mom had a collection of copper molds for her weekly Jell-O salad, and this week she had used the cluster of grapes.

The timer went off on the oven, announcing that the refrigerator rolls were ready, and Dad and Jonathan automatically moved from the family room to the dining room. Dad pulled out his wide captain's chair, and the rest of them followed suit, taking their places around the table. Jonathan had eaten many Sunday dinners with the Grahams while he was growing up next door. He fell right into his role as well.

"Let us pray," Dad said. Meri listened to his words. Over the years she hadn't paid much attention to his mealtime prayers, but today she listened. Despite his eloquent flourish to the simple words, Dad's true heart shone through when he prayed. He was a man who loved the Lord and deeply desired that others would come to know God by making a personal commitment to Jesus Christ.

Meredith had made that commitment when she was nine. One Sunday, after a dinner not unlike this one, she had followed her father into the living room, where he had stretched out on the couch for his usual Sunday-afternoon nap while Mom did the dishes.

"Daddy?" Meri had asked, approaching him cautiously. His eyes were closed, and his right arm was over his head with his wrist resting on his forehead. She remembered the moment distinctly.

"Hmm?" her father responded without opening his eyes.

"I want to go to heaven, Daddy," she said.

He slowly opened one eye and looked her over.

"Like that missionary said in church this morning. All of us are sinners and need God's free ticket to get to heaven. I want that ticket."

Dad opened both eyes and turned his head toward her. His arm was still across his forehead. "Do you believe that Jesus is God's Son?"

"Yes."

"Do you believe he died for your sins?" The arm came down to his side.

"Yes."

"Are you willing to confess your sins to him and ask him to come into your heart and take over your life?"

"Yes."

"Then go to your room, kneel by your bed, and tell that to God. After you pray, come back and tell me what happened."

Meredith remembered being so surprised at her dad's instructions. She had expected him to take her by the hand and pray for her. At the least, he could have smiled or kissed her forehead and told her how proud he was that she was making this big decision. Instead, he stayed on the couch, still lying down, and watched her go upstairs to her room.

On the bumpy throw rug beside her bed, Meredith knelt. She folded her hands and rested her elbows on the edge of her bed. Meri didn't remember what she prayed that day. She was pretty sure she had all the steps right. Ask forgiveness, invite Jesus to come into her life, then thank him. After the amen she waited. Her father had told her to come back and tell him what happened. Nothing seemed to be happening. She waited a little longer. Her room remained silent. The only tingles she felt were in her legs where the circulation was pinched off.

Finally, convinced she had done something wrong, Meri went back downstairs to sheepishly admit to her father that she had failed in her attempt to become a Christian and secure her ticket to heaven.

He was still lying there, with his arm over his forehead, but his eyes were open, and he was watching her come toward him. Meri sat down cross-legged on the floor in front of him, and with her head hanging down, she said, "I prayed, and nothing happened."

"Nothing happened that you could see or feel," her dad corrected her in his rich preacher's voice, now toned down to touch the heart of his youngest daughter. "But everything happened inside the forever part of you that you can't see or feel. You just became a Christian, Meredith. You are a daughter of the King. Your name was just written in the Lamb's Book of Life. You are now a joint heir with Christ. Your sins have been cast as far as the east is from the west."

Meredith looked into her father's kind face. All his big words confused her. "Am I going to heaven when I die?"

He smiled. "Yes. By surrendering your life to Christ, you just entered the kingdom of God, and his kingdom is eternal."

Her father reached over, and with strong, supple fingers, he took her chin in his hand. "Welcome to the family of God, my dear child."

Meredith felt a little dissatisfied. "Why didn't you come with me and pray with me?"

"You just made the most important decision of your life," he said. "This is between you and your Father God. He will always be there for you. I won't always be here. From the very start you must learn to depend completely on him and not on people who will end up leaving you or disappointing you."

"But I don't know if I prayed right."

"Anytime a heart opens to Christ, it's a right prayer. The words don't matter. God already knows what you're thinking. He knows everything."

Meri looked down again and admitted to her father, "But I didn't feel anything. Shouldn't I feel something when I make the most important decision of my life?"

"Sometimes people do, and sometimes people don't. The facts are never changed because of feelings. The Bible makes it clear that once you invite Christ into your heart he will never leave you. You may always rely on that unchanging fact."

Meredith believed his words. After all, her father was in the business of getting people into God's kingdom. He would know.

"Remember," he said, "this is just the beginning. Now your relationship with God must continue to grow. Do you still have the Bible we gave you last Christmas?"

Meri nodded.

"It's up to you, not your Sunday school teacher or anyone else, to take God's Word and hide it in your heart. Do you understand that?"

Meri nodded again, solemnly.

With all the instructions given, Dad's face broke into a big smile. He leaned over and kissed Meredith on the cheek. "I love you, honey. The angels in heaven are rejoicing over you right now." His eyes grew misty, and he said, "You will never know how magnificently my heart is rejoicing over you at this moment as well."

She basked in his touch and his words of approval. Then she skipped out to the backyard and sat in the swing for a long time.

As the poignant memory began to fade now while Meredith sat at the dining-room table with an empty plate in front of her, she wished the old swing set were still in the backyard. She would sit in the swing again this afternoon and lose herself in her thoughts.

Mom rose to clear the plates. Shelly helped her and returned with an apple pie that had been warming in the oven.

"I saw the sign up for the loganberry farm when we were at Whidbey yesterday," Mom said. "The sign said they would open on June first this year. Isn't that early for loganberries?"

"It's been unusually warm," Meri said, entering the conversation for nearly the first time during the meal. "They also sell other berries at the stand. I don't know what's going to ripen first this year."

"I'm ready to make some berry pies," Mom said, pressing the knife into the homemade crust. "I'm hoping the blueberries will be sweeter than they were last year. It was not a good blueberry year."

Meri was amazed that, despite the crisis with her parents, all they talked about was berries. She reminded herself this was the way her mother coped best, and Meri tried to honor that.

The apple pie was delicious, as always. The rest of the dishes were cleared with precision. Dad excused himself from the table by placing his cloth napkin, folded and tidy, next to his plate. Mom would wash it even though it was unsoiled. He pushed back his chair and said, "Excellent dinner, Ellen. Thank you." Then he took the eighteen steps from the dining-room table to the living-room couch like a man under the pull of an irresistible magnet. Within three minutes his light snoring ruffled the air.

The women began the cleanup in the kitchen. To the delight of Meri's mom, Jonathan ordered her out of the kitchen, saying he would help clean up. Mom didn't leave the kitchen and go relax as Jonathan had ordered, but she did sit down and put her feet up.

"It was really nice of you three to come today," Mom said. "I know your father appreciates it."

"We wanted to be here," Jonathan said, washing the china with much less finesse than those fragile dishes were used to. "This is an important crossroads for you and Perry. Shelly and I have talked about it, and if we can help in any way, you know we're here for you."

"That's kind of you, Jonathan, but I'm sure there's nothing you can do."

"Even so," Shelly said. "Keep it in mind. If you end up moving out of this house, you might need a place to stay for awhile, and we have room."

"In your little cabin?" Mom said with a laugh. "I hardly think so. Meredith has twice the space you two have."

All eyes turned to Meredith as she pulled a dry towel from the bottom drawer. "Oh, of course," she said, quickly entering into the charity of the moment. "You're welcome to come stay with me. Anytime. As long as you like. I'd love to have you." She wasn't sure why her heart was pounding so wildly. Maybe because she was unaccustomed to lying.

"I'm sure none of your hospitality will be necessary. We are in no rush to sell this house. Who knows? We might end up finding another pastorate here in town."

Meri knew that wasn't likely. She hoped their moving in with her wasn't very likely either.

Chapter Nineteen

After the dishes were done and the kitchen cleaned, Shelly lured Meredith away from the others by saying she wanted to pick some flowers from Mom's garden and needed help.

Mom's garden was practical. She had built terraces years ago and kept all the flowers in nice neat rows and sections. The garden wasn't particularly beautiful to look at, but the abundance of flora it produced graced every room of the house nearly nine months out of the year.

Shelly picked up Mom's gathering basket from the corner of the mud room, and Meri followed her out to the garden. Neatly tucked inside the basket were Mom's garden gloves and a pair of clippers.

"If you're going to talk to me about convincing Mom and Dad to live with me, save your breath," Meri began before they even reached the terraces. "I didn't mean it when I said they would be welcome anytime."

"Don't worry," Shelly said. "They would never do that.

They like their privacy and schedule too much to become dependent on anyone. I was thinking we could put them up at camp in one of the staff cabins. For a short time. Mom didn't seem too interested."

"I'm trying to be more understanding of Mom now that I know what a stressful time she's going through, but honestly, Shelly, she would drive me crazy."

"Don't worry!" Shelly said again. "But I don't want to talk about Mom. I wanted to tell you what Jake said about you last night."

"Oh, pu-leeze," Meri said. "When are you going to stop with the matchmaking? Did he tell you his view of love? That one would stop you dead in your attempts. He thinks falling in love is a chemical reaction. That's all. His views are about as romantic as cold fish-head soup."

Shelly laughed. "Where did you get that?"

"From the cold fish himself," Meri said, reaching over and dead-heading some of the shriveled-up daffodils Mom seemed to have missed. "He, Helen, and I had a little discussion at my house Friday night. Jake seems to think the spiritually correct route to marriage is to make a logical choice in a suitable life partner and then commit to that person. Feelings shouldn't be involved."

"That's not such a radical notion," Shelly said, snipping a bunch of pansies low at their base. "Jonathan and I made a logical commitment to each other when we got back together and before we became engaged. It's part of the process."

"Yes, but you and Jonathan were also in love. You knew you were. Everyone knew you were. You had lots of feelings between the two of you. That's how I want it to be for me. I want some man to be absolutely taken with me, and I want to be wild about him, not logical and calculated as Jake says it's supposed to be if it's to last."

Shelly flung her long, fawn-colored hair over her shoulder
and took a good look at her little sister. "You already are wild
about him, aren't you?"

"Jake?"

"Yes, of course, Jake. I can see it on your face, Meri. Now I
know why you were always badgering me about admitting that
I was still in love with Jonathan. It shows up in a woman's face
when she says his name, doesn't it?"

Meri let out a sigh and sat down on the weathered railroad
tie that held the second level of the terrace in place. "You know
me," she began her unplanned confession to her sister. "I don't
get crazy about men. I've held out for a hero. I'm pure as the
driven snow. I've prayed for my future husband for years. I'm
trusting God that he has one perfect Mr. Right just for me and
that he'll bring him into my life when the timing is right. I also
believe what everyone has always told me about love: When it's
right, you'll know it."

"Well, everyone is wrong," Shelly said flatly. "You don't
always know when it's right. At least I didn't. It took me five
years to admit that Jonathan was right for me."

"You guys were a special case," Meri said, plucking a weed
from the soil beside her.

"Everyone is a special case," Shelly said. "And now do you
want to hear something that will freak you out?"

Meri shrugged.

"I don't believe there is only one man for one woman."

"What is that supposed to mean?"

"You just said that you believe God has one perfect Mr.
Right for you. First of all, nobody is perfect. So don't hold your
breath waiting for someone perfect. And second, I agree with
Jake. Marriage is a commitment. I don't believe there is only
one perfect man waiting for you, Meri. I think you could end

up marrying one of many different men and be very happy and satisfied if you're both deeply committed to each other."

"This is too much," Meri said, getting up and pacing back and forth on the garden pavers. "Of all people, how can you say such a thing? Jonathan is the one and only for you, and you are the one and only for him."

"That's how it turned out. But if he had ended up marrying Elena, I believe the two of them would have been very happy if they both were committed to their vows."

"Oh, come on," Meri said. "They would never have lasted. His heart was yours from the start."

"But when I left Seattle, he slowly made room in his heart. Then when Elena came along there was enough room for her to fit in there comfortably without ever bumping into me." Shelly put down the basket and batted at a fly eavesdropping on their chat. "Jonathan and I have talked about this before. He agrees. The larger portion of love is the choice. What makes it real is the commitment to honor and nurture that choice."

"You're bursting all my bubbles," Meri said flatly. "Whatever happened to heart-stopping, spine-tingling, take-your-breath-away love? And please, oh, please don't you dare say that's just a chemical reaction—because I might be forced to take these clippers to your hair if you do!"

Shelly paused before letting a wide, welcoming smile draw up the corners of her mouth. "Does he take your breath away?"

"Who? Jake? No, of course not!"

Shelly raised her eyebrows. "Stop your heart a little? Give your spine a little tingle?"

Meredith held up her chin. "I find him intriguing."

Shelly laughed. "Intriguing? That's the exact word he used to describe you when Jonathan asked him last night. Jake said you weren't like any woman he had ever met and he found you intriguing."

"Is that a step up from 'original'?"

Shelly smiled. "You know what I think? I think spine-tingling romance is much more than a chemical reaction. I think it's the icing on the relationship." She raised her eyebrows and gave Meredith a knowing look. "Believe me, there is nothing like having your breath taken away and then having it given back to you by your true love."

Meri knew this was the voice of experience speaking.

"But you can't live on icing," Shelly said. "Spine-tingling comes and goes. It's the commitment that builds the real base for love."

"You're telling me you don't get tingly anymore? You're married one year and all the tingles are gone?"

"I didn't say that!" Shelly laughed, and her cheeks turned rosy. "It's only getting better, believe me. All I'm saying is if you plan for the commitment, the tingles will come."

On her way home, Meredith mulled over her sister's words. She drove her Explorer onto the ferry and walked up to the top deck, eager to feel the wind in her hair. To her surprise, it was cold once the boat moved out on the water. Shivering cold. The sun, which had been the area's guardian for so long, was now being replaced by huge clouds that carried rain in their dark hems. It would be wonderful to have some rain again, but as Meri clutched her arms and headed back inside the ferry, she thought of how much she was going to miss the sun and the clear blue skies.

By the time she was off the ferry and driving home on Whidbey Island, the clouds were letting out their hems. Great drops of rain spattered her windshield. Meredith switched on the radio, hoping to catch a weather report. A familiar love song was ending.

"When I see you, that's when I know
Love like this is ours alone.

When I touch you, that's when you see
Your lips were meant for only me."

"That's pretty self-serving," Meri muttered, switching to another channel. The next song was an oldie.

"Girl, what you do to me is better than
The perfect wave
On the perfect day
On the perfect beach,
So come here, baby,
And do it all over again."

"Good grief," Meri muttered, dialing in a western music station.

"You left me
And here I stand
Heart in my hat,
Hat in my hand."

She couldn't bear to listen to the rest. The way that song was unfolding, Meri was sure it would contain a tender reference to either this country boy's truck or his dog before it was over, and those two items were at the very bottom of her list of favorites.

Of course, she knew most songs were written about love. That's what kept the whole industry going. It had never occurred to her how much those songs were based on feelings and selfish desires. She had never heard a song that said anything like

"Even if you get hit by a semi
And your face is mashed
And you're in a wheelchair,
I'll still love you
Just like I love you now."

True, songs like that might not hit the top of the charts, but still, it made her think about how slanted the whole industry was toward romance. Subconsciously she had been influenced over the years by those songs as she formed her concept of love.

She wondered if Jake and Shelly had more of a point than she wanted to admit. Suddenly Meredith felt more grown-up. It was more than turning twenty-five and seeing her parents move toward retirement, although both factors certainly played a part in what she was going through. It was also that her dream-world image of what it would be like to meet a movie star had been so shaken when she had met Jake. And her idealized view of love had taken a serious blow in the past few days.

Meredith pulled up in front of her house and hurried into the cottage through the pelting rain. Inside, the air felt close and stuffy. The morning had been hot, but she hadn't left any windows open. Now the rain had turned the air humid, and the house smelled of mildew. Meri left the front door open so the chilling breeze could run through and freshen up the place. She checked her phone messages and changed into sweats and her favorite slippers.

Elvis was swimming contentedly in his bowl. He bobbed eagerly to the surface when she sprinkled his dinner on the water.

"Would you like to go back upstairs with me, Elvis?"

Closing the front door and heading for her office loft with Elvis under her arm, Meredith knew it was time to throw herself into her work. True, it was Sunday night, and she should finish her Sabbath rest from work. However, she couldn't wait until Monday morning to read one particular manuscript.

Digging halfway down through the pile of manila envelopes, Meredith came to the two packets bearing Helen's New York return address. The first manuscript was from an author Helen had pitched to Meredith several times. She put that one back into the middle of the stack. With curiosity driving her, Meredith pulled out the other manuscript and skimmed Helen's cover letter.

Yes, yes, you told me it's a honey, Meredith silently answered as Helen's praises of Jake and his screenplay dripped off the cover letter. *Now show me what he's got.*

Turning to the three-page synopsis, Meredith carefully read Jacob's own words describing the journey of Young Heart to the city called "Fullness of Joy." Throughout the journey, Young Heart faced choices. How he responded at each crossroads led him on to the next challenge until he finally reached Fullness of Joy.

Sounds like a video game.

At the end of the summary, a Scripture reference was listed. Meredith reached for the hardback reference Bible she kept on her desk and looked up Psalm 16:11. She read it once to herself and then again, aloud.

"You will show me the path of life; in Your presence is fullness of joy; at Your right hand are pleasures forevermore."

Meredith sat back and let the words sink in. *Is this his philosophy of life? Pleasures are only to be found in heaven? Does he think life is nothing more than a journey of choices, commitments, and trials? So the joy doesn't come until we go to be with the Lord?*

Meredith agreed with the concept. After all, the verse did emphasize the pleasure and joy we would one day experience in heaven if we trusted Christ and surrendered to him in this life. But something seemed to be missing. Other parts of the Bible talked about how wonderful life was…didn't they?

She felt like Pollyanna, ready to go on a hunt for all the "glad" verses in the Bible.

"First things first," Meredith told herself, moving from her desk chair over to her comfy reading chair. "Let's see what you have to say, Jake Wilde. Or is this Jacob Wartman speaking?"

Putting her feet up on a stack of manuscripts and settling in with the pages, she said with a smile, "Okay, you cold fish head, prove to me you have a heart after all."

Chapter Twenty

 es, Helen," Meredith said the next morning on the phone, "you were right. I already told you you were right. It is a honey. Now I'm telling you, it's almost there, but something is missing."

"I don't see how you can say that," Helen responded. "Gabriel Kalen is behind this project, and it's going into video production in a few weeks. I told you I have a firm offer from Medina & Beckmann Publishers, but when I talked to Jake this morning, he didn't want me to respond to them until after we had heard from you. He would rather be with G. H. Terrison, for obvious reasons."

Meredith flattered herself for a moment that she might be the obvious reason. Then she remembered Gabe Kalen's close association with her publishing company.

"Look," Meri said diplomatically, "I stayed up until midnight reading the screenplay over and over, trying to figure out what's missing. I couldn't figure it out. It's good, Helen, but it's not great. Not yet."

"Aren't you being a little too rigid here, Meri?"

"All I know is that Terrison doesn't pay me to find good books. They pay me to find great books."

"Are you saying you don't want this project?" There was such an edge to Helen's voice that Meri was sure Helen had dyed her hair jet black today and was wearing black high heels to match. The two of them had dickered well in the past. This was not uncomfortable for either of them. This was business.

"I don't know yet," Meredith said.

"And when do you think you will know?" Helen asked. "You've had the manuscript for well over a week, and as I said, we have another offer from Medina & Beckmann."

"I know, Helen. Just give me two more days. I want to think about it. Can your client wait two more days?"

Helen let out an exasperated sigh. "Wednesday morning you will receive a call from me at eight o'clock sharp."

"I don't get to my office until nine," Meri said with a playful chime in her voice. "Why don't I call you?"

"If you don't call by nine, I'll call you," Helen said.

"Okay," Meri agreed.

"Fine," Helen stated. Then, changing her tone, she said, "So how was your weekend?"

Meri told her about her dad's forced resignation and how he had made the announcement from the pulpit on Sunday.

Helen fired up again. "See? That is why I am a nonpracticing Protestant. Things like that happen all the time in the church, and I can't stand it. It's so unfair to your parents after they've given their whole married life to that church. What are they going to do now?"

"They don't know yet. There was some uncomfortable talk

about my inviting them to live here if they had to sell the house."

Meredith expected Helen's sympathy.

"That's not such a bad idea."

"Tell me you're not serious, Helen."

"Sure. Let your parents have the cottage in the woods. They can sit on the porch and watch little bunny Foo-Foo hop through your vegetable garden. And you—" Helen paused for effect—"you come to New York to get a real life."

"I'm going to hang up on you now, Helen."

"It's a thought," Helen said.

Before Meri could think of a witty response, the call-waiting click sounded in her ear. "I have another call. I'll talk to you Wednesday morning."

"It'll be afternoon by the time you call, but to keep my client happy I'll wait for you."

"Good-bye, Helen."

Meri was on the phone all morning with a string of business calls. When she took a break to get something to drink, it was almost noon. Then she realized she hadn't checked her e-mail yet today. Since she normally had several messages, she decided she had better look right away. A memo was awaiting her from one of the editors at Terrison announcing a publications meeting the next morning at ten o'clock in Chicago. It was not the usual monthly meeting at which the acquisition editors presented their most promising projects. Shawn was calling this unscheduled meeting because he had found something he really liked and wanted to zip it through the committee immediately. Such meetings didn't happen often. The company policy was that if the manuscript was great, it would be great a month later when the committee held its regularly scheduled meeting.

Meredith decided to take advantage of the opportunity. She went to work sending her own e-mail memo to the committee members stating that she had an urgent project and time would not allow them to wait for the June meeting. She faxed copies of the summary and proposal to all the committee members and then made a call to Helen.

When Helen's voice mail picked up the call, Meri said, "Look how good I am to you, Helen. It's not even Wednesday, and I'm phoning you. I put my neck on the line for this honey of a project, and I slipped it into an emergency pub meeting tomorrow. It has to get past this bunch anyway. I thought we'd take advantage of the situation to speed up the process. You may tell your client that I'm going to give this project my best pitch at the meeting tomorrow, and if they go for it, we can talk numbers tomorrow afternoon. Are you happy now? Oh, and by the way, something is still missing, and I intend to discover what it is and fix it as we go along."

Meredith hung up and set to work doing her least favorite part of the job. She had to make up a budget sheet. What would the length of each book be? What would the paper cost be? How many books would be run in the first printing?

It took her all afternoon. She typed up everything and faxed it off to her associates so they would have the proposal first thing in the morning.

To Meredith's surprise, when the conference call came the next morning, the committee wanted to discuss her project before Shawn's. She sat back in her desk chair and listened to the others enthusiastically approve the project. Only one editor had a concern, and that was the timing of the release. Could they finish the books to launch them alongside the videos? Would the producer be willing to hold the videos, if need be, to get the books ready?

"I can find out," Meri said. "The biggest concern I have is

that we find the right assistant or ghostwriter for this project. As I mentioned, it's in screenplay form now, and some basic elements are missing for it to work as a book series."

"Why don't you ghost it?" suggested a voice over the speaker phone.

"Because I've never done ghosting before," Meri said.

"I'll do it!" a female editor offered. "I'd love to meet Jake Wilde and work side by side with him late into the night."

"Me too," another woman chimed in. "Maybe we could make it a group project for all interested female editors."

A rumbling of spicy comments and some laughter sounded in the background. That was the part Meri liked least about these conference calls. She could never catch all the innuendos and side jokes. It especially bothered her today because the comments were about Jake. None of them knew he was a real person who embarrassed easily. They thought of him as an unattached movie star, which made him fair game. What would they think if they found out this icon had left a grape on her pillow?

"Let's get back to the business at hand," the managing editor stated firmly. "We are in agreement that you should proceed with this series, Meredith. Make sure you budget for the ghostwriter and have Jake's agent contact the producer so we can work with them on the release of the books and videos."

"Okay. Great."

Shawn's project didn't meet with as much interest, and he was asked to put it on hold. When she hung up, Meredith realized how timely and unusual it was that Jake's project was given the go-ahead so quickly.

Helen was, of course, delighted. She promised Meri a box of Godiva chocolates for all Meri's extra efforts.

Meredith went to work on the project. In the busy days that followed, along with her regular workload, she championed and babied Jake's books through all the necessary hoops and loops. Helen remained their go-between until the day before Meredith was to leave for the writer's conference in California.

She was in her room packing for the trip when the phone rang.

"Meredith?" the rich voice asked.

"Yes?"

"How are you? This is Jake."

She sat on the edge of her bed, crumpling her stack of blouses and not caring a bit. "I'm doing great. How about you? I hear from Helen that everything we've done so far in negotiations has been okay by you."

"Yes," he agreed. "It's all fine."

She wondered if that was a hint of nervousness in his voice or if it was the poor phone connection. Meredith tried to relax and keep the conversation light. "You caught me in the middle of packing for this conference. Are you ready to go?"

"It's practically in my backyard, you know, so that means I don't have to pack the way you do."

There was a little pause.

"It sounds as if it's going to be a good conference," Meri said. "Are you teaching some workshops? Or are you the keynote speaker for one of the dinners and I should know that already?"

"I'm only doing one workshop," he said. "I still haven't figured out why they asked me to come. I'm a novice myself in this field."

"Yes, but a famous novice, and I'm sure that counts for something."

Again, a pause.

"How are the videos coming along?" Meri asked. "I haven't talked to Shelly lately. She was keeping me updated on your plans to film at Camp Heather Brook. Is everything still on schedule?"

"More or less. We've run into some difficulties with our cast."

"Oh?"

"We need a Maiden of the Waterfall," he said. "We had an actress all set, but she received a better offer and left to do a film in Spain. So we've begun some of the studio work, and we have the film crew in place for the next month and a half. I'll feel better when we have all the parts cast."

"I can't imagine how much work that must be," Meredith said, walking over to the dresser, where she balanced the phone on her shoulder and started pulling out her shorts to see if any of them would be worth packing for Los Angeles.

"It's a lot," Jake agreed. "But you've been doing a lot on the book end of the project. When Helen sends me updates I'm amazed at how much goes into book production. Thanks for all your hard work."

Meredith smiled. "You're welcome. Thanks for thanking me. It seems those are words editors rarely hear. I appreciate your saying something." She wasn't sure if she should bring up her concerns about the missing element in the books. Helen hadn't indicated that she had said anything to him. Still, was it fair for him to think that everything was fine the way it was?

"I was wondering," Jake said, "if you had some free time during the conference. I'd like to have a chance to talk with you about the books."

"Sure," Meredith said. "I think it would be good if we could talk through a few things up front. As Helen, I'm sure, told you, we've hired a terrific ghostwriter who has had experience in transforming screenplays into novels."

"Yes, that's what Helen said."

A pause. This time Meri waited for him to speak first.

"So, we'll get together, then."

"Yes. That will be good."

"Maybe we should set a time," Jake suggested. "If this is like other conferences I've attended, time can get away."

"Good idea. I guess evenings would be the most open time."

"Evenings are fine."

"How about Tuesday evening?" Meredith suggested. "My workshop ends that day at four thirty."

"I won't be free until around seven," Jake said. "Would you mind if we met in the hotel lobby a little after seven? I'll treat you to cheesecake."

Meredith smiled. He must have remembered she liked cheesecake.

"Sounds scrumptious," Meri said. "A little after seven in the hotel lobby."

"Great."

A pause.

"Well," Meredith said, not sure why he wasn't ending the conversation, "I'll see you then, unless we run into each other before."

"Okay." Jake paused again. "I just thought of something. It might be a little easier, you know, if I could pick you up in front of the hotel. If I come in…"

"Good thinking," Meredith agreed. She could see him being swamped by autograph seekers in the lobby. The two of them might never make it out for cheesecake.

"I know that's pretty tacky, asking you to wait out on the curb."

"Don't worry. It doesn't bother me. I'll be there a little after seven, then."

"Terrific," Jake said. He sounded relieved, as if he had just asked a girl out to the eighth-grade dance and, beyond all his wildest hopes and dreams, she had agreed to go with him.

"I'll see you in a couple of days, then," Meredith said brightly. "Thanks for calling."

"I suppose I'd better let you get back to your packing."

"It's a monster of a task. I'm not used to dressing up much. That's one of the perks of working at home; slippers and a robe go a long way as career apparel." Meredith giggled at her own comments.

Jake laughed with her. It seemed he had been waiting for Meredith to give him something to chuckle about. But his laughter lasted much longer than necessary for the silly comment she had made.

"I suppose I should ask since you're on the line," Meredith said, "what's the weather been like?"

"Warm. Some hazy afternoons. It's cool at night, but not cold. Mostly low eighties, I'd say."

"It's been raining here for a week straight," Meredith said, peering out her bedroom window. In the waning light of dusk, the rain was still coming down steadily. "I'm looking forward to sunshine."

"It's been nice here," Jake said.

Again they each waited to see who was going to speak next or suggest they end the call. Meredith took the initiative this time. "I'd better get back to packing. I have an early flight in the morning."

"Okay," Jake said.

"I'll see you in a couple of days."

"Tuesday," he repeated.

"Bye."

"Good-bye, Meredith."

She hung up and smiled, savoring the sound of her name on his lips. *This is pretty promising. Sure, it's a business meeting, but he wants to get together. He initiated it. He even thought of the cheesecake! Of course, we both understand up front that he is allowed no tingles.*

She giggled. "That doesn't mean I can't enjoy a few myself, does it?"

Chapter Twenty-One

Meri put down the phone. Humming softly, she went through her stack of shorts, trying to decide which ones she would be willing to be seen wearing in public. The black linen ones had potential. Now, what shirt would she wear with them? And the bigger question, what would she wear Tuesday night? A summer dress maybe.

She flipped through the few dresses still on hangers. None of them jumped out and said, "Take me to cheesecake!"

The clothes on her bed looked frumpy and outdated. She hadn't bought herself anything new this spring, and the newest outfit she could see was a long, navy blue, cap-sleeved dress with buttons down the front. She had only worn it once because she didn't like the way the line of buttons twisted when she walked.

This is pitiful! Why didn't I go shopping last week? I wonder if I can get away from the conference on Monday to buy something.

The phone rang. She considered letting the answering

machine pick it up, but since this was Sunday night, it would be someone from her family or a friend. Probably Shelly was calling since Meredith had tried to phone her that afternoon and hadn't caught anyone at home.

Feeling cheerful, Meredith playfully answered the phone, "Hello, you have reached Meredith's answering service. If you would like to leave a message, please chirp like a bird at the sound of the beep. Beep!"

After a pause a rich male voice said tentatively, "Chirp?"

Meredith swallowed her giggles. "Jake?"

"Meredith?"

"Yes." She freed her laughter and tried to explain. "I thought you were Shelly."

"Oh. I was wondering," Jake said slowly. "You said you have an early flight. What time do you arrive tomorrow?"

"Around ten-thirty, I think."

"Is someone picking you up from the airport?"

"I don't think so. I understood we were supposed to catch the hotel shuttle at the airport."

"I see," he said.

"Why do you ask?" Meredith ventured.

"Well, if you'd like, I could pick you up. I thought maybe you could stop by the studio. We aren't filming tomorrow morning, but you could see the set design."

"That sounds great! I'd love to see the studio." She hoped she didn't sound too enthusiastic. "Let me check my ticket and give you the info. I could meet you at the curb in front of baggage claim, if that would be easiest for you." Meredith pulled her ticket from the leather briefcase Shelly had given her. "I arrive at LAX at 10:10 from Seattle. Should I meet you outside of baggage claim around ten thirty?"

"That would work."

"Great. How fun! Thanks for thinking of this, Jake."

"Good. Then I'll see you tomorrow morning at ten-thirty. I drive a tan-colored Ford Explorer."

"You're kidding! That's what I drive."

"I know. I saw it the night Helen and I were there."

"Isn't that a coincidence," Meri said.

"Yes," he agreed, his voice matter-of-fact. "I'd better let you get back to your packing."

"Okay. See you tomorrow. Bye, Jake."

"Good-bye, Meredith."

Oh, I love the way he says that! "Good-bye, Meredith." My name rolls off his tongue like honey.

"Meredith," she repeated aloud, trying to catch his inflection. She lowered her voice a notch and slowly spilled out the word, "Meredith."

Tomorrow I'm going to see Jake, and he's taking me to the studio. She smiled broadly at her bedroom mirror. *This is the face of a happy woman!*

Behind her, in the reflection of the mirror, she spotted the mound of clothes on her bed. With a groan she turned to face all the pitiful rags. "Now what am I going to wear tomorrow?"

Three hours later, Meredith sat on her bedroom floor surrounded by every article of clothing she owned. There were piles here and stacks there. She had created a mess, but nothing had made it into her suitcase yet.

I realize there are greater problems in this world than my clothing crisis, but right now world hunger pales in comparison to this. What am I going to wear to a Hollywood studio?

Upset with herself for being obsessed with her appearance, Meredith decided to take a different approach. "Jeans," she declared to the heaps of clothes. "I'll wear jeans tomorrow. Jeans go with everything, anytime, anywhere, in any part of the world, right? Now, which top?"

When Meredith stepped off the plane in sunny southern California the next morning, she wore her black jeans with a wide black belt and a short-sleeved, black mock turtleneck. A row of hoop bracelets jangled on her arm as she slung the leather bag over her shoulder and headed for the baggage claim on the lower level.

She had gotten three hours of sleep the night before since she had to be up at five to make her plane out of Seattle. The catnaps on the plane had helped some, but she knew her eyes were puffy. She was glad she could hide behind her sunglasses at least a little longer.

Her luggage came through with the first batch on the conveyor belt. She stepped outside, scanning the area for a tan Explorer. It was parked twenty yards away, right by the curb with its blinkers on. Meri felt her heart pounding as she pulled her wheeled luggage toward Jake's car. She went up to the passenger door and, with an eager tug, opened it and said, "Hi!"

The overweight man in the driver's seat was not Jake.

"Oh, excuse me. I'm sorry!" She slammed the door and began to hurry away.

"No, wait," the man called after her. "Are you Meredith?"

She stopped and looked back at the stranger, who was hanging his head out the passenger window. "Jake sent me," the man said. "He got held up at the studio."

Meredith returned, feeling the warm, red glow that must now be staining her cheeks a deep shade of rose.

"I'm Chad," the large man said. "You need a hand with your luggage?"

"No. I'll just put it in the backseat here." Meredith placed her luggage inside and then settled herself into the passenger's seat. "How are you?" she asked the unlikely chauffeur as he pulled away from the curb.

"Fine."

"That's good."

Chad drove silently, and she decided not to disrupt his concentration since the traffic was thick exiting the airport. They entered the freeway, and Chad turned on the radio to a rock station. Apparently he liked his music loud. Driving with one hand on the wheel, Chad hung his left arm out the open window and pounded on the door to the music's beat. For the next half hour Meredith received a crash course on all the current rock hits in L.A., accompanied by Chad, the would-be drummer.

The breeze from his open window blew her hair like crazy and filled her nostrils with the acrid scent of fuel emissions rising in the warm, thick, morning air. She didn't know why she couldn't bring herself to ask this guy to turn on the air conditioner.

When they arrived at the studio, she was surprised at how boring it looked. They entered the first building in a row of what looked like three warehouses. A red light was hung over the door, and a bold sign read Do Not Enter When Red Light Is On. The red light was off.

A welcoming blast of cool air met Meri when she stepped into the studio. A narrow pathway led to the back corner of the building. All along the narrow path were thick cords taped to the floor with duct tape. Some of the cords were blue, some black, and some green. On the right wall were stacks of huge pressed-wood boards folded up, lights on tall metal stands, and ladders. More cords hung from the very high, dark ceiling. The studio was completely different from what she had pictured. Nothing was glamorous about any of it so far.

Chad led her through a set that was a kitchen, complete with kids' artwork on the refrigerator. It seemed smaller than a real kitchen, and there was no ceiling. Hot lights bore down on the dull linoleum floor. They walked out the kitchen door and into what looked like a props junkyard. The huge, open, middle area of the studio was surrounded by different stage walls fencing it in. Meredith guessed that each of those walls framed a set just like the kitchen they had walked through.

She wanted to stop and have a look at all the crazy props that had been laid to rest here in this no-man's-land. A Tiffany lamp stood next to a stuffed gorilla and a recliner chair with a large basket of silk tulips on the seat. A coat rack held a leather jacket, a jump rope, and a baby blanket. A basketball and a painting of a sailboat were beside a patio table that was loaded with trinkets like at an estate sale.

Meredith had seen this kind of colorful mayhem only once before, in the drama-department props closet at her high school. But this studio was that prop closet's mother ship. Walking through the middle of all this imagination waiting to be used filled Meredith with excitement.

They turned a corner, and there stood Jake. Meredith saw him first. Her heart flip-flopped. Jake had on khaki shorts, a blue denim work shirt, and his camel-colored loafers with no socks. His sunglasses were around his neck on a black leather string. He held a clipboard in his hand and was going down the list of items with a man who was holding a can of Diet Coke in one hand and a three-foot, multicolored butterfly in the other.

Glad I didn't dress up for this.

She smiled and waited for Chad to announce her. Chad didn't say a word. He walked past Jake and went to an ice chest on the floor, where he fished out a couple of drinks. He came back and handed a dripping Cactus Cooler to Meredith.

"What is this?" she asked quietly.

"Soda," Chad said, giving her a strange look.

"Oh. I've never heard of this kind of soda."

He looked at her even more strangely, as if she had just arrived from Mars. Jake must have heard them talking because he looked over and caught Meri's eye. His expression seemed to brighten. He said a few more words to the man with the butterfly and walked over to greet her.

"Hi," he said. "I see Chad found you okay. Sorry I couldn't be there. Thanks, Chad."

"No prob'," Chad replied, popping the lid on his drink and walking away now that he had been dismissed by the boss.

"It's good to see you," Jake said.

Meredith smiled. She wondered if she looked silly with her sunglasses on top of her head. Did her eyes look too puffy? Why was he smiling at her so warmly? Was he just happy to finally be in his own comfort zone with her?

"This is quite a place," Meredith said, unlocking her gaze and taking a sweeping glance of the studio. "I've never been to Hollywood before."

"I hate to disillusion you," Jake said, "but technically we're not in Hollywood. We were able to rent this studio for five hundred dollars a day less than the same size studio in Hollywood."

"Sounds like a good choice." She snapped open her can of soda and took a cautious sip. It was sweet. Very sweet. Sort of an orange soda with a twist of 7UP and lots of sugar.

"Did Chad give you the tour already?"

"Not really. He's not much of a talker."

"No, I guess he's not. Let me show you around." Jake gently touched Meredith's elbow and directed her to the right. He let go immediately, but the memory of his touch lasted for the rest of the tour.

As Jake took her through all the sets and described each scene that would be filmed and where, she wondered what he was thinking. Was there a glimmer of a chance that this love legalist might actually be experiencing a little bit of heart flop-ping himself? The way he had looked at her when she first came in was not at all the look of a man who is only interested in business.

Or am I making this up in my overactive imagination? Do I want him to be interested so badly that I'm willing to convince myself he might be?

But what if he is? How can anyone start a casual friendship with a man like Jake Wilde? And what about all the business arrangements? Will I jeopardize my professional integrity if I become involved in a relationship with this guy?

What am I thinking? He hasn't given any indication that he's interested in me. And I know how interested he is in a relationship! Commitment first, then feelings. This does not appear to be a man who is in a position to make a commitment to anything but his work.

There, that makes it clear. Nothing is going on between us, and I have no reason to concoct something in my imagination because it will be one-sided. My side. And my side doesn't need to get its hopes up and its feelings hurt.

"So that's about it," Jake said as the tour came to a close. "Are you hungry?"

"Yes, as a matter of fact, I'm very hungry." The pretzels and orange juice on the plane had burned off long ago.

"We have a caterer who brings lunch in for the crew," Jake said, glancing at his watch. "They should be ready to serve in about twenty minutes. Could you stick around for lunch, and then I can have Chad drive you over to the conference."

"Aren't you coming?" Meredith asked. The thought of being carted across town by Chad was not appealing.

"My first workshop isn't until tomorrow morning," Jake said, walking over to the back wall of the studio and hanging the clipboard on a peg. A time clock and a bulletin board loaded with notices were also on the wall. "I have an appoint-

ment with our casting director this afternoon and then a meeting with the wardrobe people. That reminds me—I wanted to
show you this."

He led her down a maze of pathways lined with cables and
cords. They entered an open area that was well lit and had several long racks of outfits. "These are the costumes for Young
Heart," Jake explained. "I thought maybe you would like to
have a look since you suggested we do photos for the covers
instead of drawings. I like the idea because I think it will build
continuity between the videos and the books."

"I think it will, too," Meredith said, trying hard to set her
mind on this as a business situation and not a prelude to a date.
It was difficult not to be a little disappointed that Chad, not
Jake, would drive her to the conference. She dreaded the
thought of spending the afternoon in thick traffic on that hot
freeway with Chad's music and drumming on the side of the
car.

"This costume was the one I had in mind for the cover of
the first book," Jake said, pulling out a hanger from the rack.
Draped on the hanger was a pair of deep green breeches with
matching suspenders. The shirt was pale yellow. "Of course, if
this works, we would like to have the cover of the videos and
the cover of the books be the same photo."

Meredith nodded.

A stagehand walked into the dressing area carrying a bowl
of something white. Black flecks were sprinkled on the fluffy
white substance.

"I think we've got it, Jake," the stagehand said. "Try this."

Jake reached for the ice-cream scoop in the center of the
bowl and scooped out a mound of the mysterious mixture. He
plopped it onto an ice-cream cone the man held in his other
hand. Jake looked at it this way and that. He touched the glob
and then nodded in satisfaction.

"That's it. Good job, Miguel. Keep it in the refrigerator, and write down your recipe. We don't want to forget the proportions this time."

"Got it," Miguel said, leaving with his big bowl of white fluff.

"He's not the caterer, is he?" Meredith asked.

"No." Jake laughed. "He's our prop man. That was our chocolate-chip-ice-cream cone for the opening scene."

"Ice cream?"

"It's actually instant mashed potatoes with shavings of black crayon for the chips. Real ice cream melts under these hot lights. Everyone knows you use instant mashed potatoes on screen for ice cream, but we couldn't get the chocolate chip shavings to look right."

"Very clever," Meredith said.

Jake looked at her and smiled proudly. "Not everything around here is what it appears to be."

"So I'm beginning to discover," she said.

Chapter Twenty-Two

She wasn't mad at Jake, she decided, as Chad drove her through the miserable traffic to the writers conference. It wasn't Jake's fault she had built up unrealistic expectations. He had never indicated that this meeting would be anything other than business. He hadn't purposely failed to be what she had envisioned. It was just so frustrating.

She had stuck around for lunch but only long enough to eat some taco salad and listen to the not-so-interesting conversations of the stagehands who shared the outdoor picnic table with her. Jake was too busy to eat and had waved good-bye when she let Chad know she was ready to leave.

Now she wasn't looking forward to seeing Jake for their cheesecake date. The invitation had felt much more promising and romantic when he had extended it over the phone. But this trip to the studio had burst all kinds of bubbles.

Once she had settled into her hotel room with the conference agenda before her, Meri realized how busy she was going to be these next three days. Besides the two workshops she was teaching, she was expected to read a stack of manuscripts that had been presented to her when she checked in. Reading the manuscripts alone would take her three days! Then conferees had made appointments to meet with her for fifteen-minute segments starting this evening after the opening session.

The only comfort Meri found as she studied the schedule was that she was free Tuesday night. That meant she could sneak off for cheesecake with Jake, even though the free time was probably designed for reading manuscripts.

Her phone rang, and she caught it on the second ring. It was an editor she had met a year ago. The two of them chatted, and then Paula got to the point of the call. "I'm in charge of the opening skit tonight, but my ditz hasn't arrived. Her plane was rerouted or something. Would you consider playing the dumb blond?"

"I'm supposed to be flattered by this offer?" Meredith laughed.

"You remember this skit," Paula said. "We did it at the last conference. You were such a good airhead. I know you can jump right into the part again. Will you, please? I'm desperate."

"Is this type casting or what?" Meri muttered. "Okay. Where do I have to be and when?"

"Downstairs, main meeting room, in fifteen minutes for practice."

"Fifteen minutes!"

"Yes, we only have an hour and a half before the opening meeting, and we have to grab some dinner before then."

Meredith cleaned up and headed for the elevator with her official name badge pinned to her flax-colored blazer that she now wore over her black mock turtleneck and jeans. She had rolled up the sleeves and given her brushed hair a squirt of perfume to freshen herself up.

"Why did I agree to do this?" she muttered. The elevator took her to the first floor, where she met her business associates and fellow actors in the main meeting room.

"Here's our lifesaver!" Paula announced when Meredith walked in. "Somebody give her the script. Let's get going."

They only practiced twenty minutes or so. It was a silly sketch about an editor meeting with different conferees and how each of them used the appointed fifteen minutes. It was intended as a spoof to show first-time conferees how to make good use of their appointments.

Meri remembered how it had gone at a previous conference and knew that all she had to do was pretend to be chewing gum, look starry eyed when the editor asked intelligent questions, and end with, "You mean you're in charge of *books?!* I thought you were in charge of *looks.* I signed up for the Patty Fay Beauty Makeover Convention. Am I in the wrong room?"

All she had to do then was to rush offstage in search of the Patty Fay group. It was silly, but it put the nervous conferees at ease, especially since all the roles were played by editors.

Meredith ate dinner in the coffee shop with her editor friends from the skit and laughed about some of the inside jokes of the industry. One publisher had released a book with the title misspelled. The *e* and *i* were transposed in the word *weird.* From the limited number of people who wrote to call attention to the misspelling, the publisher guessed most of America didn't know how to spell *weird.*

Paula confided that she was thinking of changing positions if any of them heard of an opening at another large house. She had been acquiring cookbooks for five years, but the publisher was cutting back to only two cookbooks a year. Now Paula reviewed science fiction manuscripts, which rolled in at an average of three hundred manuscripts per month. It wasn't her idea of a good time.

One of the men asked Meri if she had any hot new products coming out. She didn't mention the Young Heart series because the signed paperwork hadn't been delivered to her files yet. Helen had said that all the contractual details were agreed on, but Meredith knew better than to brag about projects prematurely.

"I'll tell you what I have," she said to the others around the table. "I have way more manuscripts than I can ever wade through at this conference. Did they load you guys up, too?"

"Are you kidding?" Paula said. "As soon as they found out I'd consider looking at sci-fi, my pile tripled. If I never had to read about another big-eyed alien who lives on grasshopper blood and mango pits, I would be a happy woman."

"Mango pits? Grasshopper blood?" one of the other women questioned.

"You have no idea," Paula said, shaking her head. "That's why I want to go back to cookbooks where grasshoppers mean minty green beverages and mango pits go in the garbage can when making tropical fruit salad."

The editors wrapped up their enjoyable conversation and moved back to the meeting room, where they sat toward the front. The conference started at seven, and after the opening remarks and announcements, the workshop leaders were asked to come to the stage and give a two-minute description of their sessions. Close to eight hundred aspiring writers had registered for this conference, which had enlisted more than fifty instructors to teach workshops. Meredith was trying to calculate how long this was going to take since their skit was the last item on the agenda.

Sliding out and making her way to the stage, she heard a slight rumbling sound throughout the auditorium. She turned to see the object of the audience's interest. Jake was walking down the center aisle, his head down slightly, that boyish, embarrassed look on his face.

I didn't think he would come after the full schedule he had today. I wonder if he's noticed me.

When Meredith reached the stage, it appeared that Jake had noticed her, all right. He came over and stood next to her in line. It was a suave move. To the casual observer, his choice made sense because there was more room next to Meredith than at the end of the line, where the others from the center aisle were heading. But Meri wanted to believe his action was deliberate.

They stood side by side, neither acknowledging the other. Meredith looked out at the room of hopeful writers and felt it safe to say that nearly every eye was on Jake. At least every female eye, and that accounted for more than eighty percent of the conferees.

"If all the workshop leaders could please scoot down a bit more, we can get everyone on the stage. After you give a presentation of your workshop, please sit down," the master of ceremonies said. "And please remember, no more than two minutes. Please!"

As everyone shuffled to the left, Meredith felt the hairs on Jake's arm as they gently brushed against her arm.

Did he notice that? It was like electricity! Is it me, or is it static in the air? This is too much. I have to say something.

"I never told you," Meri said quietly without turning to look at Jake. "I got your grape. Very creative."

"You liked that, huh?" he whispered back, leaning just close enough for her to smell the cocoa-butter scent of his skin.

Meredith smiled to the sea of faces in front of them and in a low voice said, "What do you think you are? The grape fairy?"

A low chuckle rumbled from his chest.

"You could write that into Young Heart as a new character. All the good souls find a grape on their pillow at the end of their journey, but the bad souls find a dried-out raisin."

Jake covered his mouth and camouflaged his laugh with a cough.

As the line moved along, Jake moved closer to Meredith. Was it her imagination? Or was he pressing his upper arm against her shoulder? The sensation of his touch was so slight and thoroughly justified that it made it hard to know if she should read anything into the gesture. The woman next to Meredith stepped to the podium and used a total of thirty seconds to describe her workshop on learning how to prepare a query letter.

Meredith was next. She reluctantly stepped away from Jake's closeness and walked up to the microphone. "I'm Meredith Graham, and I'm representing G. H. Terrison Publishing. I'm an acquisitions editor of children's books. We're always looking for bright new ideas and manuscripts that are well written. My first workshop tomorrow afternoon is entitled 'Getting Your Foot in the Door.' I'll be telling you what to do and what not to do when you're trying to get an editor's attention. My second workshop on Wednesday morning is called 'Learning from Your Mistakes.' I'll be showing you how to take a returned manuscript and fix it so you can resubmit it. Thank you."

The obligatory round of applause followed Meri as she walked down the three steps from the stage to return to her seat. She glanced at the audience and wondered if it was her imagination or if everyone had suddenly perked up and leaned forward.

Jake's voice rolled through the speakers and surrounded the eager listeners. "Good evening. My name is Jacob Wilde." A cluster of young women in the far-right corner of the room immediately began to clap, whistle, and stomp their feet.

When the ruckus died down, Jake continued his presentation. "I'm teaching a workshop on Wednesday morning entitled 'The Basics of Writing a Screenplay.' I'm currently involved in producing a video based on a screenplay I wrote. I look forward to seeing some of you in my workshop."

A murmur of admiration rumbled through the crowd as Jake stepped down. Instead of returning to wherever he had been sitting before, he came over to Meredith and, with a smile, asked quietly, "Mind if I sit with you?"

All the seats in her row were empty at the moment since her friends were still up on the stage. Without a word, Meredith motioned for him to sit. She was aware of the stares of everyone in the auditorium. Jake looked as if he was pretending to pay attention to the workshop leader who was standing at the podium.

When only three people were left to make their speeches, Jake leaned over and whispered to Meredith, "Would you do me a huge favor and walk out of here with me after the last person is finished?"

"I can't. I have to stay. I'm in a skit," she whispered back.

Jake thought a moment and then whispered, "As soon as the skit is over, would you mind if we walked out together with our arms around each other?"

Meredith turned and looked into his cocoa brown eyes. He was only inches away, and she felt all her chemical reactions happening at once. Her heart stopped, her spine tingled, and her breath disappeared. She asked, "Why?"

His eyes looked at her, pleading. "It's for cover. If they think I'm with someone, they aren't as forceful about cornering me."

Meredith gave him a perplexed look, still not understanding why he would ask her to be his bodyguard.

"I admit it," Jake said out of the corner of his mouth. "I'm a coward. You can make fun of me later, but just say you'll protect me."

Meredith laughed softly. "You big baby."

"Is that a yes?"

She nodded.

A few minutes later the skit was announced. Meredith rose to join the others onstage, and Jake grasped her wrist. He gave it a squeeze as she slid past him. She turned to look at him, surprised by his gesture. "Don't forget about me," he said. The look in his eyes was genuine fear.

Meredith paused and decided to let the feelings of her heart be known. She leaned closer and said, "Don't worry, Jacob Wilde. I will never, ever, be able to forget you."

Chapter Twenty-Three

*A*ll the way to the stage, Meredith clenched her teeth. A chorus of accusing demons huddled close to her. *"Ha, ha!"* they cajoled. *"Look what you've done! You opened yourself up to a man, and now he's going to stomp on your heart. You fool!"*

The skit was announced, and Meredith tried with all her might to ignore the heckling that was at full volume inside her head. She worked to get into her character while she stood in the background, chewing her pretend gum, checking her nails, and flicking invisible fuzz balls from her jeans.

When Meredith heard her cue, she stepped forward to meet the editor. "I'm so excited to meet you!" Meri blurted out. "This is, like, totally a dream come true!"

"Why, thank you," the patient editor said, motioning for Meredith to sit across from her at the table on the stage. Meri continued to gush and flatter the editor, all the while chewing her invisible gum and flipping back her hair. She crossed and uncrossed her legs, giggled and periodically flicked fuzz balls from her clothes.

"I just totally can't believe I'm here!" Meredith cooed. "I always wanted to come to one of these conferences, but I never thought I'd actually make it to one—and one in California even!"

"Yes," the editor said graciously while checking her watch. "We only have a few minutes left for our fifteen-minute meeting. Was there something specific you wanted to discuss?"

"Well, I guess the first thing I should tell you is that I just love, love, love your makeup!" Meredith said.

"Why, thank you," the flattered editor responded.

"I mean, I like all of it. Your eyeliner, your foundation, your lipstick. Oh, and I love, love, love, and I do mean love, your perfume."

The editor checked her wrist by taking a sample whiff and seemed surprised, as if she wasn't wearing perfume. "Thank you again," she said.

"And I can tell how well your cleansers work for you," Meredith went on. "I mean, look how smooth and even your skin tone is. It's, like, totally awesome."

"Yes," the editor said, touching her cheek with a look of confusion. "Well, as I was saying, did you have a book proposal you wanted to discuss?"

"A book?" Meredith took on her very best airhead expression.

"Yes, a book. These fifteen-minute interviews are set up so you can meet with editors to discuss book ideas."

"Books? You're in charge of *books?!* I thought you were in charge of *looks*. Isn't this the Patty Fay Beauty Makeover Convention?"

"Why, no."

"I can't believe it! How did I end up in the wrong room?" Meredith bolted out of her chair and, with a dazed look, exited, searching for the Patty Fay Convention.

The editor played her last bit by pulling a large mirror from under the table and looking herself over. Then, with a shrug, she called out, "Next prospective author, please!" She froze in place, and the skit was over.

Meredith returned to her seat to find Jake standing in the aisle waiting for her. As soon as she was close enough, he slipped his arm around her shoulders and whispered, "Walk me out now, okay?"

Still in the acting mode, Meredith put her arm around his middle. She looked up with all the charm she possessed and said, "You know they're all going to be asking about us now."

Jake took long, quick strides to the back of the auditorium. "And just what are you going to tell them?"

"The truth," Meredith said, feeling way too perky for her own good. "I'll tell them you're crazy about me, but you're just too legalistic to admit your feelings."

They were at the back door now. Jake pushed it open for her. The minute they were outside the meeting room and out of sight of the large audience, Jake pulled his arm away. Meredith let go, too.

"I have to run," he said, his cheeks flushed.

"That's it? You parade me up the aisle and leave?" Meredith spouted.

"I'm sorry. I have to—"

"I know, I know. You have work to do; people waiting for you. 'There was a man all alone; he had neither son nor brother. There was no end to his toil, yet his eyes were not content with his wealth. "For whom am I toiling," he asked, "and why am I depriving myself of enjoyment?" This too is meaningless—a miserable business!'"

Jacob stopped to stare at her with an incredulous look on his face. "What are you talking about?"

"Nothing," she said. "It's just that next time you need someone to put your arm around, pick someone who doesn't have a heart."

He waited for an explanation.

Meredith was beginning to feel sick inside. She had laid out her feelings, and he had walked over them, with his arm around her. It was all part of an act. And it made her mad. Mad at him, but mostly mad at herself.

"I have to go. Good-bye, Meredith," he said. Without looking back, Jake took off at a fast clip.

"See what you've done?" the row of accusers began. One by one they railed her for letting her feelings show and for being so bold. *"No wonder the guy ran away. You not only embarrassed him but you also terrified him." "What kind of a Christian woman are you? He probably thinks you go after men all the time."*

Meredith forced herself to walk, not run, to the elevator. She pushed the button over and over, begging it to arrive before her tears did. The merciful lift carried her to her floor where she rushed to her room and bolted the door behind her. Her heart was pounding, and the tears were now stinging her cheeks.

"Why am I doing everything wrong, God? This connection with Jake has been doomed from the start. Why can't I leave well enough alone? He's going to cancel our cheesecake date, isn't he? I can't believe my emotions are running amuck. Is this what happens after years of stuffing my emotions because there weren't any guys I was interested in? Suddenly, one intriguing man steps into my life, and I'm a ranting, emotional idiot."

Meri threw herself on the bed, disrupting the stack of manuscripts in her fall. She wanted to have a good cry, but all that dribbled out were a few tears.

"This is ridiculous," she said, sitting up and wiping her eyes. "I am a mature, responsible woman who has much more control of her life than this. Stop acting like a child. It's no longer allowed. Not with your mother; not with Jake or with anyone else."

She got up and looked at her reflection in the mirror. She could use a little lipstick and a touch-up with her mascara. Glancing at the clock on the nightstand, Meredith did a quick makeup refresher and finished her private pep talk.

"In ten minutes you have your first meeting with a potential author. This is what you came for. This conference is not about you. It's not about Jake. It's about your job for Terrison Publishing. You are here to instruct and to acquire new manuscripts. Get a grip, Meri Jane. Go back down there with your head held high, and do your job."

Meredith accomplished everything she told herself to do in her pep talk. But she wasn't prepared for all the questions the conferees threw at her, not about Jake, but about getting their books published with G. H. Terrison. Never before at a conference had she been so inundated with questions. She guessed it was because only one other acquisitions editor of children's books was attending this conference, and he didn't arrive until tomorrow.

Fortunately, she was passionate about what she did because the eager-to-learn conferees kept talking with her long after the last appointment ended. Not until she was back in her room late that night and slipping into bed did she realize how exhausting all this was, even without the confusing emotional outbursts with Jake.

Why in the world did this guy think he had the right to use her as a bodyguard to escape the auditorium? He could have left easily without her so-called protection. By exiting with his arm around her, he had given everyone at the conference the distinct impression that she and Jake were together. That may have been a convenient camouflage for him, but it was unfair to her.

In the dark and silent room, Meredith lay on her back and wrote imaginary letters to Jake on the ceiling. She told him he was unfair, inconsiderate, and cruel to use her the way he had. She used the word *defraud* and wrote with her invisible ink in bold letters, "You had no right to use me in a way that benefited you but gave me false impressions and put me in a compromised position. Now it's up to me to explain to all these people that there's nothing between us."

As the fire from within her dispelled with each hot word she penned across the ceiling, a timid question rose to the surface. "That is the truth, isn't it? There is nothing between us, right?"

She had a fitful night. Her business association with Jake meant she would be in contact with him a lot more in the months to come. Why had she jeopardized all that by saying she would never forget him and then telling him he was crazy about her but too legalistic to admit it?

Sleep came only in ragged patches. If she had had enough time to gather the patches through the night, she might have been able to stitch them all together and have sufficient covering for her weariness. As it was, she got up at seven and stayed in the hot shower long enough to develop wrinkled toes. It helped to perk her up only a little.

When she finally made her appearance for her first appointment with a conferee at nine o'clock, she was once again assaulted with questions about every detail of publishing. For some reason she felt stronger this morning than she had last night, so she had no trouble giving shorter answers to the inquiring minds that wanted to know.

Meredith found she had a break for an hour and a half before her next round of interviews. She retreated to her room, ordered a chef's salad, and pulled a chair out on the tiny balcony so she could start to read her stack of stories.

The peace and quiet did her good. This was what she was used to, burying herself in mounds of stories. Refreshed and ready for round two, Meredith returned to the general meeting area, where she had several more meetings before she had to teach her first workshop.

It felt funny standing in front of a roomful of curious faces. One hundred twenty people attended her workshop, twice the number she had been told to expect. She didn't know how many of them had come to learn about writing and how many were Looky Lous who wanted a closer view of the woman who put her arm around Jake Wilde.

Before she started her workshop, Meredith decided to make one of her bold moves. She assumed many of them wanted to know about Jake. "As you know, I left the auditorium last night with Jake Wilde. Let me make a few comments just so we can get on with this workshop. I am a business associate of Jake's."

She wanted to scold her audience and say, "The reason he had to have protection when he left the auditorium last night was because of the way you people chase him." But she knew that didn't sound professional. It also meant she was defending Jake, and she refused to do that.

"If I've learned one thing from Jake, it's that actors are no different than anyone else. They have their strengths and weaknesses like all of us. Jake has also taught me that being an actor is something you do; it's not who you are. In the same way, I hope many of you who haven't published yet will become authors. When you do, please remember that being an author is what you do. It's not who you are."

The conferees silently checked those around them. None of them seemed prepared for her opening statements, but a few of them began to take notes.

"Now, if you'll check your syllabus, you should find the outline for this workshop on page seventeen in the yellow section." Meredith switched into instructor mode. Teaching workshops was something she loved to do, and she had taught this class, "Getting Your Foot in the Door," three times.

The hour zipped along, with the last fifteen minutes used for questions, which this group had lots of. When she finished, a long line of conferees waited one after the other to have a chance to talk to her. They stood there listening to her pointers on how to get published. Then one of the organizers came up and diplomatically let Meredith know that the next class was scheduled to start in this room in five minutes and the instructor was waiting outside for her to finish.

Meredith apologized and took the opportunity to gather her briefcase to return to her room. She made it as far as the lobby, where a group of six continued to ask for her advice and describe their projects to her. She listened patiently and made suggestions, which they thanked her for.

Four of the conferees who were asking questions entered the elevator with her and followed her down the hall to her room, still talking. They would gladly have come in, if she hadn't tactfully let them know she needed to read manuscripts.

Closing the door behind her and taking a deep breath, Meredith was shocked to see that it was already six thirty. A phone message was waiting for her.

When she pushed the button to play back the message, Jake's rich voice greeted her. Meredith found herself smiling when she heard it.

"Hi, this is Jake. I'm just checking in to let you know I'll be a little late for our cheesecake break tonight. I hope it's okay with you if we meet out front at seven thirty. If not, here's my cell-phone number."

There was a pause, typical of Jake's phone conversations. Then he added ever so cautiously, "I'm looking forward to seeing you. Good-bye, Meredith."

She pushed the button to replay the message. Leaning closer to the phone as if she could better capture the meaning of his words by hovering near the source, she listened carefully. "I'm looking forward to seeing you," his voice repeated. "Good-bye, Meredith."

That "good-bye, Meredith" got her every time. How did he do that? *Good-bye* seemed like the saddest word a man could say to a woman. It wasn't that way with Jake. Was it the tone of his voice or how he drew out her name that melted her heart?

At least he still wants to go out tonight. And he said he was looking forward to seeing me. Did he slip and say that? Or is he allowing himself to feel something for me?

Meredith hurriedly decided what to wear. It was an outfit she had ordered last summer from the closeout section of a catalog. She had never worn it, partly because of the color. It was turquoise. But this silk pantsuit with a sleeveless, embroidered top seemed perfect for a night on the town in southern California with Jake Wilde. When Meredith saw how it set off her blond hair and ocean green eyes, she felt confident.

If this doesn't turn his head, I give up.

Chapter Twenty-Four

Hurrying to the lobby at seven twenty-five, Meredith was about to rush out to the curb when someone called her name. One of the conferees she had talked with earlier had spotted her.

"This is my friend Marsha," the conferee said. "I told her what you said about sending in the entire manuscript if it's short, but she had some more questions for you."

Meredith listened carefully and gave a few pointers before checking her watch. It was seven thirty.

"I need to go. I have an appointment."

"Just one more question," the woman said. "In your workshop you told us to watch for trends and send in ideas when they're current and not after everyone else has already done them."

"Yes," Meredith looked past the woman out the front of the hotel. She thought she saw a tan Explorer pull up.

"Can you tell us how we're supposed to find out what these trends are?"

"You can see trends develop by reading and listening to what people are talking about. Read books, magazines, newspapers, and even the ads that come to your house in the mail." She looked past the woman again. "I mentioned all this in the workshop."

"I know, but my friend wasn't there, and I didn't remember."

"Perhaps you would like to get the tape. I understand they're taping each of the workshops."

The lobby door swung open, and Jake walked in, wearing a pair of tan casual slacks and a light blue, striped, short-sleeved shirt. He took off his sunglasses and looked around. When he spotted Meredith, a spontaneous smile spread across his lips.

He must like turquoise. This is good.

"Ms. Graham?" A man came up behind Meredith with an envelope in his hand. "I have a manuscript here I didn't submit during registration because I didn't think it would be a match for your house."

Two older women were with the man, and suddenly Meredith had a crowd keeping her from Jake.

"After I went to your workshop, I felt certain this would be a good match for G. H. Terrison. I know they asked us not to do this, but would you consider taking this manuscript from me now? You can call me after you have a chance to read it, since I know you have to read all the other manuscripts first."

Meredith looked at Jake, who stood a few feet away, covering his grin with his hand. No adoring fans were flocking to him as they had both expected. All the action was around Meredith.

"Actually, they made it clear that we're not to take any of what are affectionately called 'black-market manuscripts.' The conference director needs to keep a tally of how many manuscripts come in. It helps them gauge how many people they'll need for staff next year."

"It's only one story," the man said. "And it's short."

"You can ask at the information booth," Meri said. "I'm not able to take it from you."

Her firm words apparently discouraged all the conferees gathered around Meredith, and the crowd dispersed. Jake approached her with a grin. "Maybe I should ask for your autograph now before you become too popular and forget you ever knew me," he teased.

"Look who's talking!"

"That's why I know what I'm talking about," he said dryly.

Dozens of people were in the lobby. Not one of them seemed interested that Jake Wilde was in their presence. Either that or no one had discovered it yet.

"Let's go," Meredith said, walking quickly toward the door. "Hurry, before anyone discovers you're here."

Jake walked a little faster and reached the door in time to open it for her. He also opened her car door. They drove off into the balmy California evening with a comfortable quiet nestled between them.

After Jake entered the freeway he said, "The only place I know that has cheesecake that might compare with the one you served us is the Cheesecake Factory in Hollywood. I hope you don't mind that it's a bit of a drive."

"No, that's fine. It'll give me a chance to apologize and yell at you," Meredith said.

Jake turned to look at her with surprise. "Do I get to pick which one I hear first?"

"No. You get to hear the apology first. I was a little too mouthy last night. I shouldn't have said a lot of the things I did."

"None of them bothered me," Jake said calmly.

"That brings me to the yelling part. It didn't bother you to walk out with your arm around me, but it did bother me. It made me feel used. I was the one doing all the flirting last night, but you set me up."

"I didn't see it that way."

"How did you see it?"

"Acting, maybe. I don't know. I honestly wasn't trying to use you, Meredith. I guess I shouldn't have involved you in my exit. I apologize."

"Apology accepted," Meredith said, leaning back and appreciating that Jake had the air conditioner on low and the windows rolled up. The radio wasn't even on. This ride was a peaceful change from being carted around by Chad.

"It feels good to get away from the convention," Meredith said, changing the tone before they became bogged down in evaluating anything else.

"I can see why." Jake looked over at her. "Your adoring fans won't leave you alone, will they?"

"How do you stand it?"

"I don't like it very much."

"I got that impression in Glenbrooke," Meri said.

"I think because Glenbrooke is such a quiet little town I caused more of a stir than usual," Jake said thoughtfully. "Here it's not such a rush, you know? Lots of actors and actresses are around town. You notice I didn't get any attention in the lobby this evening. They were all flocking around you."

"That's because they want something from me. They want their books published, and I'm the gatekeeper."

"You handled it with ease, I noticed."

"Oh, you think so?" Meredith laughed her magnificent, light, airy laugh. "That's because you don't know what I was thinking."

Jake laughed along. "Don't be so sure of that! I've hidden many an unkind thought while signing autographs. There's something about being presumed upon that I have a hard time with. It's as if some people think I owe them something simply because they recognize me."

"That does seem to be how it is," Meredith agreed. "I never thought much about it before."

"A year ago I was in a small coffee shop in Pasadena. After I finished my coffee and pastry, I realized I'd left my wallet at home. It's a mom and pop place run by a German couple. The Frau literally took me by the arm into the kitchen and commanded me to wash dishes."

Meredith laughed. "What did you do?"

"I washed dishes," Jake said with a shrug.

"I can't believe that."

"That was a year ago. Then *Falcon Pointe* came out, and a few weeks later I stopped by the coffee shop again. The same woman recognized me. Can you guess what happened?"

"She wanted your autograph."

"That was only the beginning! She had her husband take our picture, which is now hanging on the wall in a nice eight-by-ten gilded frame. She loaded me up with her freshest rolls and coffee cake and told me anytime I came in the coffee would be free."

With more silvery laughter, Meredith said, "You did tell her you were the vagrant who washed her dishes, didn't you?"

Jake shook his head. "I couldn't bring myself to remind her."

Meredith looked at Jake thoughtfully. She again noticed his birthmark below his right ear. It was sort of shaped like a bird's nest. At least that's what it looked like to her. But then, she realized she was a person who saw the portrait of Elvis in the wood grain of her kitchen cupboard. In a sweet, silly way, the bird's-nest birthmark comforted her. Jake was not only one hundred percent human but he also had a God-given tattoo that represented to Meredith all that was free and safe in her forest. She was beginning to let herself feel that way with him.

"I have a friend who made it big in Hollywood," Jake continued. "And he got smart. He carried around business cards with his name embossed on one side and his signature preprinted on the other side. Whenever he was approached at shopping malls or restaurants, he pulled the cards from his pocket, and people walked away happy."

"Are you going to buy some cards like that?" Meredith asked.

"I don't think I'll need to. My popularity seems to be waning. And I don't mind a bit. Did you notice last night that nobody followed us out of the auditorium? I think that's a pretty good indication that I'm on the way out."

"Is that what you want?"

Jake nodded and looked over his left shoulder to change lanes. "I'm much more interested in directing and producing at this point in my life. Acting is hard work. I don't think I have the stomach for it."

Meredith was surprised at his words. "It seems producing and directing would be hard, too. Lots of long hours, tons of responsibility."

"True, but something about the creative process energizes me. With acting you have to take someone else's idea and create a character that reflects what others had in mind. I guess I like the creating side of it more."

"Because you have an imagination," Meredith suggested softly.

Jake thought a minute. "Maybe that's it. I also have an interest in seeing kids stretch their imaginations. That's why I wanted to write this screenplay. What Clive Staples did for opening up imaginations more than fifty years ago has yet to be duplicated, in my opinion."

"Clive Staples?"

Jake glanced at Meredith and smiled. "That's what I affectionately call Lewis. C. S. Lewis. Didn't you ever wonder what his initials stood for?"

"No, I guess I never did. I always thought his name was Jack."

"That's what his friends called him. I looked it up when I was in junior high when I did a report on one of the Narnia tales. I decided then that anyone who could be christened 'Clive Staples' and find a way around such a name was my hero."

Meredith asked cautiously, "Is that because of your last name?"

"Yes," Jake answered quickly. "Being a 'Wartman' was about the worst curse a kid in junior high could have. That and having red hair."

"Your hair is really red?"

"It's brown with a deep red sheen to it. I don't know how to explain it. It's a strange, unnatural color. I couldn't stand it as a kid." Jake pulled off the freeway and stopped at a red light in a business district lined with tall buildings.

"Mine's a dull, mousy brown," Meredith suddenly confessed. "I started coloring it when I was in eighth grade, and my mom threw a fit. She got over it quickly, though, because I was the youngest of four daughters, and I think she and Dad had run out of steam when it came to upholding the family image. I colored it again four months later an even lighter shade of blond, and it's been this color ever since." Meredith felt her cheeks beginning to blush. "I can't believe we're sitting here telling each other about our hair-coloring histories."

Jake laughed. "You forget, I've seen you in the middle of one of your coloring rituals. It wasn't a secret to me."

Meredith laughed, finding herself more embarrassed over the circumstances of their initial meeting than she had been at the time.

"I think," Jake said, pulling into a parking lot and waiting for the attendant to come to the car, "anyone who colors her hair has great imagination."

Meredith liked his words. She liked his stories and his easygoing style. She especially liked his hair. "Let me get your door," Jake said, reaching for his black leather satchel.

He opened Meredith's door and took the ticket from the parking attendant, leaving his keys in the car. They walked a few short blocks past small shops and cafés with outdoor seating.

"Where are we?" Meredith asked. It seemed to her this street could be downtown Whidbey Island, yet the tall buildings looming in the late-evening sky behind the cute shops made it feel as if they were in a little hollow of the big city.

"Rodeo Drive is that way," Jake said, motioning with a nod of his head. "This is Beverly Hills."

"You're kidding."

"Not what you expected?"

"I'm not sure what I expected."

"I don't hang out here much, so I won't be a very useful tour guide, but I have been here for cheesecake, and it's worth the trip."

Meredith noticed the clusters of people sitting outside the cafés they passed and strolling along window-shopping in the cool night breezes. She was dressed just right. People were flashy here, well dressed and stylish. One woman they passed wore a wide straw hat, a black shorts outfit, and sunglasses, even though it was dark. She had on gold sandals with spiked heels, and her tiny white poodle was on the end of a silver leash. It was hard not to stare at people as they walked by.

Jake opened the door to a restaurant, and they approached the hostess station to put their name in. People were everywhere, standing and waiting to be seated.

"It'll be about fifteen minutes, Mr. Wilde," the hostess said.

For a moment Meredith was impressed that the girl knew who Jake was, but then Meri realized he had given the name when he had asked for a booth. She couldn't help but glance around. The place had to be crawling with well-known people. She thought of trying to sneak a peak at the waiting list to see if she recognized any names. But it didn't appeal to her the way it would have several months ago. Her image and her thoughts about movie stars were different now. They deserved a night out for a slice of cheesecake without being made a fuss over, just like anyone else.

"Would you like to wait outside?" Jake suggested.

"Sure."

They slid through the crowd, and Meri noticed his black satchel again. Was this supposed to be a business meeting? Meri tried to rein herself in. Everything about their ride over had felt like a date. She was enjoying every minute of being with this man.

Don't put your heart out there so quickly. Slow down. Be cautious. He's never indicated he's interested in this being anything more than a business relationship, has he?

Meredith's counterego chirped up, *"He said on the phone message that he was looking forward to seeing you."*

Yes, she argued back, *but Helen says that, too. That could be a business line.*

A moment of silence fell on the battlefield of her mind, and then her counterego fired its fastest cannonball. *"Do mere business associates usually leave a grape on your pillow?"*

Chapter Twenty-Five

hey were seated at a window booth about twenty minutes later. Meredith felt nervous. Their conversation outside had been about a dozen unrelated things, like what kind of warranty she got with her Explorer and how her parents were doing since her dad's resignation.

The menu was handed to Meredith. It was a tall, extensive listing of all kinds of foods.

"Have you had dinner?" Jake asked.

She couldn't remember. At the moment she didn't feel very hungry.

"Please, order whatever you'd like. It's my treat."

Meredith scanned the long list and stopped at the bottom with a grin. "They have muffins, Jake," she said, looking at him over the top of the menu. "I still owe you a whole, unsmashed one."

Jake's smile spread across his face. He leaned forward and said, "Do you know that you are the only person in the world who has ever caught me with a prank like that?"

"Really?" Meredith sat up straighter and squared her shoulders to demonstrate how proud she was of her success.

"You're quite original."

She made a smirk. "So I've heard."

"You don't think of that as a compliment?"

Meredith shook her head. "It ranks right up there with 'but she's got a great personality.'"

Jake laughed. "No, not at all," he said. "Do you know how few creative people are left in this world? So many conformists and imitators. You're genuine. Original. It's very rare."

"So now I'm rare," Meredith teased. "Do you want to cut right to the bottom line?" Her nervousness and insecurities were putting her mouth into gear before her mind had a chance to review and approve the words. "Go ahead. Say it—I'm the strangest person you've ever met. I walk around looking like a green-faced alien; I do puppet shows on the floor of truck cabs; I smash food in people's faces; I dance with blow-up mannequins. What did I leave out?"

"You play a very convincing ditz in conference skits."

"Yes, I play a very convincing ditz." Meredith felt insecure. She would give anything to appear sophisticated and elegant like the people around her in this restaurant.

"Those are all things you do," Jake said, leaning forward and warming her with his kind, brown eyes. "That's not who you are."

Meredith swallowed his words. They went down hard. He was right. Before she had a chance to respond, the waiter stood before them.

"Have you decided?"

"I'd like a cappuccino," Jake said. He looked at Meredith.

"I'm afraid I haven't had time to decide."

"Something to drink, then?"

"Um, yes. I'll have a latte. Decaf with skim milk."

"A 'why bother,'" the waiter repeated.

"A what?"

"A 'why bother.' That's what we call decaf with skim milk."

"You're right," Meredith said quickly before he walked away. "That's too boring. Could you change that to one of these?" She pointed to a list of specialty coffee drinks at the bottom of the menu. "How about a Black Forest?"

"Sure. That's a mocha latte espresso with cherry and whipped cream."

"Sounds like a lot of bother," Meredith said. "I'll take it."

Jake seemed to be covering his grin with his hand as he examined the back side of the menu where the dozens of flavored cheesecakes were listed. "I've had the lemon raspberry," he said. "That was killer."

"Look at this list!" Meredith silently read all the kinds of cheesecake and settled on chocolate chip. Jake ordered the key lime. The waiter brought their coffees, took their orders, and returned a few moments later with two huge slices of tall, fluffy cheesecake.

Meredith took a bite and said, "You're right. This is a close second to Rondi's cheesecake." She went for a second bite and nearly choked on it when she saw who was stepping up to their table. It was Clint James.

Clint had been her favorite movie star when she was in college. He appeared in five films during her four years of college, and she had seen every one of them at least half a dozen times. What put Clint at the top of her movie-star list was that he had appeared as a child actor in her favorite sitcom. Every Friday night when she was growing up, Meredith would plant herself in front of the television at eight o'clock and wait for her weekly "fix" of Clint James. She had spent her hard-earned allowance on posters of this teen star, who was at least seven years older than she. The posters were purchased from her friends at school and sneaked home, where she hid them in her room, begging Shelly to keep her secret. The Graham daughters weren't allowed to waste their time or money on such "idol worship."

Now, here the flesh-and-blood idol stood, right next to their table. Clint slapped Jake on the back and said, "I thought that was you, Wilde. What are you doing slumming around these parts?"

"Clint," Jake responded, putting out his hand to shake. "How have you been? I heard that deal with Left Coast Productions looks like it's going through for you. Congratulations."

"We'll see," Clint said, turning his focus on Meredith. "Final papers haven't been signed yet." He let out a string of four-letter words. "They don't know what they're doing over there. I don't think there's half a brain between the whole lot of them."

More expletives came spewing from his mouth, and then, with his finely chiseled face turned toward Meredith, he asked, "And who is this?"

"Clint, I'd like you to meet Meredith Graham. Meredith, this is Clint James."

Meredith found she felt no frenzied awe at meeting and shaking hands with Clint James. His breath smelled of alcohol, and he held her hand way too long for a simple handshake. She actually had the urge to wash her hand after he gave it back.

"Did Jake tell you yet that he owes his success to me? I'm the one who got him the part on *Falcon Pointe*."

Meredith smiled politely. "He hadn't mentioned that yet."

"Come on, Jake, you're turning into a big disappointment."
Clint put his arm around Jake's shoulder and placed a few
punchy cuss words on the table before saying, "You're sabo-
taging a perfectly good career. I hand you Hollywood on a silver platter, and you turn down the sequel. You're an ingrate,
that's what you are." The swearing went on for two more sentences as Clint roughed up Jake with his accusations about
throwing away the opportunities of a lifetime to write some
cheesy screenplay for kids.

Meredith was amazed at how well Jake took the chiding,
which was loud and obnoxious.

Clint turned his attention back to Meredith. "Is he showing you a good time? Because if you're ready to dump this
loser, you can come with me, pretty Meredith. We're headed
down to Malibu. Jake never wants to go to these parties with
me, but a beautiful woman like you shouldn't be stuck all night
with a loser like Jake." Clint reached for Meri's hand in a gesture of persuasion.

It had a negative effect on her. She pulled her hand away
and said calmly, "I'm afraid I'm a bigger loser than Jake. You
see, I once admired you, Clint James. I even thought I wanted
to meet you someday. That was before I knew you were a
drunken, swearing womanizer. Thanks for the shot of reality."

Clint looked shocked. Meri turned away from him and
concentrated on her cheesecake as if he weren't there.

She could hear Clint slapping Jake on the back and saying,
"You sure know how to pick 'em, Wilde."

Jake remained silent. Meredith could hear Clint walking
away. She wondered what the people around them were thinking. It didn't matter. She didn't care what anyone thought. This
had been a crossroads in her life. All the directness and confidence she had when it came to publishing matters had found
their voice in the everyday side of her personality. Helen would

have told her she was "empowered." She felt free, free to be her original self without being controlled by what other people thought. At this moment she believed she could even stand up to her mother.

When Meri finally looked up at Jake, he was watching her. It seemed he was still trying to decide if he appreciated her reaction or if it bothered him.

"There aren't a lot of Christians in this industry," Jake said slowly, speaking with kind, quiet words. "Most of the people I hang out with are a lot like Clint."

"And that makes it okay?" Meredith challenged.

"I guess what I'm trying to say is that not everyone has the same standards or lifestyle that I do, but I'm still good friends with a lot of them. Sometimes they open up and ask me about my faith. It gives me a chance to tell them about my relationship with Christ."

Meri felt convicted for her brashness. "I apologize if I was out of line. Do you think I just ruined a friendship for you?"

"No. I doubt he'll even remember meeting you. No offense. It's not because you're not memorable, because you are. It's because he's a little too high to have recollection of this by tomorrow morning."

Meredith put down her fork and looked at Jake. *Memorable. Original. Are these the only feelings he has for me?*

It suddenly occurred to Meredith, in the wake of her newfound freedom from being awed by movie stars or controlled by other people's opinions, that she could control her feelings for Jake. She didn't have to go around spouting her emotional interest in him, as she had done last night. Or teasing him by telling him he was crazy about her but not willing to admit it.

She could hold back and have a little discipline in this emotional area of her life, too. She had held off for a lot of years from trusting a guy enough to offer him the key to the garden of her heart. Why should it be any different now just because her heart pounded, her spine tingled, and her breath left whenever he entered the room?

Those are chemical reactions, Meredith told herself firmly. *Jake was right. Shelly was right. I can tell Clint James to bug off. I can hold my own with a swarm of writers at a conference. I can live by myself and plant my own vegetable garden. I can certainly grow up emotionally and stop making a fool of myself with Jacob Wilde.*

"You have some business you want to discuss?" Meredith said, taking Jake by surprise.

"Yes, I do. We don't have to jump right into that unless you want to."

"Might be a good idea," Meredith said.

"I have some questions on one of the points of the contract," Jake said, reaching for his briefcase. "I was going to send it to Helen, and I still can, but I thought since you were right here, it might be helpful if I heard it from you."

"Fine," Meredith said. The gushy, being-out-with-Jake, just-the-two-of-us feelings she had experienced on the way over were quickly dispersing as she took on her acquisitions-editor role and Jacob became only a client to her.

He pulled a few papers from his satchel, and they went over them line by line. Meri explained the franchise clause of the contract to the best of her ability and wrote down the phone number for Dan, the legal advisor at the publishing house.

Jake finished his cheesecake. She ate about half of hers and drank most of her Black Forest coffee. It all seemed to have lost its flavor when she rebuked her feelings and toned down her approach with Jake. She felt heavy. Maybe a little sad.

After Jake paid the bill and she properly thanked him, they headed back to the car.

"Are you okay?" Jake asked.

"Yes, fine."

"It just seems like you became quiet after Clint left."

Meredith walked beside Jake another half block and then stopped. He stopped, too. They were in front of a beauty supply store, and Jake looked in the window of the closed shop as if Meredith had stopped because of something she saw in the window. Then he turned to look at her face.

She tried to keep a cheerful smile there to greet him. "I started thinking about what you said at my house about relationships being based on logical commitments rather than emotional responses."

"Yes," Jake said, looking confused.

Meri looked down and then back up. "I agree with that. I've been giving in to my emotional responses far too many times. The flirty things I said to you last night, the way I ripped on Clint. I don't need to be so controlled by what I feel. I'm ushering in a new era in my personality." She spread her arms open. "This is the new, improved Meredith Graham. A wiser, less ballistic woman." She slapped her forehead with her hand. "What am I doing?"

"What are you doing?" Jake asked.

"I'm trying to…"

Jake waited for her to finish.

"You don't know what it's like to…"

His eyebrows went up, and he waited.

Inside Meredith a volcano was about to explode. She wanted to tell this man that she was crazy about him, she loved being with him, and she wanted to kiss the little bird's nest on his jaw and make all kinds of commitments to him. But if that was all a chemical reaction, then, according to Jake's philosophy, it was invalid.

She was telling herself not to listen to her feelings and to take slow, steady steps of logical relationship progression. Let God work out the details.

Besides, she pointed out to herself, how could a woman of such passion ever be happy with a cold fish head like Jake? But he wasn't cold. He was really kind, tender, and caring about his drunken movie-star friends.

Maybe it was she. Jake just wasn't interested in her the way she was in him. She didn't make his heart zing the way he did hers.

It was exhausting work to keep a volcano from erupting.

Meredith drew in a deep breath. "I don't know what I'm saying. Don't listen to me. Let it go."

"Are you sure? It seems like something is really bothering you."

She wanted to yell back, "Something *is* bothering me! It's you! You're driving me crazy!"

But all she said was, "I'm sure. Forget I said anything."

They began to walk again. After about six feet, Jake stopped and said, "Meredith, there's something I want to ask you."

"Yes?"

"It's pretty important," Jake said. "I don't know how you'll feel about this. I've gone back and forth trying to decide if I should say anything."

"It's okay. What do you want to ask?"

Jake drew in a deep breath and said, "Let's go to the car. I think you might want to be sitting down when I ask you."

They walked briskly toward the parking lot, neither of them speaking.

Meredith suddenly understood why Shelly said she hated Meredith's cat-and-mouse games. They were fun only for the cat and absolutely no fun for the mouse.

Chapter Twenty-Six

They were in the car and pulling out of the parking lot before Jake sprang his question. "It's really not a big thing. Well, maybe it is and maybe it isn't. I don't know. I just don't know how you'll feel about this, and it's highly unusual that I would ask you."

"I'm sure it's okay," Meri said, her patience wearing thin.

"You have the freedom to tell me I'm crazy," Jake began.

Do I also have the freedom to tell you you're driving me crazy?

"When I saw you in the skit last night, I had an idea. Do you remember my saying we still needed to cast the part of the Maiden of the Waterfall? I was wondering if you would consider testing for the part."

Meredith looked at him with little emotional response. It was possible she had used up all her fiery emotions in trying to deny her feelings for the past half hour.

"What's involved?"

"You would need to come to the studio tomorrow or the

next day and read the part. We'll tape you and run it past the casting director. The part isn't very large, but it's crucial we get someone right away because we start to film in a week. The scenes with the Maiden of the Waterfall are in the first filming sequence."

"Sure," Meredith said with a shrug.

"You'll do it?" Jake looked at her and back at the road. "That's great! Of course, I can't guarantee you'll get the part since the casting director has final say, but I think you have the right look and the right voice. You proved last night that you can act. I think it might be a good match."

"What time should I come to the studio?"

"I can have Chad pick you up. Or better yet, how's your schedule tomorrow after twelve-thirty?"

"Open. I teach my last workshop at eleven."

"That's when mine is scheduled, too," Jake said. "This will work out great. I'll take you with me after we finish our workshops, and we can get you back to the hotel whenever you need to. The screen test should only take an hour or so."

"Fine," Meredith said, still unemotional about the invitation.

She remained unemotional for the next twelve hours. Jake dropped her off at the hotel at almost eleven. She thanked him, and they agreed to meet in the lobby tomorrow as soon as their workshops were over. Meredith returned to her room and read manuscripts until two-thirty in the morning. She made it to her first morning appointment at nine-thirty a little groggy and met with people until her workshop at eleven.

It was easy to pour herself into her topic, "Learning from Your Mistakes," since she felt she had made countless mistakes with Jake. As she told the students in her workshop, "Don't be afraid to make mistakes. Just don't be a fool and make the same mistake twice." She wondered if that applied to relationships as well as publishing.

Could she possibly erase all her crazy rantings of the night before and start fresh with Jake today? She had to believe that was possible; otherwise everything else in her workshop would also be false.

She wouldn't be a fool and make the same mistake twice. She would calm her emotions when she was around Jake and remind herself over and over that it was merely a business arrangement. They met in the lobby, and Jake hurried her to the car, joking that he didn't want any of her devoted students to follow her. He chatted all the way to the studio about the part of the Maiden of the Waterfall, saying his explanation of the background would help her prepare for the role.

"Do you remember the daughter of Ramandu in the *Voyage of the Dawn Treader*?" Jake asked. "Her father was a star at rest. Every morning the birds would bring him a fire berry from the Valley in the Sun. He would eat the berry and become younger."

"I don't exactly remember that part," Meredith admitted.

"His daughter ended up marrying Prince Caspian. She welcomed Prince Caspian and his crew on their journey to the Utter East. A great banquet table was spread for them."

"Yes, I remember. The three Narnian lords had fallen asleep at the table."

"That's right. Think of the daughter of Ramandu when you read for this part. The costume will be a long, flowing blue gown with sparkles. Just like a waterfall."

"Hence the name, Maiden of the Waterfall."

"Exactly," Jake said. "I should have told you to wear what you had on last night. That was a perfect look for this screen test."

Meredith now wore a classic business suit: linen skirt, silk blouse, and matching linen jacket. It was the color of butter and didn't show off her hair and eyes the way the turquoise outfit had. But the buttery vanilla color matched how she felt while riding to the studio with Jake. Bland. Neutral. Inoffensive to anyone.

At the studio Meredith was shown into a small soundproof room. She was given half an hour to read over the two pages of dialogue and was offered a bottle of spring water. When everything was ready, she stood in front of the video camera and read the part for the cameraman, with Jake standing right beside him. Jake kept smiling, offering nonverbal praise. Meredith had a hard time getting into the part. She stopped the test before they were halfway through.

"I'm sorry. I need another minute here."

"No problem," Jake said.

The camera stopped, the red light went off, and someone walked in the door. It was Chad. He had a message for Jake.

"I'll be right back," Jake promised. "Go ahead if you're ready."

Meredith read the first few lines again and tried to clear her thoughts. She didn't really feel nervous. She didn't feel much of anything. Only relieved that Jake was no longer in the room watching her.

"Ready to roll?" the cameraman asked.

She nodded.

"From the top. And action," he said.

A short man stepped in front of Meredith and held up a board saying, "Meredith Graham, Maiden of the Waterfall, Take Two." With a brisk slap of the board he stepped away, and the camera moved in closer.

"Hail, young traveler," Meredith began, feeling freer and more into the part. "From where have you come?"

A reader sitting in a chair to the side read the part of Young Heart. Meredith allowed her facial expressions and body movements to reflect her response to what Young Heart was telling her.

"Then you have chosen well. Enter now into the Vale of Peace. Your journey ahead will hold many more adventures. You must be rested before you can embrace them."

She made an elegant, welcoming gesture with her arm and open hand. "Come, Young Heart. Drink of the living water until your soul is quenched. Eat of the bounty prepared here for you."

Young Heart then questioned how he could know if this was yet another trap like the many he had already faced.

"You cannot know," the Maiden of the Waterfall responded gently. "You may only choose to enter or be on your way. Belief offers no guarantees until after the traveler has entered in wholeheartedly."

She read for another five minutes, feeling captivated by this character she was portraying. It suddenly mattered very much that she get the part.

"And cut," the cameraman said after she delivered the last line. He stepped from behind the camera and said, "That was good. The boss will like this one."

Meredith gathered her things, still feeling her heart in a flutter from having put so much into the reading. She chatted with the woman who was sitting in the chair and had been reading the lines to her.

"Should I wait here?" Meredith asked.

"Might as well. Jake will be back eventually. Have you done a lot of this?"

"What? Acting? No. None."

"Really?" The woman in the chair seemed impressed. "You have the right look and the right voice for this part. I think you can feel pretty confident that you'll get it."

Jake hurried in the door with a clipboard in his hand. "Are you about ready to roll in here?"

"Already got it," the cameraman said, nodding at the camera. "When do you want to see it?"

"Get it ready for Jan, and we'll view it up in her office." He turned to Meredith. "That was quick."

Meredith nodded.

"Do you want to go on back to the conference center, or can you stick around here for a while?"

She checked her watch. "I'd better go. I have a stack of manuscripts to read before my evening appointments."

"Next conference," Jake said, stepping closer, "tell them you can't read manuscripts. You're only there to teach. That's what I did."

"Sure," Meredith said with a tease edging into her voice. "You're not an acquisitions editor. That's why they invited me to come. I buy books, as you well know. I can't make any demands and say I'm a famous actor like you."

"Not yet," Jake said, giving her a wink, which she alone noticed. "We'll decide after we view the tape if you're going to be a famous actress or not."

Chad drove Meredith back to the hotel. He spoke three words the whole way. This time she asked him to leave the windows up and the air conditioner on. She also asked if he would mind turning off the radio. She had brought manuscripts with her, and she wanted to do some reading. Chad complied, but she could tell he wasn't happy about it.

Meredith read through two manuscripts on the ride back and marked her comments on the editor's form that accompanied each manuscript when it was returned to the conferee through the central station. The system was a good one, and Meredith found she wasn't as overwhelmed as she had thought at first. Fifteen more manuscripts waited for her back in the room. If she read for about four hours tonight, she could probably finish them all. Then she would meet with her next round of appointments, starting at nine in the morning and going through one fifteen.

Changing into shorts and a T-shirt, Meredith hauled a chair out onto her tiny balcony so she could sun her white legs. Just as she settled in and picked up the first manuscript, the phone rang.

"Hello. Is this *the* Meredith Graham?"

She recognized Jake's voice but wasn't used to his chipper greeting. "Hi, Jake."

He paused before saying, "I think I have good news for you. You got the part!"

"Really?" She had been trying not to think about it since she was hoping for it, and that made it all the more probable, in her estimation, that it wouldn't work out. She knew all about how deferred hope makes the heart sick.

"We'll need you to come down tomorrow and get fitted by Muriel in wardrobe. I should have thought of it today to save you the additional trip."

"That's okay. I'll be free most of tomorrow afternoon, and my plane doesn't leave until seven-thirty tomorrow night."

"Muriel is only here until four tomorrow. Should I send Chad over for you?"

Meredith sat down quickly on the edge of the bed. The news hit her, and she felt a little weak kneed. "No, I'll rent a car. That way I can drive myself to the airport. I don't think Chad wants to see me ever again."

"Papers need to be signed, of course, and Gina in makeup wants some Polaroids."

"Papers?"

"Your contract."

Suddenly the roles were reversed in their relationship, and Meri was the one feeling at a loss. "Do I need an agent?"

"Do you have one?"

"No, but I know a few."

"It's up to you. It's a standard contract for nonunion actors. For the size of your role and your experience, I'm afraid you won't have a lot of negotiating power, if that's what you're thinking."

Meredith started to laugh and flopped onto her back, laughing at the ceiling where she had written that nasty letter to Jake a few nights ago. All her fierce words had been erased.

"No, Jake, I'm not thinking of negotiating anything. This is all so out of the blue. I didn't expect it to work out."

"It's a nice surprise for both of us," Jake said. "We start to film in Glenbrooke on Monday."

"Monday!"

"Yes. We need you there for at least two days, but plan on three or four since it's the first few days of filming. A lot can go wrong."

"Okay. Got it. Tomorrow I'll drive to the studio about two o'clock, I'll meet with Muriel, sign some papers, let Gina take some Polaroid shots of me, and get myself to LAX by six. It could happen."

"It could and it will. You're a lifesaver, Meri. Your screen test was perfect."

He had never called her Meri before, and she wasn't sure she liked it as much as when he said Meredith, and it rolled off his tongue.

"I like this character. She's going to be fun to play."

"I think so, too," Jake said. "Now, how about going out to dinner with me? We can celebrate."

It was Meredith's turn to pause. A waterfall of thoughts and feelings cascaded over her, nearly drowning her on the bed. If she didn't finish reading all the manuscripts tonight, she would never be able to leave the conference by one o'clock tomorrow. She was flattered that he wanted to celebrate with her, but what if it turned out to be an emotional mess like last night at the Cheesecake Factory?

"I'd better not," she said slowly.

Jake waited.

"I have a huge stack of manuscripts to read, and I really have to do them tonight."

"I see." The disappointment was evident in his voice. "I hope they go quickly for you."

"Thanks," Meredith said, biting her lower lip and wondering if she had made the right choice.

"I'll see you at the studio, then, tomorrow. Do you remember how to get here?"

"Yes, Valley View exit, right?"

"Right."

"I'll see you sometime close to two o'clock," Meri said. "Bye, Jake."

"Good-bye, Meredith." For the first time, his farewell sounded sad.

Chapter Twenty-Seven

*M*eredith read like a crazy woman. She ordered in room service, missed the evening session, and kept reading and writing her editor's comments until well after midnight. Of all the ideas she had seen during the conference, only one proposal sounded like a book G. H. Terrison Publishing might be interested in. Meredith wrote her comments on that one last. She asked the writer to make a few changes and then send the revised copy to Shawn in the Chicago office.

She felt wonderful having all the manuscripts now in a tall "out" stack. At home the out stack grew this tall, but more were always coming in.

She fell into a deep sleep and dreamed of waterfalls and a fair maiden rowing across the lake in the same boat she and Jake had shared for their morning picnic. When the alarm sounded the next morning, Meredith tried to pull her dream with her into the waking world. But like all things made of feathery-light vapors, her dream fled before it could acclimate to the harsh realities of the world. The sweet images slipped back to her dream world.

It occurred to her in the shower that Jake had not appeared in her dream, at least to the best of her recollection. Did that mean he didn't have access to the garden places deep inside, as she thought he did? Had Jake only seemed wonderful and intriguing because she willed it to be so? Maybe nothing had been there to begin with, no chemical reaction even.

All the analyzing gave her a headache.

Dressing quickly and packing her clothes while her hair dried, Meredith realized she was going to be late for her nine o'clock appointment. There was nothing she could do about it. She hoped she could make up the time elsewhere in the morning and not have to reschedule anyone for the afternoon.

By the time she arrived downstairs in the meeting area, it was 9:10. She saw a small woman sitting alone at the table that had Meredith's name on the placard. With sincere apologies, Meredith met the older woman and shook her hand. When the woman said her name, Meredith thought it sounded familiar. Then she remembered.

"I have something encouraging to tell you," she said. "Of all the manuscripts I've read here this week, yours was the only one I thought might be a match for our publishing house. I have it right here."

The woman looked as if she might cry as Meredith handed her the manila envelope with the editor's notes on the cover. "I've made a few suggestions. I'd like you to make those changes and then send it to the editor I listed for you. Be sure to include a self-addressed, stamped envelope. This is no guarantee that we'll buy your book, but it's a lovely story, and I think it has a lot of potential."

"Thank you," the woman said, rising and bowing to

Meredith. It appeared to be her Asian custom. Meredith nodded her head back and congratulated the woman again for her fine work.

"Thank you," the woman said again. "You have given me hope."

As she left, Meredith imagined how hard it must have been for a woman of her age to come to a conference like this and try to beat the odds of getting a book published. It did Meri's heart good to know that at least one person would leave the conference with some hope. Hope was a good thing.

The appointments continued, one right after the other until almost noon, when Meredith had a fifteen-minute break. She went to the rest room and then grabbed a candy bar from the machine by the phone. The next three appointments went by like clockwork. At one fifteen, she was checked out of the hotel and sitting in the rental car she had arranged to have waiting for her. Everything was clicking right along.

She eased the car out of the hotel parking lot and headed for the studio. It was hard for her to analyze how she felt about Jake at the moment. Somewhere inside, a spring of logic rose up, and she began to evaluate and comment on each of her thoughts in the same way she had made orderly logic of the stack of manuscripts she had waded through during the past few days.

First, you just turned twenty-five. This panic over your singleness was bound to hit you. Jake just happened to be around when the panic hit.

Second, you wanted Jake to be the answer to all your prayers. You willed yourself into your emotional responses.

Third, you tried to make something out of nothing. Only God can do that. Saving a grape as if it had special meaning is ridiculous. You were setting yourself up for disappointment.

And fourth, this is not the time in your life when you need to be looking for a lasting relationship. Wait five more years.

Meredith watched the car in her rearview mirror as she changed lanes.

Okay, three more years. In three years, you'll have established yourself with Terrison Publishing well enough so that if you want to take some time off to get married and have babies, they'll let you work part-time and welcome you back after the kids are in school.

Letting out a sigh and merging onto the freeway, Meredith told herself she was right in her four logical laws. It made good sense to guard her heart as she had all these years. When the time was right, she would know it, and right now wasn't a convenient time to start a relationship with a man who lived a thousand miles away and was in the middle of working day and night on his video production.

We'll see each other a lot over the next few months with the books and the video. If I had let my emotions get carried away, it would have only made things more complicated for us to maintain our professional relationship. I'm glad I started to think clearly before it was too late.

Meredith found the studio with no problem and walked into the building at exactly 1:50. She headed for the back corner where Jake had showed her the wardrobe on her first visit. Muriel was waiting for her and was delighted that Meri was early. Handing Meri the blue diaphanous gown that had been created for the actress originally cast as the Maiden of the Waterfall, Muriel showed Meredith to the small dressing area. Meri put on the spectacular gown.

No mirrors were in the dressing stall. Only pegs to hang clothes on. Meredith gave up trying to zip the dress and stepped out, asking Muriel to help her.

With her face to the full-length mirror by the door, Meredith admired the costume while Muriel worked to fasten it in the back. The color was a softer blue than turquoise, more of a robin's-egg blue. The fabric was as sheer as a whisper with a thin, matching lining. The bodice was showered with tiny glitters and elbow-length, billowing sleeves. The soft blue fabric drifted in layer upon layer down the long skirt, cut in angles like feathery fairy wings. The most amazing part was that it fit so well. Muriel went to work pinning the sides, which needed to be taken in just a pinch. She directed Meredith to stand on a carpeted box to check the hem. It wasn't a straight hem but was pointed all around from the many layers of sheer blue fabric that cascaded to the floor.

Muriel fussed and pinched and stuck Meredith twice by accident. The seamstress was determined to mark the waist so she could cinch up the skirt at the waistband.

Meredith watched her reflection in the mirror and felt sure she was Cinderella, and at any moment the little mice would come skittering in to help Muriel sew this enchanting dress.

There was a knock at the door. No mice appeared. Only Chad, the big rat, telling Meredith that she needed to stay there so Gina from makeup could come take some "Roids."

A few moments later a redheaded Gina appeared in shorts, clogs, and a pink T-shirt that said "Mr. Bubble." She had to be one of the plainest women Meredith had seen during her time in Los Angeles. Gina didn't wear a drop of makeup, and her eyes looked wide and bulgy like a frog's. She didn't appear to have any eyelashes. Her eyebrows were either blond and very faint or she had none.

"Good," Gina said, checking the light above her head before coming closer to Meredith. "Stand just like that. I need one serious." She clicked the Polaroid camera and pulled the photo out slowly. "Here, hold this a second. Now, one smiling. Very good. Hold it."

"Do you need one with the wig?" Muriel asked.

"Wouldn't hurt," Gina said. She had a lovely voice with an accent. Australian, maybe?

Muriel took the developing picture from Meredith's hand and told her to step down. "Now bend down," Muriel ordered. "Watch the pins."

Too late. Meredith had already harpooned herself on the right side. Muriel lifted an extremely long white wig and placed it on Meredith's head. It felt like it weighed a hundred pounds.

"Tuck your hair behind your ear," Gina instructed. She came forward and began fidgeting with the wig, trying to get it straight. The white wavy hair tumbled over Meredith's shoulders and down her back until it touched the ground. Muriel pulled some of the long strands over the front of Meredith's dress.

Meri looked in the mirror and smiled. "I look like something from a fairy tale," she said, amazed at how much the wig transformed her appearance, especially with the dress.

"That's the idea," Muriel said.

"All I need is a wand."

"No wand. Sorry." Muriel tried to tuck Meredith's stray blond hairs under the wig on the side. "We'll do a proper cap and all for you when the time comes. This is good enough for now."

"It's good enough for me," Gina said, snapping a few more pictures, one from the center and one from either side. "Are you allergic to any cosmetics that you know of?" Gina asked.

"Not that I know of."

"All right, then. My work here is finished. I'll see both of you Monday on location."

Muriel helped Meredith take off the heavy wig. Meredith immediately felt cooler and lighter. "I'll help you with the dress, too," Muriel offered. "Those pins might be a problem."

Meri had just removed the dress and was in the stall

putting on her clothes when there was another knock on the door. This time it was Jake, not Chad, who entered. She hurried to pull on her jeans skirt and T-shirt.

"Do you need to make many alterations, Muriel?" Jake asked.

"Enough," the practical woman said flatly.

"Did Gina take the shots yet?"

"She just left."

"Great. Where is our Maiden of the Waterfall?"

"Right here," Meredith said, shaking back her mussed hair and opening the door to the dressing stall.

When their eyes met, Jake's smile spread across his face. His gaze softened. He definitely gave her a tender, appreciative look.

And why shouldn't he be appreciative? I just saved him from holding up production while he tried to find a Maiden of the Waterfall.

"Do you have a minute?" Jake asked. "We have some paperwork to go over."

Meri glanced at Muriel, who gave a silent nod that she was finished with her. "Sure. I'm all yours."

Oh, that was good. I'm all yours. Why couldn't you just have said "yes"?

Jake led her upstairs to a long, narrow room that had been transformed into office space. The place was crammed with four desks, a copy machine, a fax machine, several computers, and a large television set in the corner.

"Not very glamorous, I know," he apologized as they slid past two other people. One was tapping away on a laptop computer, and the other was on the phone. "These guys can't wait for us to go on location so they can have their space back. Let's sit at the desk in the corner."

Jake cleared a place on the desk and pulled some papers

from the drawer. "This is the standard contract. You're welcome to take it with you, but we need it signed before we start to film on Monday."

Meredith nodded.

"Here's our production schedule and your script. The script is the same as the one you read for the screen test. There aren't any changes yet. Did I leave anything out? Oh yes, Monday. The crew will all be in Glenbrooke by Friday or Saturday at the latest. If you could get away for the weekend and come, it would be helpful. I'm asking all actors to be there by Sunday afternoon. I want to catch the morning light, so plan on being in makeup at three o'clock on Monday morning."

"Okay," Meredith said, taking in all the information. "Anything else?"

Jake paused and looked at her. He leaned forward across the desk and lowered his voice. "I've been thinking about something you said, and I think you might be right."

Meredith couldn't imagine what she had said. The only thing that came to mind was when she told him he was crazy about her but too legalistic to admit it.

"You said something was missing, and I think you're right. But I can't figure out what it is."

Meredith didn't know what to say. Something was missing from their relationship? What relationship? They weren't having a relationship. When did she say something was missing?

"I went over the script again last night, and I can't see it, but I know what you were saying. There is something missing in the story."

Oh, the story!

"If you have a chance to give it another look, or if you even have time to think about it in the next few days, and see anything we could improve on, would you give me a call right away?" He handed her his business card. "My cell-phone number is on the back. Call me anytime." That warm grin rose on his handsome face, and he said, "I'd love to hear from you. Anytime."

Chapter Twenty-Eight

$\mathcal{L}$ate Friday night Meredith held Jake's business card between her thumb and forefinger and examined it the same way she had examined the grape. She hadn't taken him up on his invitation to phone during the past few days simply because she had so much to do. Work and calls had to be caught up, and she had had lengthy conversations with Shelly and Helen about this Maiden of the Waterfall twist of events. Helen had recommended that a lawyer in Seattle look over the acting contract, and Meri had met with him that morning. He advised her to go ahead and sign and charged her a hundred bucks for his time.

Then she had packing to do. Not only clothes for the week she planned to stay in Glenbrooke, but also all her business paraphernalia. She had her calls forwarded to her cell phone and packed her computer and two boxes of manuscripts. She decided she didn't want to leave Elvis at home alone again, so she arranged his fish bowl inside her small ice chest and secured it on the floor of the backseat, where she thought he would feel the least amount of bumps.

Everything was set. She was ready to sleep and then hit the road when her alarm went off at five in the morning. She would arrive in Glenbrooke close to noon on Saturday, giving her a chance to settle in at Kyle and Jessica's.

Something inside her wanted to call Jake. She looked at his cell-phone number on the back of his business card, closed her eyes trying to memorize it, then checked it again. What would she say if she did phone him? Since saying good-bye to him in L.A., she had put him out of her thoughts and emotions. He wanted to know what was missing in the screenplay. She still didn't know. She had no reason to call.

Turning off the light and praying in the stillness of her bed-room, Meredith fell into a deep, sweet sleep. The alarm jolted her out of bed at five, and she went into action, readying all the last-minute things. She decided to throw in a warm jacket and went to the guest-room closet to pull it out. When she opened the closet door, Guard Man Fred popped out, scaring the stuff-ing out of her.

"What? You want to come with me so we can play a joke on Shelly? Okay. Glad you thought of it, Fred." Meredith packed the inflatable dummy into the backseat, laying him on his side so he could keep an eye on Elvis in his ice-chest domain.

She hit the road right on schedule, made the early ferry, and didn't hit any traffic through Seattle, which amazed her. By the time she arrived in Portland three hours later, she was ready for a stretch. She pulled off the freeway and bought gas. As the attendant filled her tank, he kept looking in the back-seat at Fred. Meredith rolled down her window and asked where she could find a good cup of coffee and some pastry. The attendant looked at her suspiciously and told her about a place called Mama Bear's. He said it was about a mile or two away on Hawthorne, but he guaranteed her they had the best cinnamon rolls in the city.

Meredith didn't mind the little jog if it meant award-winning cinnamon rolls. She found the bakery in a row of charming shops and parked a few doors down in front of a flower shop called ZuZu's Petals. Before she got out, she decided she had better cover up Fred so passersby wouldn't notice him lying there. The only thing she had handy was a black garbage bag. She opened the back door and quickly put the bag over Fred's head and pulled it down. It only came to about his knees, but she figured it was okay. Nobody would notice jeans and two feet with ratty tennis shoes. It was the face they always noticed, and that's what startled people.

She locked the car and stepped into the bakery. The warm, welcoming aroma of cinnamon greeted her, and she drank of its fragrance deeply. A round woman in a bright apron called out, "Good morning." The apron was green with yellow pears all over it. It reminded Meredith of her lemon apron at home, and she had to force herself to shake away the image of Jake in her kitchen wearing her lemon apron.

Meredith ordered a regular coffee, milk, and a cinnamon roll. The roll was huge and delivered warm on a plate with a fork. She moved to the register where a cute teenage girl with wild, curly blond hair took her money. The girl had on the same bright apron and a row of jangling silver bracelets up her arm that clinked merrily like a wind chime when she gave Meredith the change. The teen's cheery smile invited a return smile from Meredith.

Ah, to be young and innocent. Now there's a Young Heart. It shows all over her face. Not a care in the world, I bet.

A jar by the register had a sign attached to it that said If You Fear Change, Leave It Here. Meredith smiled and dumped her change into the tip jar. She took her roll and coffee to a side table and went back for the milk. Glancing up at the clock on the wall behind her, she noticed it was a brown bear with the clock's face on his tummy.

Nine forty-five. I have plenty of time.

She enjoyed every bite of her roll and watched the young girl at the register. A line of customers had formed, and every table but one was taken.

In the back of her mind, Meri started to put a few thin strands of an idea together. Maybe what was missing from the Young Heart script was that it was only about a boy. What about bringing a girl into the story?

Meredith couldn't quite put all the pieces together, but she knew the granule of a good idea was there. The soft, female element would give the story much more dimension. With a final glance at the girl at the register, Meredith headed for her car, eager to return to the road. When she exited Mama Bear's, she noticed a crowd of people gathered around her car. A short, spunky woman with jet black hair stood by the side of Meri's Explorer. She held a baseball bat and was ready to swing at the back window.

"Hey!" Meredith yelled, running to her car. "What are you doing?"

"Is this your vehicle?" a man in the crowd asked.

"Yes! What's going on?"

Everyone looked at her and at each other, none willing to speak up.

"I've called the police," the feisty, dark-haired woman said, still wielding the bat. She looked willing to swing at Meredith.

"What's the problem? Did I park in your space?"

"You have some explaining to do when the police arrive,"

the woman said. "Watch her. Make sure she doesn't bolt."

Suddenly it dawned on Meri that all these people were peering in the back window, looking at Fred with the garbage bag over his head. She broke into her shimmering laugh, and everyone looked even more frightened. More people gathered.

"That's my Guard Man," Meredith said lightly. "He's one of those inflatable travel companions. I'll show you." She stepped through the crowd and unlocked her back door. Lifting Fred and pulling off the garbage bag, Meredith showed him to the leery bunch of spectators.

A ripple of laughter made its way through the group.

"Charlotte," one woman said to the feisty gal with the bat, "you have definitely had way too much coffee this morning. Anyone could tell it was a mannequin."

Charlotte looked humiliated. She put down the bat. With a shrug and a weak giggle, she said, "Sorry."

"That's okay." Meri opened the front door and positioned Fred in the passenger seat, complete with shoulder-strap seat belt. The crowd dispersed, and Charlotte went back inside ZuZu's Petals still arguing with the other woman that she had had no way of knowing it was only a dummy.

Eager to get out of the Saturday-morning hubbub on Hawthorne, Meri drove back to the freeway and didn't stop again until she reached Glenbrooke. All the way down, she thought about how to add the female element to Young Heart.

Kyle was the only one home when Meri arrived in the early afternoon. He helped her carry her things in and had a good laugh over Guard Man Fred. Meri decided to leave Fred in the car so she could take him over to Shelly's that evening. She hoped to get some work done before then. Kyle offered Meredith his office and set up an extra table for her to use as a work station. Elvis's fishbowl was the first thing she placed on the corner of the table.

As she set up her laptop computer and plugged her phone in to recharge it, she asked Kyle, "Do you by any chance happen to have a copy of *Pilgrim's Progress* by John Bunyan?"

Kyle smiled. "What language would you like it in?"

"What?"

"Up there," he said, pointing to a row of books on the top shelf. "It's been my hobby ever since we moved here. I've collected thirty-four copies. Seven of them are in different languages." He seemed proud of his collection, and rightly so.

"I only need one copy. In English, please."

Kyle slid the wheeled ladder over to the top shelf and came down with a 1902 leather-bound edition. "It's the newest version and has the sturdiest binding," he explained.

"Thanks. This is perfect."

"Can I get you anything to eat or drink before you plunge into your project?"

"Something to drink would be great. I can get it."

"No, let me." Kyle returned in a few minutes with a plate of cheese, crackers, and apples, a liter-sized glass bottle of sparkling mineral water, and a glass filled with ice.

"Such service!" Meri remarked. "Thanks, Kyle."

"No problem. I'm on my way over to the camp. Jess and Travis should be home soon. I'll leave her a note that you're here."

Meredith went to work, reading over the screenplay, looking for a likely place to insert another character. She envisioned a traveling partner for Young Heart. But how would that work?

There was a tap at the door.

"It's open. Come in."

She heard footsteps and thought Kyle had returned, so she didn't look up from the papers.

A rich voice behind her said, "He looked lonely in your car, so I brought him in."

Meri turned to see Jake standing there with his arm around Fred. She burst out laughing. Fred's baseball cap was on backward, he had on Jake's sunglasses, and his shirt was unbuttoned and hanging out. His arms were posed in a folded position, making him look like a rap singer.

"All he needs are baggy pants and a few gold chains and we can put him on the cover of an album. What do you think?" Jake was enjoying this moment.

"I think you're a little crazy," Meri said.

"From the queen of crazy, I'll take that as a compliment." Jake let go of Fred, and the unsupported mannequin flopped over. "The guy can't hold his root beer," Jake quipped.

"Help him find a nice quiet corner to sit in," Meredith said. "I'm working here."

"So I see," Jake said. "Should I take him back to your car?"

"Good idea."

Jake returned a few minutes later and stood before Meredith's newly set up desk. He tapped on Elvis's bowl and watched him swim around, unaffected. Meredith kept working as if Jake weren't there.

"Your diligence is very impressive, Miss Graham. However, a wise person once reminded me of the words of Ecclesiastes, chapter 4, and I quote loosely, 'There is no end to her toil, yet her eyes are not content with her wealth. "For whom am I toiling," she asked, "and why am I depriving myself of enjoyment?" This too is meaningless—a miserable business.'"

"I've heard that somewhere," Meredith said, looking up with a coy smile.

"I was hoping you had some free time this afternoon," Jake said. "We're all set up at the camp, and I told the crew to take the rest of the day off." He sat down on the leather couch across the room from her, and then, apparently not content just to sit, he kicked off his loafers, stretched out, and stuffed a throw pillow under his head.

"It's good for a person to cease from her toil and experience a little of life's enjoyments," Jake continued. He folded his arms across his chest and closed his eyes. "So how 'bout it?"

"You look like your greatest enjoyment in life right now would be a nap," Meredith said, intrigued at how easily he had just made himself at home.

"*Nap...nap*. I know I've heard that word before. What does it mean? I can't seem to remember."

Just then they heard little footsteps pattering across the hardwood floor. Jessica's quick, motherly steps weren't far behind.

"Travis," she called out as the toddler came bursting into the library.

"Hey, Travis," Meredith said. "What are you doing?"

He stopped and stared at the two of them, his little eyes like two blue marbles.

"Hello!" Jessica called out as she caught up with her son. "I saw Kyle on my way in. He said you're all set up here. That's good." Jessica came over to give Meri a warm hug. "You know you're welcome to stay as long as you want."

"Thanks. You guys are so gracious. I love being here."

Travis followed his mom and grasped the hem of her shorts. He popped his first two fingers into his mouth and stared at Jake.

"You remember me, don't you, Tiger? I was here last night. I'm the one who gave you the ride in the spaceship." Jake sat up and opened his arms, inviting Travis to come to him.

Shyly, Travis moved toward Jake, pulling his mom with him as he went. When Travis reached the couch, Jake broke his frozen pose and lurched forward, scooping up the delighted Travis and turning him upside down, making loud spaceship sounds. Jake stood up and lifted Travis in the air, taking him for the spaceship ride of his life. Travis was all glee and no fear.

The scene brought laughter to both Jessica and Meri.

As Meri watched, a long-held image in the back of her mind vanished. A new picture took its place. Her picture of the perfect husband, the frugal, balding man who looked just like her dad, was replaced with a new image. The image was Jake, right now, right here, exactly like this.

God, will you be merciful to me, please? Take this man away from me right now! Get him out of my life. I'm trying so hard not to have feelings for him, but how in the world am I supposed to remain immune to this? I'm only a woman, God. And I don't have a heart of steel.

Chapter Twenty-Nine

It took a full five minutes for the space commander to run out of fuel and bring the little rocket in for a landing on the couch. A few minutes of tummy tickling followed and then the firm words of Mother. "Come on, Travis. It's time for me to read you a story."

Meri guessed that was a ploy to get him in his room, all settled down and sleepy so that he would be more willing to take a nap. Jessica and the reluctant Travis left, and Jake returned to his reclining position on the couch.

Without looking up from her papers, Meri said, "Sure is hard to get any work done around here."

Jake closed his eyes and let his rapid breathing slow down. "I love little kids," he stated. "I want at least a dozen."

Meri was startled by his comment but gave a quick comeback. "You know what they say, 'First comes love, then comes marriage, then comes the baby in the baby carriage.'

That progression might be a little confusing to someone who doesn't believe in love."

Jake opened his eyes and turned his head toward Meredith. "I never said I didn't believe in love. I said I don't agree with the notion of falling in love and letting that be the basis for a relationship."

Meredith didn't reply.

Jake sat up. "Is that why you call me a cold fish head?"

Meredith looked shocked. "I don't call you a cold fish head!"

"That's what Shelly said."

"You can't believe everything you hear." Meredith felt herself blushing. She was furious with her meddling sister. How could a sister do that?!

"I'm not a cold fish. I'm picky."

"So am I," Meredith shot back.

"There are too many traps out there when it comes to relationships."

"Too many losers," Meredith echoed.

Jake leaned forward, his hands on his knees, his voice rising. "A marriage relationship is based on a lasting commitment, not on feelings."

"Without feelings we wouldn't be human."

"With feelings we make weak and foolish decisions."

"If God is in control, everything that happens comes from his hand."

Jake stood to face her, a worthy opponent in the war of words. "If we are depending on him, we don't have to rely on frail emotions."

"He made our pickin' emotions!" Meredith shouted, standing to face Jake.

Jake paused. With a calmer voice he said, "I believe in commitment."

"I believe in love," Meredith retaliated.

"God calls us to a life of commitment."

"Then why didn't he say, 'These three remain: faith, hope and love. But the greatest of these is commitment'?"

Jake stared at her.

She stared right back.

Neither of them spoke.

Meredith sat down first, a nonverbal gesture of her victory.

Jake laid down and drew in a long breath. He put his arm over his forehead and kept breathing deeply.

Meredith picked up the copy of *Pilgrim's Progress* and began to scan the pages, trying to get her mind back on her task. She was still, above all, this man's editor. Best to let sleeping dogs lie, so to speak.

"You know," Jake said calmly, "love is more than an emotion. It's a choice first. That choice leads to commitment."

Meredith had to smile. This guy worked hard to come to that conclusion. The truth was, she agreed with him. Should she give him the satisfaction of knowing that?

"You're right," she said sweetly.

"You agree with me?" he asked, opening one eye.

"Yes, of course. One hundred percent."

"Then what were we fighting about?"

"Was that a fight? That wasn't a fight. You should see me when I fight! It's a grand and glorious sight."

Jake shook his head. "You are by far the most alive woman I have ever met."

"Alive?" Meri echoed. "That's good. We can put that right up there with 'original.'"

Again, Jake seemed stumped. He had run out of verbal ammo and seemed eager to close his eyes and go back to his napping.

Meri smoothed the pages of Kyle's treasured book and started to make notes of some of the key points in *Pilgrim's Progress*. The main character, Christian, began his journey after reading in the Bible that he was condemned to die because of his sins. He met Evangelist, who directed him to the narrow path. With a heavy burden slung over his shoulder, Christian took to the narrow path, where he was met by many who opposed or questioned his quest. His burden was swallowed up by a sepulcher when he came to the cross, confessed his sin, and surrendered to Christ. The rest of the journey was full of ups and downs as Christian pushed on toward the Celestial City.

She silently read the portion where Christian and his companion, Hopeful, were about to enter the Celestial City. "The pilgrims saw the City was built of pearls and precious stones. The streets were paved with gold. Reflections of sunbeams off the natural glory of the city made Christian sick with desire. Both he and Hopeful cried out, 'If you see my Beloved, tell him I am sick with love.'"

Sounds like a rather emotional reaction from a guy who's supposed to be on a quest of commitment! She checked the author's note at the back of the book to verify her recollection. Yes, John Bunyan wrote this classic during the twelve years he spent in prison for preaching without permission from the established church. He wrote those words around 1647.

Looking over at Jake, who was asleep on the cushy sofa, Meri thought, *You're wrong, Mr. Logic. Love sickness and falling in love isn't a modern American malady. It's been around for a long time. If John here can quote Song of Solomon and get away with it, there's something to it that's bigger than both of us.*

It struck Meredith that just as *Pilgrim's Progress* was an allegory of a Christian's journey through life, maybe falling in love was also a living allegory of how it will be when we reach heaven and can fall into the arms of our relentless lover, God. The spiritual life of love and the physical were not so vastly separated as she once thought. She remembered how Jake hadn't wanted to hold hands at dinner when they prayed because he didn't want to "confuse" the physical with the spiritual. Maybe the physical and spiritual were already so interwoven it wasn't possible to dissect them or limit them by saying one was good and one was bad.

She noticed how peaceful Jake looked at the moment. He had his hand up over his forehead and looked just like her father taking a Sunday-afternoon snooze on the couch. Here was living proof of a physical and spiritual life all intertwined.

Suddenly, like a swirling, rushing wind, a strong impression came over Meredith, taking her breath and tingling her spine. Her heart began to pound. This was the man she had prayed for all these years. She was in love with Jake Wilde, and nothing or nobody could change that. Not even Jake. She couldn't shut down her emotions. Everything within her declared that she was in every way—physically, emotionally, spiritually, and mentally—sick with love over this man.

Why are you telling me this, God? What kind of joke are you playing here?

A strong thought came to her on the heels of her doubts: *Rest in hope.*

She sat still. Had God just spoken to her? It seemed so clear. That phrase, *rest in hope,* sounded familiar. Meredith reached for her reference Bible and looked in her trusty concordance. There it was. Psalm 16:9. Funny, that was the same chapter Jake's key verse for his Young Heart story came from.

Meredith read the verse to herself while Jake slept deeply.

"Hope," she whispered in the stillness. "Rest in hope." *I can do that. I can rest in you, Father. And I can hope.*

It struck her that Hopeful was the name of Christian's travel companion. She skimmed the story, reading how Faithful had been his constant companion in the beginning, but then Hopeful took over and completed the journey with Christian.

Meredith started to get excited about this concept, even though she wasn't completely sure why. *Faithful. I've been faithful. I've saved myself for the right man. I've been obedient to God's Word. Now Hope will become my companion. That's what's missing in Young Heart's journey! He's trying so hard and being so diligent with each foe he faces, but he doesn't have Hope.*

Meredith turned to a fresh page of paper and went to work, sketching out her ideas in long, flowing sentences. She found this method more freeing to her creative senses than typing it on the computer. Within an hour, she had the solution and felt giddy over how it all came together.

Turning on her computer, she prepared to put her scribbles in order. Her laptop made a chirping sound when it turned on. It was enough of a noise to wake the sleeping giant. While he had slept, everything had changed for Meredith. She had realized and admitted that she was in love with this man, she had sensed a fresh word of encouragement and direction from God, and she had solved the problem of what was missing in Young Heart's story. Fresh in spirit and fully alive, Meredith greeted him with an eager, loving smile.

Jake, on the other hand, looked startled when he awoke. Apparently he had been so deeply asleep, he didn't remember where he was. When he looked at Meredith, it was as if she had appeared out of nowhere. Glancing around quickly and moistening his dry lips, Jake tried to focus on Meredith.

"Did you have a good nap?" she asked.

"Huh? Ah, yeah."

Meredith giggled to herself at how drowsy Jake was. No wonder he had fled from her room in such a panic that first time they saw each other. This guy could fall asleep in a second and sleep like a rock. She wondered if Eve had been met with as charming a reception when God woke Adam from his deep sleep and pronounced that since it was not good for man to be alone, this was the helper he had made suitable for him.

It became apparent all too quickly that although Meredith had heard voices and seen visions during this past hour, no angels had appeared to Jacob in his dreams. He seemed almost irritated that he had slept so long.

"I don't know what happened," he said, sitting up and running his fingers through his hair.

"You were tired," Meredith suggested. "You've been going pretty hard and fast for a long time."

"Did I talk in my sleep?"

Meredith laughed. "No. Do you usually?"

"I've been told I do." Jake let out a huge yawn. He glanced at his watch again. "I have to get back to the camp in about an hour. Do you want to ride over there with me?"

"Sure. First I have an announcement to make."

"Oh yeah?" Jake stood and put his arms over his head. He stretched his stiff neck and rotated his shoulders.

"I'd like to suggest a new character in the video series and in the books."

"A walk-on part, right? No lines?"

Meredith shook her head. Her smile was firm. "I know this is going to be a big hassle, but I'm convinced this is what the story needs. I'm committed to helping you rewrite."

"You're committed to helping rewrite," he repeated. He made it sound like a joke.

Undaunted, Meredith pushed forward. "Young Heart needs a companion on his journey, in the same way that Christian had Faithful and then Hopeful as his traveling companions. Young Heart needs a companion who will bring to his journey the softer side of grace and mercy in the midst of all his trials."

Jake nodded slightly as if he was tracking with her.

"He needs Hope."

"Hope," Jake repeated.

Meredith held up her rough pencil sketch of what she thought the young female companion should look like. "Hope."

Jake sat down and put his head in his hands. "Do you realize what this means? We have to find an actress, rewrite the entire screenplay, delay the filming, and who knows what else."

"Yes," Meredith stated calmly. "I know."

Jake looked at her. She could almost see the zillion thoughts racing through his mind.

"It's your choice, of course," Meredith said. "I only offer this as a suggestion. You have a good story here. It will make a good video and book series. If you add Hope, I believe you will have a great story, and you'll double your audience appeal."

Jake kept staring at her, still thinking all this through.

"You're right," he finally said. "I don't want to change everything, I don't want to halt production, I don't want to lose any money, but you are absolutely right."

Meredith gave him a comforting grin. She knew she was right. Deep inside she felt good. Better than she had felt emotionally, spiritually, mentally, and physically in a long time. She was in love, and in her heart, she was resting in hope.

Chapter Thirty

*T*t took only ten days for Meri and Jake to rewrite the script. They worked side by side day and night. Kyle had let them take over his office, and they transformed it into a dual work space. From the start, Meri and Jake meshed. Ideas from one of them sparked ideas in the other. Their working habits and styles blended, as did their thought processes.

Meri took the time off work as her two-week vacation. Because she had never taken any vacation time since she started her job, it was no problem. Jake sent the crew home and immediately faxed the studio with specifics for cast selection and wardrobe preparations. Jessica and Kyle kept them well fed, and Travis visited them regularly, looking for spaceship rides from Jake and giving Meri sticky, wet kisses on the cheek.

Only once did they take a genuine break. One Friday night, a little more than halfway through the rewrite, they decided they desperately needed a change of pace. It seemed even their tolerance levels were the same when it came to how much they could cram through their imaginations. And Jake was a man with imagination. Meri knew there were many more stories inside him that needed to be written. She served as a propelling force to get his ideas going.

Their break was for dinner at Jonathan and Shelly's. When they walked in, they found that Shelly had tied Bob Two to a post in the backyard so as not to disrupt the evening.

"Did Mom get ahold of you?" Shelly asked.

"No."

"She just called here and said the board offered Dad a part-time position at the church as the visitation pastor."

"Did he take it? It seems as if they're just tossing him a bone after how everything went down."

"Mom was happy about it. They will stay in their house, and supposedly Dad will work fewer hours. She's going back to see Molly next week."

"I'm glad it's what they want," Meri said with a sigh. "I'm all in favor of people getting what they want."

At the dinner table, Jonathan asked if Jake and Meredith were ready to strangle each other yet, having worked so long in close quarters.

Jake looked surprised at the idea. "No, it's going unusually well. I feel I'm along for the ride. Meri's mind is like a waterfall, fresh, flowing, always spilling over. I just get in my little raft and go for a tumble."

Meri gratefully absorbed his words. For all the closeness of their days and nights of working together, Jake had made no romantic gestures. Meri didn't feel the need to try to convince Jake that they should have a relationship or to wrestle with understanding or expressing her feelings. In every way she was at rest in hope.

Jake cut off a piece of the tender T-bone steak Jonathan had barbecued for him and said, "If I were rewriting this script by myself, it would take me a year. Maybe two years. It's astounding how much we've accomplished in such a short time."

"You know what they say," Shelly interjected. "Two are better than one, because they have a good reward for their labor."

"It wasn't 'they' who said that; it was God," Meredith said. "I know that verse."

"You know a lot of verses," Jake said. He turned to Shelly and Jonathan. "We'll be writing away, and all of a sudden Meri will add this great line. I'll say, 'Where have I heard that before?' and she'll go to her concordance and find it."

"It's one of the drawbacks of being a P.K.," Shelly said. "I have the same problem. I know thousands of verses but none of their addresses."

"Meri is the only person I know who can breeze her way through a concordance and find what she's looking for in a minute flat." Jake gave her a warm smile.

It seemed to Meri that he was beginning to feel something for her. Respect and admiration, if nothing else. Those were good cornerstones for a relationship.

By the time they finished the final revisions on the following Wednesday, other details had fallen into place for the filming. The casting director had sent a batch of videos for Jake to review for the part of Hope. Meri and Jessica both sat with Jake to review the young actresses on the tapes. The fourth one they saw was far and away the best choice. Jake immediately made a call to set all the wheels in motion.

"Are we actually ready to call the crew back?" Jake asked as he paced the office.

"I think so," Meredith said, surveying the mess all around them. "Can we call for a Dumpster to clean this place out?"

Jake was already on the phone, calling the studio to verify that they were ready to call the crew back. When he hung up the phone, he clapped his hands together, grabbed Meri by the shoulders, and did a little dance. It was the clumsiest, most two-left-footed dance Meri had ever seen. She burst out laughing and bumped into a wastebasket, knocking it over.

"You are a klutz!" she told him.

"But I'm a happy klutz," he said, letting go of her shoulders and righting the wastebasket. "The crew will be back up here by Saturday morning, and we should be able to start shooting on Monday, if our little Hope is ready. I think it's time to celebrate!"

"As long as it's not dinner and dancing," Meri teased. "I'll take the dinner but pass on the dancing."

"How about a picnic at the waterfall?"

Meredith felt her hopes rise. He wanted to go back to their spot. With the pressure off, they could relax and talk. Wonderful conclusions could be drawn when a man had a chance to reflect and eat at the same time.

"I'll see if Jess and Kyle want to come with us." Jake hurried from the office.

Meri kept her brave smile showing as he left, but her heart was fainting. *I've been very patient, Lord. Nearly two weeks alone with this man, and I'm desperately in love with him. I've kept all my love hidden away. Why can't he see how perfect we are together? Lord, when will you open his eyes?*

She comforted herself with the thought that God must have put Jake's emotions in a deep sleep. She tried to convince herself that everything God had revealed to her that afternoon in the library was still true, even though Jake hadn't yet responded.

What was that saying Dad used to tell us? "Never doubt in the darkness what God reveals to you in the light." I won't doubt. I'll stay faithful, and I will rest in hope.

By six-thirty the extended party had gathered at the water-fall and spread a grand picnic. Jake had invited Jess, Kyle, and Travis. They, in turn, had invited Kyle's brother, Kenton, and Kenton's wife, Lauren. Meri had called Shelly, and she and Jonathan showed up with Bob Two. The June evening was perfect, and the abundance of food amazing considering the quickness with which it had been prepared. Jonathan and Kyle went swimming; Bob Two jumped in with them. Jessica tried to restrain Travis, who was wailing that he wanted to go with his daddy.

"I'll take you in, Tiger," Jake said, pulling off his T-shirt and slipping out of his loafers. He pulled off his leather belt and emptied his pockets onto the blanket. Scooping Travis up in his arms, he waded out slowly.

Jake's wallet had fallen open when he tossed it, and Shelly was the first to notice the picture beside his driver's license. "Meri," she said, picking it up and taking a closer look. "That's you. Where was this taken?"

Meredith grabbed the wallet. The picture appeared to be cut from a larger photo. She was sitting in a rowboat with a big smile on her face. The morning sun poured through the trees, showering her with golden radiance. It was a stunning picture. And it was in his wallet. Glimmers of hope raced down Meri's spine.

"Here," she said to Shelly calmly.

Shelly handed the wallet to Lauren and Jessica. Kenton looked over their shoulders. "That's a very good picture," they all commented.

"Are you two getting pretty close?" Lauren asked. She looked quickly at Shelly and Jessica to make sure she wasn't out of line in asking such a question. "I mean, of course you are. You're a writing team now. Words can draw two people together very tightly."

Shelly leaned a little closer and seemed ready to hang on every word of Meredith's answer. Shelly had reminded Meri more than once during this past week and a half that she had been extra good about not asking how things were going between them. She had promised Meri she would wait until Meri had something she wanted to tell her.

Meredith Graham, the queen of coy, slipped off her sandals and tucked her tank top into her jeans shorts. "Anybody else going in?"

"You're going in with your clothes on?" Shelly asked.

"They'll dry. Life is too short to sit on the shore and only wonder." With that, Meri stood and with light steps entered the water.

"I was never such a free spirit," Meri heard Jessica say. Slowly walking in, Meri felt the water reach her knees. Jake was a few feet away, in water up to his waist, holding Travis and dipping his little bare legs into the water.

With one graceful motion, Meri stretched out in the water. She caught her breath at the shock of the cold water. Closing her eyes, she submerged, feeling the chill as it penetrated every pore.

I am alive! I am fully alive, and I love experiencing every sensation there is on this planet!

Surfacing for a breath of warm air, Meri found to her surprise that Jake was right beside her. Kyle had taken Travis from him, and Jonathan was on his way out of the water.

"Come with me to the waterfall," Jake said. His wet hair was slicked straight back, and drops of water glistened on his eyelashes. Meri thought she had never seen a more appealing sight. It was all she could do not to take that handsome face in her hands and kiss those perfect lips.

They swam together in steady rhythm, the roar of the waterfall growing louder as they approached. Jake pointed to the side and then yelled, "Let's try to go behind it."

Meri followed. They broke through the pounding water, receiving a full, freezing scalp massage in the process. Then they discovered a little pocket where the stones were worn away. A space of about a foot lay between the cold, gray rock wall and the sheet of water. Meri and Jake shivered, treading water while the pounding waterfall echoed in their numb skulls.

Meredith laughed. She couldn't help it. This was such a wild, invigorating experience. Jake laughed with her. They didn't say a word.

Unable to stand the cold another minute, Meri bobbed her way out, under the pelting water. She swam as fast as she could with Jake right behind her, both eager to get out and warm up. Shelly tossed Meri a tablecloth they hadn't used, and she wrapped herself in it. She sat on the shore shivering.

"What a rush!" Jake said, flipping his hair back and wiping his face with his hands. Jonathan tossed him a towel.

"It's used," Jonathan said. "Better than nothing."

Jake dried off and wrapped the towel around his shoulders. "Could you hear us laughing?"

"It sounded really strange," Jess said. "As if the waterfall had come to life and was laughing."

"That's it," Jake said, looking to Meri for support. "We'll have Tom do that. We'll record your laughter and get him to mix it with the sound of the waterfall. What a great idea." He sat down beside Meredith, closer than he ever had before. "What would this project have been like without you? I don't want to know." He put his arm around her shoulder appreciatively and gave her a buddy squeeze the way a coach congratulates the kid who just made the best play of the day.

Everyone was watching. The women gave Meri subtle sympathetic glances. They could now see for themselves how close she and Jake were. It was all business and no romance at all. "Such a pity," Meri could almost hear them say.

"Yeah, Jake," Shelly said, jumping in with both feet, "where would you have been on this project without Meredith? And a bigger question is, where will you be the rest of your life without her as your partner?"

Everyone looked at Shelly, surprised at her bluntness. Then they looked at Jake, then back at Shelly.

"You'll have to excuse my wife," Jonathan said. "She was absent on subtlety day."

"Jonathan!" Shelly said, swatting him. "Why did you say that?"

"Why did you say what you said?"

A spat ensued. Meredith thought, *Oh, great! Instead of helping nudge Jake in my direction, these two are only proving his theory that falling in love is a chemical reaction that wears off, and these two are about to hit their expiration date.*

"We're ready to head back," Jessica said. Travis was sitting contentedly in her lap, sucking his first two fingers. "I have a sleepy boy here."

"Yeah," Kenton quipped, "and Travis should probably get to bed, too."

The gang gathered up the remains of the picnic and made their way back down the trail to the cars. Shelly and Jonathan emerged from the hushed forest trail holding hands and appearing to have made up. Not that it mattered to Meri if Jake noticed their starry eyes. She had a calm, settled confidence that when the time was right, Jake would wake up. If they were going to get together, it would be God's doing and not anyone else's.

Chapter Thirty-One

$\mathcal{A}$ s the days wore on, Meredith was beginning to rethink her option of having her sister help out a little on this going-nowhere romance. Maybe with a few extracurricular lessons in subtlety, Shelly could have a more positive influence on Jake.

The crew arrived Saturday with the new actress and her mom. Filming began Monday, and Jake was on the go all day, every day. Meri used the time to catch up on her work for the publishing house. With the changes in the script, Jake didn't plan to film the waterfall scene with Meri until the fourth day of shooting. It turned out to be the fifth day because it rained on Wednesday.

The cast all hung out at the lodge on Wednesday, waiting for the rain to clear and acting thoroughly bored. Meri took Guard Man Fred out of her car and thought she could play a little joke on Chad. She had intended to use Fred to surprise Shelly, but teasing Chad would be much more fun. They told Chad a cast member was waiting in the van for a ride to the airport.

Everyone watched as Chad ran outside the lodge in the rain and got into the driver's seat with Fred strapped into the passenger's seat. Chad started up the van and pulled out.

"He's not much of a conversationalist," Meredith said with a giggle. "Chad probably won't notice that Fred doesn't talk until they reach the airport and he finds out that Fred doesn't move either."

The crew peered through the curtains at the lodge. Brendon, the child actor who played Young Heart, was the first one to see the returning van. Chad drove back up to the lodge, parked the van, got out, came inside without a word to any of them, and went back to work on his newspaper crossword puzzle. Everyone busted up. Everyone but Chad.

The next day they were filming in the woods. Brendon and Emilie, the girl cast as Hope, played a trick on Jake. They had gotten into the helium tanks in props, filled some balloons, and then sucked in the helium. When they took their mark, and Jake called action, their words came out as squeaky mouse sounds. Meredith noticed how well Jake rolled with the joke in the midst of all the frenzy to get back on schedule.

Meredith liked Brendon and Emilie and thought they were perfect for their parts. When they asked to borrow Fred to play a joke on someone, she agreed and handed him over to them.

Thursday night during dinner at the lodge, Jake sought out Meri to ask if he could speak to her. They stepped out of the dining room into the hallway.

"How are you doing?" Jake asked.

"Great. How are you doing?"

Jake nodded. "It's coming together." He looked down at his feet and then back up at Meri. "It's been so busy, I haven't had a chance to talk with you in more than a week. I mean, I've seen you around, but it's not at all like it was the week before."

"No, it's not. You've been running at full speed. I didn't want to get in the way."

Jake's eyes searched hers. "Thanks," he said.

"For what?"

"Thanks for coauthoring the screenplay with me. Thanks for being honest and telling me what was wrong with it, even though you probably knew I didn't want to hear it. Thanks for being there for me."

"It was all my pleasure," Meri said. "I'm sure you have many more stories in you that need to come out. This is only the beginning for you. I honestly feel honored to have been a part of the process."

He looked thoughtful. "You're amazing. You know that, don't you?"

"Sometimes I forget," Meri said playfully. "So it's nice to be reminded every now and then. Thanks."

Jake smiled. "Hey, I wanted to tell you I was able to get the budget adjusted. There's a check coming for you to cover your time and work as a consultant on the project."

"I didn't expect any payment."

"I know. But you earned it. You earned twice what I have to pay you. Three times."

"Thanks," Meredith said. "I appreciate it."

It was silent for a moment. He kept looking at her as if he had something more he wanted to say but couldn't figure out how to say it. He was like an actor who had forgotten his lines and was keeping his eye on the target but had an ear to the prompter in the orchestra pit, waiting for a cue.

When no words came to his lips, Meredith said, "Have you had a chance to eat yet? It's pretty good tonight. Pork chops."

"No. I'll be there in a minute. Could you tell them to hold some dinner for me?"

"Sure." She turned to go. If he thought this close encounter was easy for her, he was mistaken. Her heart was pounding, and her eyes were tearing up. How could he be so close and not be able to say anything personal like "I've missed you. I want to be with you"? Those phrases burned the roof of her mouth as she kept them inside.

"Meri?" he said.

She turned, blinking away the tears and putting on a smile. He was standing where she had left him, looking lost and unable to move from that spot until she released him.

"What kind of perfume are you wearing? I've wanted to ask you that for a long time."

"Beautiful," she said.

A thin smile played across his lips. He took a step forward from his spot and said with a nod, "And I think you are."

He turned and walked back into the lodge. Now she was the one with her shoes glued to the floor. That was the closest he had ever come to anything romantic. Her hopes soared.

At 3:00 A.M. on Friday, Meredith showed up at the camp, ready for makeup. It promised to be a perfect day, and everyone was in good spirits. It took almost an hour to apply her makeup and to secure her wig. She waited in line at the wardrobe trailer until Muriel was ready to help her into the beautiful blue dress. Chad met her at the trailer door and drove her to the end of the waterfall trail in a golf cart. He didn't say anything.

Two stagehands were at the end of the trail ready to help her down to the platform they had built at the water's edge. She walked slowly and carefully, terrified that she would step on the end of her long wig and pull it off her head.

She took her mark at six o'clock. The early sunlight was filtering through the trees at a perfect angle. More than thirty people were gathered around the lake, all with a specific task. One camera was mounted on a tall crane with a cameraman seated behind it. Another was strapped to the shoulder of a man in orange shorts. She wondered if there was some significance to the color of his shorts. She didn't see Jake anywhere.

Meri had to stand in place for what seemed like a long time. Muriel came over and fluffed up her shoulders. Gina came over and touched up her makeup. Shelly came over and offered her a drink of water through a straw in a paper cup.

"You look incredible," Shelly said. "I know you described this outfit to me, but when I saw you, I felt like asking you to grant me a wish! You look beautiful."

Meri smiled. "What is your wish?"

"I think you already know," Shelly said.

Meri nodded. "A baby," she whispered.

"No," Shelly said, looking surprised. "We can wait on that. It's actually a lot better that we're not expecting a baby now. My wish is for you and Jake to get together."

Meredith hadn't expected her sister to say that, and she was deeply touched. "One wish, and you wish it for me! What a sweet sister you are."

A loud voice boomed through a megaphone, "Quiet on the set." The man handed the megaphone to Jake.

"Okay. Good morning. Is everyone here?" His eyes scanned the area until he spotted Meredith across the lake from him, standing on her platform. Jake lowered the megaphone and stared at her. Everyone watched his reaction and then looked at Meredith to see if something was wrong. She stood in her spot, feeling self-conscious because of the outfit and wig.

Tom called over to Jake, "Oh, Captain, our Captain, are you still with us?"

Jake pulled his eyes off of Meredith. He seemed dazed and not quite sure where he was. To Meredith, it seemed he was acting the same way he had the two times she had seen him wake up from a nap.

"Yeah, I'm fine. I think we're ready to roll," Jake said into the megaphone. "Are you all set, Maiden of the Waterfall?"

"Yes," Meri called out across the water.

"Young Heart and Hope? Are you two ready?"

"We're ready," Brendon called out from the edge of the woods.

"Quiet on the set."

The crew went through all the usual pre-roll-'em routine, and for the first time, Meri felt nervous. She quickly went over the lines in her head. She swallowed rapidly and licked her lips. Tom, the sound man, was only a few feet away, holding a microphone on a long boom out of camera range.

Jake called, "Action," and Young Heart and Hope came trudging from the woods in ragged costumes. They played well the parts of two children who had been on a long journey and were startled to find such a pleasant haven at the end of the trail. Stopping, they looked at each other, not sure what to make of the glorious waterfall and lake.

"Hail, young travelers." Meredith began her lines. Her voice came out clear and not at all quavering like she felt. "From where have you come?"

"We've been through the Forest of Truth," Young Heart said. "Each of our words was weighed, and we found many of them too heavy to carry."

"Please tell us who you are," Hope said. "And what is this beautiful place?"

"I am the Maiden of the Waterfall," Meredith answered. With a graceful sweep of her hand, she said, "And this is the Vale of Peace. Your journey ahead will hold many more adventures. You must rest before you can embrace them."

She made an elegant, welcoming gesture with both arms, offering open hands. "Come, Young Heart. Come, Hope. Drink of the living water until your souls are quenched. Eat of the bounty prepared here for you."

Young Heart blocked Hope, who was about to run to the water. "How can we know if this is another trap like the many we have already faced?"

"You cannot know," the Maiden of the Waterfall responded gently. "You may only choose to enter or to be on your way. Belief offers no guarantees until after the travelers have chosen to enter wholeheartedly. I offer you all that is mine to give, and I offer it with all my heart."

"Cut!" Jake yelled.

Everyone, including the cameraman, seemed surprised. It was all going so perfectly. All eyes were on Jake, who was looking down at his feet. Meri bit her lower lip. Had she done something wrong? What was it? He had been watching her through the camera monitor, which meant he had had an up-close view of everything she did.

"Everyone take a break," Jake called out. "Go. Everyone off the set. Be back here in exactly fifteen minutes. Everyone except the Maiden of the Waterfall."

Oh no! He's going to fire me! I didn't think I was that bad.

Meredith nervously shuffled from one stockinged foot to the other. The confused cast and crew began to head back up the trail to the snack cart Shelly had set up at the fork in the forest trail. As the crowd dispersed, Jake came toward Meri with small, staccato steps. It was as if he didn't want to come to her but something was pushing him. Or was it Someone?

By the time he reached her, only two people were in the Vale of Peace. She had never seen the expression he now wore on his face. He looked happy, sad, relieved, and afraid, all at the same time.

Jake stepped up onto the platform and stood before her, drinking in her appearance as a man who has been lost in the desert drinks gratefully from a redeeming cup of water.

She didn't say anything, she didn't ask anything, and she

didn't try to explain anything. Meredith had a fair idea of what was going on inside Jacob at this moment. She had waited a long time for God to move, and now that he was, she wasn't going to interrupt.

You just woke him up, didn't you, God?

Jake looked down at her hands. He slowly reached over and touched her right hand. He stroked his thumb over her smooth flesh and drew her small hand to his lips, where he kissed her bent fingers like a hero in a Victorian drama. Lowering her hand, he kept hold of it and looked into her clear eyes.

"Completely against my will," he began in a low voice, "I have fallen in love with you."

Meredith's heart began to pound wildly. She waited for him to go on.

"When you said your line just now, it all became so clear. I've been a coward. I wanted a guarantee that what I've felt for you all these weeks wasn't a trap. You just said it. There are no guarantees. I may choose to enter or be on my way."

He lifted her hand to his lips and timidly kissed her fingers again. "Meredith, I choose to enter into a relationship with you. Everything you've said all along is right. Love is more than a logical choice."

He closed his eyes and swallowed hard. "I'm in love with you," he said, opening his brown eyes and inviting her to melt into their softness.

"And I am in love with you, Jacob." Meredith did something she had longed to do since the first time she had seen his handsome face. She raised her hand and stroked his cheek. Her finger touched the bird's-nest mark on the side of his jawline. "I choose to enter wholeheartedly into a relationship with you. I know there are no guarantees, but my heart is filled with hope for us."

Jake smiled. "I'm in love with you," he repeated.

"So you've said," Meri said with a gentle laugh.

"I'm crazy, out of my mind in love with you," he said, breaking into laughter. "I never thought this would happen to me."

"What are you going to do about it?" Meredith asked playfully.

"I'll show you what I'm going to do about it." Jake took her face in his hands and tilted her chin up ever so gently.

Meredith slowly closed her eyes and felt his lips touching hers. With all the hope she had been storing up inside, Meredith let her lips kiss and be kissed by the only man who had ever tossed grapes into her mouth. The only man who had ever quoted verses back to her. The only man who ever made her spine tingle and her heart pound, just as they were doing now.

They drew apart slowly, the invisible glow of their love encircling them with faith and hope.

Just then a loud cheer rose from the forest. With their arms around each other, Jake and Meredith turned to see the cast and crew yelling and waving their arms in celebration. A large, long, odd-shaped object rose from the mouth of the trail and floated above the lake like a balloon. It was all beige with a splotch of white around the middle and was tethered on long ropes like an entry in the Macy's Thanksgiving Day parade.

Meredith noticed Brendon and Emilie standing at the opening of the trail. Chad was beside them, holding the ends of the long ropes.

Jake was the first to figure out what it was. He laughed hard. "It's your old boyfriend, Meri."

"Fred! Oh, my poor Guard Man, what have they done to you?"

Poor Fred couldn't answer. He was already at the top of the

tree line, full of helium and wearing only his painted-on underwear.

A bellowing "oops!" resounded from the opening of the trail as Chad leaped into the air. He was trying to catch a rope that had broken loose, launching Fred into the heavens.

"Sorry, Meredith!" Chad called out. "I'll buy you another one."

"You really think you need another Guard Man now that your social life has taken such a turn?" Jake said, brushing back a strand of wig hair from Meredith's cheek.

"Oh, my poor Fred!" Meredith watched him float lazily toward the fluffy white clouds and disappear from view. "I'll miss him terribly. You might as well know it now, Jake. Fred was a much better dancer than you."

Before Jake could defend himself, Meredith tilted up her chin and invited him to silence her teasing lips with a kiss, which he did better than any movie star ever could have.

Dear Reader,

Sometimes I wish Glenbrooke were a real place. If it were, I would go there.

I'd share a cup of Irish Breakfast tea with Lauren. I'd dream a sunny afternoon away in Jessica's backyard hammock. I'd persuade Teri to make a batch of her tamales. I might go for a ride on Jonathan's zip line or play a flute duet with Meredith. And I'd definitely join in the next time the gang takes a picnic out to the waterfalls.

Glenbrooke represents to me the sweetness of life: family, friends, enduring memories, and the comforting evidence of God's love. Through the midst of it all, hope comes tiptoeing in, wearing feathery, gossamer blue and sprinkling wish dust all over us. What would we do without hope?

Real life is hard. While I was writing this story, my dad suffered a stroke that left him paralyzed on the right side. His speech was taken from him and his vision impaired. For many long days we sat beside his hospital bed, praying, waiting, and asking lots of questions. God's greatest gift to us during that time was hope.

"Rest in hope," "My hope is in you, Lord," "I hope in your Word," "It is good that one should hope and wait quietly for the salvation of the Lord," "Christ in you, the hope of glory." I found my Bible to be full of words of hope, and I underlined them all.

It's been almost nine months since my dad's stroke. He's improved only a little. Still we have hope. It is a tender gift from our heavenly Father and is strong enough to carry us through. But our hope is not for this life only. No, our hope is based on God's eternal promises. My dad surrendered his life to Christ years ago. So did I. We rest in confident hope that the next time we do walk side by side, it will be on streets of gold.

Glenbrooke isn't a real place, but heaven is. The hope of my heart is that you will be there too.

Always,

Robin Jones Gunn

Meredith and Shelly's mom knew all about feeding the multitude on Sunday after church services. She also knew all about having it ready to eat within minutes after they came home. My mom did this for years as well. She had a wonderful, big, roaster pan that she would fill with a roast circled by potatoes and carrots. When we walked out the door for Sunday school in the morning, she'd set the oven on 300. By the time we came home, Sunday dinner was ready.

Even if you don't own a roasting pan, here's how you can make Sunday Pot Roast any day of the week.

MOTHER GRAHAM'S SUNDAY POT ROAST DINNER

A few tips:

–Select a fresh roast, not frozen.

–The best cuts for roasting are the rib and loin.

–One pound of boneless meat will serve four people.

Plan on roasting beef for 20 minutes per pound. Internal temperature of meat should be:

–140 degrees for rare

–160 degrees for medium

–170 degrees for well-done

Remove roast from the refrigerator at least 1/2 hour before preparing for cooking. Rinse meat, trim off excess fat. Season liberally with salt and pepper and a bit of garlic. Less tender cuts of meat may be improved by marinating for several hours.

There are many types of bottled marinades available, or you might like to try the following old-fashioned quick marinade:

    1 cup French dressing with garlic

    1 tablespoon mixed dried herbs or

    2 tablespoons mixed, chopped fresh herbs

Place roast in a large roasting pan in a preheated oven (275 to 300 degrees). Add eight to twelve carrots that have been topped, washed and cut in half. Scrub six large potatoes, cut in half or in fourths and place them around the roast. If the meat was not marinated, you may want to pour a cup of beef broth over the roast and the vegetables. Other vegetables, such as celery, turnips, and onions can be added, but allow for additional cooking time.

Roast is done when internal temperature matches desired temperature listed above. Carrots and potatoes should be soft all the way through. Leftovers make a delicious stew!